# BURN THIS CITY

*BRENDA POPPY*

First published by Glass Fish Publishing 2020

*Copyright © 2020 by Brenda Poppy*

This novel is entirely a work of fiction. The names, characters and incidents portrayed in it are the work of the author's imagination. Any resemblance to actual persons, living or dead, events or localities is entirely coincidental.

First edition
ISBN: 978-1-7356181-0-4

*www.glassfishpublishing.com*

*To my husband, Robert, and my family,
without whose support this book never
would have come to be.*

*And to all the dreamers out there, the lovers of
books, the writers, the artists, the
storytellers. You are part of something
beautiful. Don't let the world get you down!*

# CHAPTER 1

Auburn sat in prison. It was, she thought, an unfortunate turn of events. It wasn't like she'd been doing anything wrong…yet. She put her head back against the cold concrete wall and considered the choices that had brought her to this moment.

There she'd been, taking a leisurely stroll through the dirty underbelly of the city, artfully skirting the pickpockets and drug dealers, when out of nowhere an entire squadron of Peace Officers had turned up and begun arresting everyone in sight. It was a travesty of justice.

But that was the way of things on Kasis. One day, when you were eating dinner with your family or tucking your children into bed (or plotting to overthrow the military dictatorship that crushed your individual rights), Peace Officers would storm in, tackle you to the ground, and throw you in a cell. Whether or not you had actually broken any laws was more or less immaterial.

And, in Auburn's case, she hadn't. Well, at least she hadn't on that particular night.

She readjusted her body on the concrete bench, trying to find a more comfortable position. After roughly 10 hours in a cell, however, she was coming to realize that comfort wasn't exactly what these rooms had been designed for. In reality, they'd been crafted to contain the strongest, most violent prisoners, which explained why concrete covered nearly every surface – the walls, the ceiling, the furniture (if you could even call it that).

The only thing not cemented in place was the door, but since it was made up of several inches of cold, hard steel, it was almost equally impenetrable. A porthole-sized window in said door provided the only glimpse into the Peace Station beyond.

Well, that wasn't strictly true. At least not for Auburn. As it happened, she possessed a certain gift that allowed her to see past her immediate surroundings. Or, more accurately, *hear* past.

Because that was what Auburn did. She heard things. The small things whispered in dark corners and the secrets shared between lovers on cold nights. That was her gift. And her curse. And, at the moment, her only way of breaking up the tedious boredom of a sleepless night in prison.

It wasn't as if she was the sole gifted citizen on Kasis. It was, after all, an uninhabitable planet. But here they were – inhabiting. It was no wonder that prolonged colonization produced...side effects. Or deviations. Or mutations. Most of the population of Kasis was generally normal. Or normal adjacent. Or perfectly normal despite some strange physical anomalies.

Then there were the others, the extremes of the spectrum, the ones whose gifts gave them power over people or objects or forces of nature. Those were the ones the Peace Force was afraid of. Those were the ones who typically occupied these cells. And, as she listened to the world around her, sending her senses past concrete and steel, those were the people she heard on the other side of the walls.

Auburn focused her attention on the cell next to hers, where the steel door had just swung open.

"Get in there!" she heard a gruff voice say as he shoved a second prisoner in with the cell's original inhabitant. The prisoner stumbled and fell, landing harshly on the hard floor before picking himself back up.

"Play nice, you two," the guard taunted before stepping outside and slamming the door shut.

This wasn't going to be good, Auburn thought, bracing herself. One of these men was going to die. Or both. It didn't matter, at least not to the Peace Force.

That's how things worked when they brought in a *freak*. The Peace Officers would beat him up, chuck him in a cell, and a few days later – or a few weeks or months, assuming he hadn't wasted away completely – they would throw in someone else to "keep him company." Both reprobates, having been pumped with a near-lethal dose of MenniK or another rage-inducing street drug, would then proceed to tear each other to bits as inhumanely as possible.

It was cheaper than a trial. And more certain of a "favorable" outcome. The process was simple, speedy, and unequivocally corrupt. That was the norm on Kasis.

She listened intently as more officers crowded around the door, preparing for the show. This was their game, their sport, their way to win or lose a few bucks during an otherwise boring workday. Because what good is a life if you can't bet on when it will come to a sudden and violent end? And these two seemed to be particularly good lives to bet on, based on the commotion.

Auburn closed her eyes and imagined a different ending, one where they didn't have to fight and die for other people's amusement. Maybe this time it would be different. Maybe they could resist the pull of the ManniK. Maybe they could live.

But, no, the drug's pull was too strong. She listened as the battle commenced, accompanied by cheers and boos from the crowd. One of the prisoners emitted a whoosh of air that sent his opponent flying. The other man retaliated, and she heard what sounded like jets of water fling the first man to the ground.

Air and water battling for supremacy. It was quite the matchup indeed.

ManniK's blind rages didn't lend themselves much to conversation, so it wasn't a verbose battle. More grunts and thuds than witty repartee. The Peace Officers outside, however, did provide some verbal interjections – interspersed with their own grunts and thuds.

"Come on! Get that water-spewing freak!" "Kick his ass to next week." "Tear that airhead to pieces!"

The tides of the battle shifted to and fro, punctuated by the sound of soft bodies colliding with hard surfaces. Auburn didn't want to listen, didn't want to hear the outcome, but she couldn't tune it out. A hiss of water. A bone breaking. A gust of air. A moan of pain.

As she listened, the noises in the room began to change, evolving from hard thuds to wet splashes. It was as if the combatants had been replaced by monstrous sea creatures battling to the death amidst the incoming tides.

Then Auburn realized what was happening. The cell was filling with water. Quickly. She looked to her own door, trying to ascertain if any water had begun to leak into the cell, but it appeared to be sealed tight, its flush metal surface acting as an impenetrable barrier through which nothing could flow. She breathed a sigh of relief. She was safe – but they weren't.

The sounds of feet on concrete drifted away as the fighters were lifted up by the rising waters and forced to swim. But even the threat of drowning couldn't stop their battle. It was like every instinct for self-preservation had vanished, leaving only anger and enmity in their wake.

Auburn was lost in the sounds, lost in the tragic story unfolding before her ears. Which was why the knock on her door came as such a surprise. She should have heard the footsteps. But who would listen for an approach when life and death were already on your proverbial doorstep?

She straightened up, got hold of her emotions, and glanced toward the door. All she could see from her vantage point on the low concrete bench was a black hat, although this was presumably attached to a gun-wielding Peace Officer.

Auburn knew she had no real power to grant – or deny – entrance, but she still mustered her most even, unfazed voice for a quick "come in." It was a good sign that they were

5

knocking. When you were slated for "company" or the Pit, they didn't bother to warn you first.

The door opened slowly, another good sign. The riotous sounds from the hall came into crisp, clean focus before sharply cutting off as the hat-clad man shut the door behind him.

They wouldn't want her to hear anything she shouldn't, now would they?

As the hat-man turned, Auburn took stock of him. He was older, with graying brown hair peeking out from beneath his cap and a back just beginning to stoop with age. And he was a detective, not a typical Peace Officer, since he wore a slightly oversized suit and brown jacket rather than the all-black military kit. And he was familiar.

"Detective Grayland," Auburn said, feigning surprise. "How nice to see you here. Come, have a seat. Can I get you some tea?" She allowed a hint of playful sarcasm into her otherwise flat voice.

Detective Grayland smiled weakly and cleared his throat. He was clearly uncomfortable and kept glancing down at his hat, which he'd taken off and was now awkwardly fidgeting with.

"I would have come sooner if I'd known you were down here," he said apologetically. "They didn't release the list of those taken in the raid until just now. I came as soon as I saw 'Auburn Alendra' on it." He finally looked up and made eye contact, as if asking for her forgiveness.

Auburn remained silent. She held onto her explanation, saving it for when it was needed. It was best not to lie until you had to. The same went with forgiveness.

"They thought there was going to be a meeting, some rebel group or other," he continued. "Apparently there'd been a tip that they'd be meeting in the Corax End. So Cross sent out all the officers within shouting distance to bring in every person they could."

Of course it had been Cross. General Illex Cross, to be precise. Him and Auburn were…acquainted.

"But what were you doing down in Corax, Burn?" he asked, softening his voice and invoking her nickname in an attempt to lighten the mood. "There's nothing down there but ManniK men and thieves hawking their stolen goods. That's no place for a sergeant's daughter."

And there was the ace up her sleeve. She was a sergeant's daughter. Or she had been, once. It seemed like a lifetime ago. But most of the officers still saw her that way, which, it seemed, came in handy from time to time.

Grayland was waiting for her to respond. She took her time, considering the man in front of her. Once upon a time, Grayland had reported to her father and had been a veritable friend of the family. Although she found it difficult to think of anyone on the force as "good," he was likely as close as they came.

So it was unfortunate she had to lie to him.

"I was looking for my mother's music box," she began, looking down into her hands as if in a fit of emotion. She'd been practicing the story in her head since she'd been grabbed, so it wasn't too difficult. "Dad sold it shortly after she died. I've been looking for it for a year with no luck. I thought maybe it had turned up in the Corax End." She looked up into his eyes, making hers round and sad. "I wanted something to remember her by."

It wasn't entirely a lie. Burn's mother had died when she was 4 and her sister 6. Lung disease caused by the high amount of pollution in the city's lower tiers. Their family had moved up to the higher levels once the children were born and her father was promoted to sergeant, but it had already been too late. Burn's only real memories of her mother were of her bedridden and weak, coughing up blood and the black grime of the city. It wasn't exactly something she wanted to remember.

But it was enough for Grayland. "Aw, Burn," he said, sitting next to her on the bench. "All you want is a piece of your mother's life and you end up getting nabbed in a pointless raid? I'm so sorry."

"Pointless?" Burn queried, trying to hide the full extent of her curiosity. "So there weren't any rebels after all?"

"Well, no. There's still plenty of riffraff to process. But it looks like it's only the usual petty grifters. I don't know where Cross gets his intel, but I bet they'll be regretting this particular tip."

Oh, they'd regret it, Burn thought. If Cross didn't get his hands on the traitor, she would. And she had a feeling she knew who it was.

She pushed that thought aside and continued the charade. "What a relief. To think I could have been so close to anarchists gives me the chills. But at least you've cleaned up some of the Corax End. Should make things quiet down for a while."

"Yeah, but I'm up to my neck in paperwork." He laughed lightly and visibly relaxed. "Come on. Let's get you out of here. I bet your sis is worried sick." He rose to his feet, his knees making an audible crack in the process.

Burn rose, too, exaggerating her stiffness. "I think we're both getting too old for this kind of thing."

"I think you may be right," he said, tapping on the door to get the officer outside to open it.

As Burn followed Grayland out, she caught glimpses of the aftermath of the battle that had raged next door. Some officers were gradually drifting away in twos and threes, discussing "technique" and fantasy criminal matchups and the best ManniK dose for the optimal fight. Others were paying up to the few victors who had bet on a no-win outcome.

As soon as they saw Burn, however, they stood up a bit straighter, hastily putting their ill-gotten gains behind them. But they hadn't moved fast enough to stop her from seeing into the room.

Water. The room was completely filled with water. And, although Burn's eyes weren't as good as her ears, she knew she had also seen bodies, masses floating strangely about the room as their blood slowly turned the water pink.

Burn looked away, steeling herself. It wasn't the gruesome nature of the scene that got to her. It was the total disregard for life and justice and...human decency. It made her blood boil. But this was not the place to make a scene, although she desperately wanted to.

She followed Grayland up the stairs, concentrating on the steps and trying to slow her breathing to an acceptable rate. Best not to look too crazed when being brought out of a cell. They might just chuck you back in and be done with it.

They finally made it to the ground floor, passing several

more stories of cells along the way. By then Auburn had properly stowed her emotions, plastering on an expression of relief and gratefulness. Which came in handy when she turned the corner and came face to face with General Cross, who had no doubt been waiting there for this very moment.

"Ms. Alendra," he crooned with sickly sweetness. "I was shocked to learn you'd been brought in as part of our raid. For the life of me I can't fathom how an error like this occurred. As soon as I learned you were here, I took every possible action to expedite your release." He smiled and Burn's stomach roiled.

Damn, he was good. Smooth, suave, and uncompromisingly corrupt. The perfect politician.

He looked the part, too. Tall, lean, and chiseled, he oozed machismo and charm. But Burn knew better. Underneath the perfect suit and the slicked back black hair was the soul of a demon, a murderer, a tyrant. It was under his leadership that the poor and deviant disappeared from their homes, never to be seen again. His rivals, enemies, and anyone who opposed his methods typically found themselves the victim of a brutal end, or framed for a heinous act, tried by a crooked court, and sentenced to the Pit.

When the military ruled your fair city, putting people like Cross in positions of power, what else could you expect? On the surface Kasis was a highly functioning and structured society, albeit with high levels of pollution. But underneath was a grimy underbelly of sanctioned murder, bribery, and corruption.

There were even rumors that Cross and his gang were behind the recent spread of tainted ManniK, which was supposedly their attempt to weed out the city's "undesirables."

But Burn's hatred went deeper than that. It was personal. Although she had no proof, she knew Cross was the one who had killed her father – or at least the one who had sent him to his death.

Arvense had been one of the good guys. Or, at least, better. He wasn't perfect, but he had a code and he followed it. He had been selected at a young age for the military track and, as soon as he'd finished school, had jumped into the service with vigor.

With a natural litheness of mind and body, he was a natural fit. He relished the hunt and was adept at uncovering both people and the secrets they tried to hide.

Arvense wasn't immune to corruption. His extensive repertoire of secrets had bought favors with powerful aristocrats throughout the city. But his targets were the rich and powerful – not the innocent, the poor, or the gifted. Coming from the lower levels himself, he had no desire to persecute them further, and he would often find ways to loosen their collective shackles, whether by forgetting debts, misplacing paperwork, or slipping meals to those lying forgotten in cells for crimes they didn't commit.

Some of his colleagues, like Grayland, viewed his acts of kindness with admiration. Most did not. A man who knows too much and doesn't observe the established order is a risky man to have in charge. So one day he wasn't. One day General Cross sent Arvense and his team on a mission from which they never returned.

Burn didn't know what one act or secret had led to his untimely demise. She had searched for months to uncover the truth with no success. But she was certain Cross was behind it. Sure, he acted contrite. He gave Arvense a hero's funeral and made sure his daughters received a sizable amount on which to live.

But it was all for show. It was the benevolence of a dictator.

Burn seethed inside as she stood before Cross. Looking into the monster's cold gray eyes was like staring into the depths of the Pit, but she forced herself to do it, keeping her face placid.

"Thank you for your concern, General," she crooned back. "I'm sure my father would have been pleased to know how much you look out for his daughters." She couldn't resist mentioning Arvense, and she thought she saw a dark shadow briefly pass over Cross' face. In an instant, however, it was gone, and he was back to his smiling self.

"It's the least I can do for the family of one of our fallen," he said, his tone cooling. "But you should take more care, my dear. This is a dangerous city. A lot could happen to a pretty girl like you." Burn shivered as chills of unease trickled down her spine.

"I'll bear that in mind. But now I must be getting home. Good day." With that she swept past the men, skirted between the bustling clerical staff, and pushed the front door open with both hands.

# CHAPTER 2

Burn walked out into the courtyard and immediately shielded her eyes. It wasn't that the city was bright; the pollution levels under the dome actually dimmed the light from the planet's twin suns. But the city's smog made her eyes sting, and the loosely controlled chaos of the Peace Sector was a lot to take in.

Normally her goggles and mask would have provided protection from the sickening air, but both had been lost during her struggle in the Corax End. It was possible the Peace Officers had recovered them, but she wasn't about to go back in and ask. So she wrapped the neck of her tunic around her nose, holding it in place while she made her way to the edge of the zone.

Kasis was a sprawling city, the only one to exist on the planet that bore the same name. But, due to the constraints of the dome that protected them from the planet's harsh atmosphere, its ground-level growth could only extend so far. So they had begun to build up. That was a few hundred years ago. Now the city was a vertical maze of shops and dwellings, tiered based on socioeconomic status and political importance.

Those that lived at the top were the military elite, the ones that made the laws and dispensed justice. From their elevated perches they could look down upon the lower ranks, judging and punishing as they saw fit.

Below them were the influential civilians – the ones who owned the factories and the supply chains that kept them running. They had less legal power, but all that meant was that the laws were made *for* them instead of *by* them.

Then there were the highly skilled – doctors, architects, robotics specialists – who earned their money legitimately (in most cases). They possessed less political sway but enough money to make sure their voices were heard.

Burn's family lived on one of the tiers below that. Their sector was mostly comprised of mid- and lower-level military operatives, along with some aspiring craftsmen and tradespeople. Theirs was an intermediate zone – not quite rich but outside the boundaries of the poor. They worked hard, survived, and likely had a friend or two high enough to get them out of a tight spot if the need ever arose.

Underneath them were a few levels of semi-skilled workers interspersed with shops and stalls. The lower you went, the shadier the wares. And the poorer the people.

Inhabiting the bottom – and most packed – portions of the city were the menial workers, the factory hands, the cogs in the machine. And, of course, the scum of the city – both literally and figuratively. Their streets and alleys were gray with the haze of soot and pollution, and little light broke through from the upper levels.

Disease and mutations were common there, creating a class that looked – and were looked upon – as subhuman. The utter poverty, paired with the peculiar deviations, bred an environment of grift and grit. It wasn't a good place to be alone – or be at all, if you could help it.

It was also home to the Corax End. The elements that made the area dicey were precisely the ones that made it a perfect place for an off-the-grid meeting. Well, until Cross had put the area in his crosshairs. Now Burn would have to find a new locale to conduct her business. It was a shame, seeing as how Corax had the best steamed buns in the city.

That thought made Burn's stomach rumble. Feeding prisoners wasn't high on the Peace Force's list of priorities. She should really be getting home.

Although most of the influential Peace Officers lived "in the heavens," as they liked to say, they ruled from the colony's center – a middle tier in the middle of the city – from which they could easily access any level or sector.

Traversing the city was…complicated. A maze of walkways and stairs allowed citizens to pass between platforms. The setup made any sort of vehicular transport difficult at best, and outright dangerous at worst. So walking it was.

The route was second nature to Burn, as she had often traveled back and forth to visit her father or bring him lunch. She wound her way through the streets and alleys, ducking in and out of passageways in case she was being tailed, which was probable. It wasn't that going home would look suspicious to anyone following her. It was more that Burn didn't want to make their job too easy. Besides, outfoxing one of Cross' cronies was fun.

Arvense had taught his daughter many things over the years, including his well-honed evasion tactics. Burn still wasn't sure if it had been a way to groom her to become an officer or a way of protecting her from them.

Well, becoming an officer was out of the question now, so protection it was. She took a couple sharp turns and backtracked a few times before stopping to pick up some bread and cheese at a mid-level stall.

She picked at the bread as she climbed the steps between zones. Her eyes were stinging by that point, aggravated by the exposure to the fine particles of dust and grime floating in the unfiltered air.

By the time she reached her platform, Burn had worked herself into a nice simmering rage. Sleep had been elusive in the cell, but she felt wide awake, pumped up by the exertion of climbing and the fresh energy from the large chunk she had eaten out of the still-warm bread.

She used her thumbprint to unlock her door, striding in and letting it swing shut behind her. A small part of her wished a Peace Officer had been there, just so she could slam the door in his face. But this wasn't the time for petty gestures. This was the time for a plan.

And, possibly, the time for explanations. Burn's sister, Scarlett, glared at her from the living room. Well, it wasn't really a living room. Sure, it was situated where living rooms were supposed to be, right off the kitchen and adjacent to the hallway that led to their bedrooms. But most living rooms weren't filled with scrap metal, discarded electronics, cables, power tools, and blowtorches. Then again, most families didn't have a girl like Scar.

Like Burn, Scar had been born special, with an extra set of skills beyond those of a typical child. It wasn't a sensory enhancement like in Burn's case. It was more an intrinsic understanding of the way things worked and how things operated, particularly machines and electronic devices. In a minute flat she could deconstruct a comms unit and rebuild it with added range, clarity, and GPS tracking for good measure. It was a skill set an elite engineer would have killed for.

Unlike Burn, however, her sister couldn't hide her gift. It wasn't just the smoke and fumes consistently flowing from their windows – or the steady stream of odd gadgets they bartered with. Scar's mutation had a physical component, as well. Maybe it was because she had spent more of her early life in the city's lower levels, or maybe it was just the way this gift worked. But whatever it was, it certainly made her stand out.

You see, Scar was made of metal. Well, not fully. Probably not even half. But enough. She had beautiful, milky skin, which seamlessly transitioned into cold, hard metal at various points along her body. Her arms changed from smooth skin to metal and back, up the length and down her shoulders, with a wide slash of silver glinting across her chest.

And some of her wiry red curls? Yeah, they were actual wire. And, if Burn wasn't mistaken, they were currently sparking. Was that new? That couldn't be a good sign.

"Where the hell have you been?" she asked, her irritation making the question sound oddly threatening. "I waited up all night for you. I thought you'd been nabbed by the force or something."

Burn cocked her head and raised an eyebrow in response. "Shit. Really?"

"The Corax End was crawling with Cross' men," Burn sighed. "They grabbed everyone they could find. I think they even ransacked the place and started a few fires for good measure. I was hauled up pretty early so I didn't see the full extent of it. But it's clearly not safe for 'business' anymore."

"Damn. That was one of our best sites. Was it a random sweep?"

"More like a planned ambush," Burn countered, shaking her head. "They seemed to know the time and general location, but no specifics. I got there early to scout it out, but they were already in place. I let the others know, but before I could get out all hell broke loose."

"I knew that new goggle patch would come in handy," Scar said with a touch of pride.

She was right – it was rather ingenious. Scar had taken their normal smog goggles and welded in an electronic patch that transmitted short coded messages between users. The message would pop up right in front of your eyes, given you were wearing your set. A retinal scan even ensured that no unauthorized parties would be privy to your communications.

"That reminds me," Burn said reluctantly. "You're going to need to take mine offline, just to be safe. The Peace Officers got a bit rowdy during the roundup and my specs were a casualty. Got another pair?"

"I'll have one for you by tomorrow. I'm working on a few tweaks to the design. Good thing I worked in a self-destruct feature in the early stages."

"My glasses can self-destruct?" Burn asked incredulously. Scar's unique inventions never failed to surprise her. She wondered briefly how she could use this new knowledge to her advantage. A small fire in the evidence room, perhaps, if that's where her goggles had ended up?

Burn shook her head to clear it. The lack of sleep seemed to be catching up with her.

While she was thinking, Scar had whipped out her computerized tab, unfolded it, and made a few quick keystrokes. "Done," she said before folding it up and stowing it in her back pocket.

Scar's speed and precision when it came to technology were remarkable. Burn often wondered if her mind functioned more like a computer than a human brain. She had a hard exterior – figuratively as well as literally – and although Burn knew her sister loved her, emotion and sharing weren't her strong suits.

"You look terrible," Scar stated, not even looking up from her work. Tact was another area she wasn't too adept at.

"Yeah," Burn replied slowly, glancing over her disheveled state. "Turns out even those high-end, luxury jail cells don't come equipped with hot water or breakfast. Next time I get arrested I'll have to speak to them about that."

A small "hmph" was all the reaction she got from Scar, whose head was now completely hidden behind her current project – some sort of strange mid-sized robot with no head of its own. Burn knew better than to ask about it, so she gave up on the conversation and trekked down the hall to her room.

# CHAPTER 3

It had come as a shock to her mother when Burn, at the age of 3, started to relay the goings-on of people several houses down with startling accuracy. And it came as a shock to Burn herself to learn that not everyone could hear everything she could. Like when the traveling baker made his way into their sector, his cart laden with breads and baked treats. Or when Mr. Strobin on the tier above them paid his weekly bribe to the Peace Officers so they would look the other way on his back-door gambling ring.

But Arvense had never seemed surprised. It was as if he had been expecting Burn's ability. After Scar, their parents knew it was possible that Burn would also be gifted. It tended to run in families, after all. Yet it was more than that. Despite having no special abilities himself, Arvense seemed to intrinsically understand how Burn's gift worked.

In the beginning, the headaches were terrible. There were times – if she went out onto a crowded street or into the market – that she thought her head would actually split open. She didn't know how to block out the voices, so they all came crashing into her head, combining into an indistinguishable racket that she was sure would drive her mad. There were days, weeks even, where she couldn't leave the house for fear that the noise would overpower her and leave her helpless.

Her father knew she could get the better of it. He worked with her every day, helping her erect mental guards to tune out the commotion. At first it took every ounce of concentration she had to shut out the unwanted noise. Even just a few minutes of it left her feeling physically drained.

As time went on, it became more and more effortless. She could start going out again, start interacting with people without constantly being interrupted by the noise. Eventually, she could even focus in on particular people and locations, almost as if she were tuning an internal radio to their specific frequency.

Little by little, she began testing her gift, poking and prodding at the edges to see where the limits were – and if she could push them. She began to shut herself away again, this time not to hide from the noise but to embrace it.

Burn would sit alone in her room, cross-legged on her bed with her eyes shut, the gentle whoosh of her breath the only sound. Well, the only sound in that room, at least. Then she would send out her thoughts, gently rolling over nearby streets and houses, now and then alighting on a familiar voice or an interesting tidbit of conversation. As she went farther, the voices became muffled and grainy, like she was hearing them through a broken speaker. Eventually, the sounds would stop completely, replaced by an uneasy silence just waiting to be broken.

It was here, at the edges, where Burn returned day after day. She would grab onto those muted voices, those half-heard sounds, and coax them to life, stoking the embers until words and phrases burned to life.

It was a tedious exercise, hardly ever resulting in anything interesting. Once in a while, however, she'd alight on a gem of information – an affair, a backdoor deal, an illicit cover-up – which her father had found useful. More often than not, she only heard the normal occurrences of life: people cooking, cleaning, borrowing an egg, bartering for bread.

At first she felt guilty for listening in to people's private lives, like she was spying on their most intimate and personal moments. In a way she was. But, honestly, unless it concerned large-scale fraud or corruption, she wasn't interested in the day-to-day lives of those she heard. She might take advantage of small things – like listening for when the local shop owners were in a good mood (and therefore more inclined to give her a good deal on merchandise). But other than that she didn't linger on most houses or people. Their business was their own and she knew better than to get involved.

Things had changed when her father died. Scar had been inconsolable, one of the few times that emotion of any sort had cracked her metallic exterior. Though younger, Burn knew she would have to be the one who took care of them now.

Scar had never been much for interacting with others, preferring the company of computerized machines to unpredictable humans. Outside, her peculiar appearance brought stares and whispers and sometimes even outright hostility. Even though she had now figured out how to strategically cover herself with specially made masks and long-sleeved clothes, she was never eager to go out, fearing people's reaction to those who were "different."

She wasn't wrong to be afraid. Fear was, after all, a powerful motivator for hatred and violence. Especially in Kasis.

So that left Burn to pick up the pieces of their lives and try to put them back together in a way that made sense in their new father-less reality. It had meant giving up some parts of who she was in order to make herself who she needed to be.

By that time, she had honed her unique skill – and had accumulated almost as many secrets as her father had. But she had never been one to act, preferring to live a "normal" life while her father used the intel she accrued. After he died, that was no longer possible. Those secrets now belonged to her – and she had to figure out how to use them.

Without the power of the law behind her, leveraging those secrets was risky. Then again, without the badge she didn't have to answer to the Peace Force – or help facilitate their corrupt machinations. There were still a few officers who had been friends with her father and looked on Burn and Scar as family. And the rest at least feigned support. It was enough. A little pity – feigned or real – came in handy. Like when you needed to get out of jail.

So instead of waking up in a cold cell with an undetermined release date, Burn came to in her own comfortable bed to the sound of a baby crying. And a couple fighting. And a teapot whistling. And so much more.

Burn put her pillow over her head to drown out the noise. She took a minute to breathe and adjust her mental shields until the sounds quieted to a murmur in the back of her mind. Mornings sucked. Or, in this case, afternoons.

Burn cracked one eye open, removing the pillow from her head and glancing out the sliver of a window in her room. It didn't really help her discern the time of day, as it looked out onto another house, but she could see that a hint of natural light was still poking through.

Their tier enjoyed a dim, hazy sunlight that made the world appear like a dream, except far dirtier. When the light from the suns died, lamps throughout Kasis would spring to life, illuminating patchwork circles on the streets and sending long stretches of the world into shadow. Several stories below, lamps were all they had. Sunlight, however brittle, never reached them.

Burn groggily sat up and rubbed the sleep from her eyes. She glanced around the small room, taking in its meager furniture and decorations. This room, the larger of two bedrooms, had been her father's. Naturally, being older, Scar should have gotten it after he died. But – due to some combination of her strange gift and her generally anxious personality – she didn't sleep much and gave the room to Burn instead.

It still felt like her father, with the same rickety bookshelf and dresser, although Burn had added a small desk underneath the window. It was a room focused on practicality over prettiness. That basically summed up Burn, as well.

It's not that she wasn't pretty. Well, she wouldn't call herself that, but she'd heard others say it once or twice when they thought she couldn't hear them.

Instead, she considered herself fairly average – average height, average complexion, average features. Her straight brown hair was cropped at her narrow chin, while her raised cheekbones and dark eyes gave her a hard, intense aura.

When she smiled, though, her whole face would transform, the sharp edges softening to gentle curves and her eyes alighting with passion. But Burn hadn't smiled like that in a very long time. To be honest, she no longer knew if she could.

Rolling off the bed, she slowly made her way to the small communal bathroom. It wasn't much, just a tiny tub with a shower, a toilet, and a compact pedestal sink. It was, however, one of the only areas in the house not filled to the brim with her sister's computerized gadgets. Only the bathroom mirror boasted one of Scar's special upgrades.

When Burn stepped in front of it, the mirror sprang to life, reflecting not only her own image, but also her current weight and health stats, headlines from the Peace Force-controlled news, and private messages synced with her goggle feed. The great thing was that if anyone but Burn or Scar were to step in front of it, they would see nothing but themselves. Handy for the occasional "random" Peace sweep.

Today, Burn's headlines included such gems as "Peace Officers Distribute Food to St. Astiphan Orphans" (probably moldy bits of bread) and "Peace Board Ratifies New Laws for Cleaner Air" (which they'd been promising for years with no actual follow-through). No mention of the Peace Force's unsuccessful raid in the Corax End last night. Of course not, Burn thought. They wouldn't want the force to look incompetent, now would they?

Her own feed, on the other hand, was full of messages either checking in on her or bashing the Peace Force for their general idiocy – or both. After scrolling through a few, she swiped them away, returning once again to her own reflection.

The night in the cell hadn't done her any favors. Dark circles had formed below her eyes, while her hair had gotten a mind of its own and was sticking straight out in several directions. She tried to flatten it down, but soon gave up and opted instead for quick shower.

A quick, freezing shower. Warm water was not a luxury their zone was granted.

A few minutes later, invigorated by the jets of icy water that had pummeled her body clean, Burn made her way to the kitchen. Scarlett was still hard at work on her robotic companion, who was now equipped with a new scrap metal head. It apparently possessed a new voice box, as well, since as soon as Burn entered the room, she heard a nasally voice shout, "Stop! No unauthorized personnel are welcome. Retreat immediately."

Burn cocked an eyebrow in Scar's direction. At first Scar tried to look innocent. But acting wasn't her strong suit. Burn continued her stare, unfazed, and Scar finally broke.

"OK, OK," she said, throwing her hands up in mock surrender. "So I may have reprogrammed an old PeaceBot control unit to work with a personal droid interface." She looked at Burn with wide, pleading eyes, like a kid asking to keep a puppy they'd found on the side of the road.

"And the PeaceBot came from where?" Burn countered. The last thing she needed was the Peace Force to track it back here, especially so soon after her arrest.

"It's probably better if you don't know. But, hey, I think it will come in handy. You know, after a few more modifications. Besides, you can't tell it's got PeaceBot parts. Well, unless it speaks. But that should be a snap to fix." Scar stared at her creation for a beat before attacking the neck region with gusto.

Burn turned to leave the room but stopped in her tracks with a sudden realization.

"Uh, Scar?" This wasn't going to be good. Her sister popped her head back up, already annoyed at the interruption. "Is there any way you could get rid of your workroom for a few days?" Burn motioned around, indicating Scar's mess of motors and computer chips and wiring.

It was Scar's turn to stare incredulously.

"It's just that, I think I pissed off Illex Cross. And that never tends to end well," Burn went on quickly, trying to explain in a way that Scar would take seriously. "I have a feeling our street is going to be subject to one of his 'random' searches. And it wouldn't be the best idea to have your gadgets lying around."

Not that the Peace Officers would know what they were. But if any items looked suspicious or out of the ordinary – or valuable – they'd be subject to seizure.

Scar sighed heavily, obviously displeased with the suggestion. But she managed to spit out a sharp "fine" before completely decapitating the robot and throwing its head on the floor.

Well, that went well, Burn thought as she dashed into the kitchen and out of Scar's direct sightline. She made a mental note to pick up some extra batteries for Scar the next time she was out. That always put her in a better mood.

She rifled through the cabinets in the small kitchen, mentally adding fruit and salt to her ever-growing shopping list. (Seriously, what kind of people ran out of salt?)

Burn and Scarlett weren't exactly the domestic type. There was a lack of anything resembling home cooking in their house, but that didn't bother them. There were enough food stalls and shops nearby that they were never in danger of starving. Plus, the shopkeepers made sure to take care of them, adding a little extra to the sisters' orders when they could.

She finally settled on a can of tinned soup, opening it and sloshing it into a pan on the stove. A few minutes later, soup in hand, she quietly snuck past her sister, who was still ignoring her, and into her room, sitting down at the desk.

Burn grabbed her computerized tab from the top drawer and unfolded it. In between bites of scalding soup, which she had somehow managed to burn, she got to work.

Her organization, as she liked to call it, was comprised of a motley crew of citizens, some gifted, some not. It wasn't really hers; it had existed before her and would continue on after she was gone. But due to her unique skill – and the information she gleaned from using it – she'd naturally assumed a leadership role.

Somewhere along the line they'd acquired a more formal name: the Lunaria. But she rarely used it, opting instead for vague titles that were less trackable and, if overheard, wouldn't lead to questions.

The Lunaria's goal was simple, or at least it sounded

simple on paper. (Not that they'd ever written it down, as that would be an act of supreme idiocy that would no doubt lead to mass incarceration if it were ever discovered.)

Their aim was to overthrow the Peace Force. Simple, right?

Not that they'd ever gotten anywhere close to achieving it. It turns out that the road to a complete government take-down starts with many, many small steps.

Like ferreting out spies in the organization.

The Lunaria were selective. Discovering their existence was hard; getting in was a different matter entirely. Due to some of their members' unique abilities, the Lunaria had a very specific set of safeguards to ensure that their secrets stayed that way.

Currently, there was only one pending member in the vetting process: Amblys. A low-key grifter, he had a unique ability which made him of interest to the Lunaria. Through some kind of speed element and an actual lightness of the fingers, he was a master thief. He'd plied his trade for years as a pickpocket, branching out now and then for larger jobs, stealing from the rich and, well, keeping for himself.

His knack for thieving would have come in handy, es-pecially when it came to getting their hands on Peace Force files. Burn wasn't a fan of Amblys' shady morals, but she had to admit that it would have been convenient to have more info on what they were up against.

The night before had been set as the start of his induc-tion process. After hearing about him through one of their contacts, the team had scoped him out for two weeks before officially inviting him in via one of Scar's untraceable goggle hacks.

They'd been planning to test him. After meeting at their Corax safe house, they were going to send him out into the city to procure a sample of tainted ManniK and bring it back for inspection. It was one of several trials concocted to verify his skill set and his allegiances. But, as it turned out, that was unnecessary. Burn had known his true allegiances the instant she'd spotted the first Peace Officer in the Corax End.

Naturally, since he hadn't been fully vetted, he'd never met any of the group in person, so their identities were safe. Only their essential "safeguard members" were set to attend his indoctrination. But even then, the group was dedicated to secrecy.

Burn wondered how long it had taken Amblys to sell them out. Had he approached the Peace Force right after they'd made contact, or had it taken him a few days to weigh the price on their heads against freedom from tyranny? She'd been naïve to think a thief would choose morality over coin.

It wasn't the first time someone had betrayed them. Just like they had rules in place for secrecy, they had rules in place when someone betrayed it. They weren't as brutal as the Peace Force; they'd never kill to keep their power. But they weren't gentle. And they gave no second chances.

Fortunately, Burn wasn't the one who would be administering this not-so-gentle lesson. But it was up to her to coordinate it. She quickly typed out a message to her top-level compatriots updating them on the situation. She sent separate messages to her two main enforcers requesting their presence at Amblys' house later that evening. She would do the talking, and they would do the rest.

Her business complete, she folded up her tab and went to work equipping herself for the day ahead. Or rather the night, as the suns would no doubt be setting soon. Mask, backup goggles, portable lightweight taser that looked like a pen. The last had been a gift from Scar since Burn wasn't a huge fan of guns. Thankfully, it was more powerful than it looked.

She pocketed a few more of Scar's gadgets, just in case. Her stomach roiled with unease – and burnt soup. This was not going to be pleasant. Contrary to popular belief, she did have a heart and even some degree of empathy, although they were buried beneath a few generously sized mounds of rubble. She wished, not for the first time, that she had been blessed with Scar's detached steel exterior – and the steel heart that went with it.

# CHAPTER 4

Burn strolled down the main thoroughfare through their tier, stopping occasionally to browse a window display. She had already picked up a few pieces of ripe fruit and some salt, stowing them in the wooden basket she carried.

She was being followed. And not very well. The Peace Force really needed to train their officers better when it came to suspect tracking and evasion tactics. Her father would have scoffed.

She spent 20 minutes making her way down to the next sector, chatting with a few familiar shopkeepers and browsing their baubles as she went. Burn was aware of one male, tall and wiry, following half a block behind her. There may have been others, but she didn't want to alert them by overtly scanning the area.

Her brown thigh-length cloak, paired with her long-sleeved light shirt and rust-colored pants, gave her a sort of urban camouflage, helping her blend into the shops and crowds around her. Bright colors made you stand out in Kasis — and standing out was something most citizens wanted to avoid.

She took her time, being deliberately slow as she made her way across streets and down stairs. She wanted them to follow. No sneaking, no hiding. Disappearing in a busy market wouldn't be difficult, but she had a better system in place.

Burn made her way to a blue-doored dwelling situated in a row of nearly identical houses. She knocked lightly, then waited as footsteps shuffled inside. After a few moments, a plump brunette opened the door. Her lined skin and the shocks of gray threading her long hair put her a few decades older than Burn, and she stood a few inches shorter, as well.

"Auburn!" she cried happily, sweeping her up in an enormous hug. "I'm so happy you're here. Come in, come in. Shall I put on some tea?"

"Of course, Meera! I want to hear everything. I have all night." With that, Burn entered the house, closing the door behind her.

Once the door was latched, Meera's smile dropped. In the blink of any eye, her attitude shifted from genial grandmother to army general.

"How many out there?" she queried as she double-checked that her shades had been drawn.

"Two," Burn answered after listening outside. The men, stationed across the street and down an alley, had just radioed in about Burn's whereabouts and her intention to stay put for the foreseeable future. They'd been told to set up camp, just as Burn had hoped.

"Do you need any supplies?" Despite her soft appearance,

Meera was all business.

"No, I'm set. Just give me a sec to change." Burn tossed off her light shirt in favor of a darker gray one from her basket. She pulled a black cloak over her head, tucking in her hair. "Hold on to this for me," she instructed Meera, giving her the basket with the discarded clothes.

Meera nodded. "How long will you be?"

"Maybe an hour. Maybe two," Burn said, making her way down the hall. Knowing better than to ask questions, Meera followed in silence.

The hall split into two rooms, but instead of entering either Burn bent down and dug her fingernails into one of the wooden planks on the floor. After struggling for a few seconds, she pulled the plank loose, then did the same with the boards on either side until the hole was large enough for her to squeeze through. Gazing down, she could just make out the shape of a ladder in the darkness.

"Put these back when I'm down," Burn said, indicating the planks. "I'll signal when I get back so you can open it up again."

Even though they'd done this before, Burn liked to go over it again. Just one misstep could land them both in serious trouble.

Burn switched her goggles to night mode before slipping into the darkness. The descent was a long one, and it was a good thing Burn wasn't afraid of small spaces, since the tight shaft boasted barely enough room to turn around. Meera, true to her word, replaced the boards above her, blocking out the only light source.

With night mode on, Burn could just see the rungs above

and below her, as well as the sharp fragments that made up the walls. As a security measure, the tiny chamber had been constructed from scrap metal. If anyone ever stumbled upon the space, without night vision and a thorough knowledge of the layout they'd run a serious risk of filleting themselves before reaching their destination.

After a few minutes of climbing, Burn finally reached the bottom, her arms aching. Before pushing the door open, she closed her eyes and listened. This passageway let out into a seedy alley a few tiers down from Meera's house, one with blessedly little foot traffic. Once she was satisfied that there was no one outside, she eased the door open and shut it firmly behind her.

On this side, the door blended almost perfectly into the block wall around it. If a certain section of the wall was pressed, however, a small biometric scanner would appear, which allowed access to the tunnel.

There were a few such houses strategically placed around the city, manned by Lunaria operatives, although this one was Burn's go-to. She always enjoyed seeing Meera, even if it was only for a few minutes.

Meera had been the one to suggest that Auburn become a member. The Lunaria were, by nature, opposed to Peace Officers or their families joining the ranks. But they trusted Meera. And she had known Arvense and his family since before Burn was born. So she knew Burn had as much reason to want the force destroyed as any of the Lunaria – if not more.

Burn double checked that her hair was hidden under the dark cloak, pulling the fabric as far as possible over her face.

Before exiting the alley, she sent a message to the others to update them on her position. With any luck, they would be a few minutes behind her, giving her enough time to scope out the scene before they arrived.

It was much darker down here and the smog was thicker, making everything appear gray and hazy. The dust and dirt hanging in the air tickled her nose, and she pulled her mask tighter around her face. There were still plenty of people ambling about, so Burn did her best to blend in with the crowd.

Despite Amblys' success at pickpocketing and minor crime, he had never managed to pull himself out of the lower tiers. She wasn't surprised. When the rich and powerful ran your city, facilitating others' upward mobility wasn't in their best interest. Her family had been lucky. Others hadn't.

Burn glanced around at the shops as she walked. Vendors with carts and stalls hawked food on sticks, not all of which she recognized – or wanted to. Other shops sold cheap goods, stolen jewelry, shoddy electronics. Here and there, scantily clad women stood on street corners selling a different kind of ware entirely, while grubby children sat with their hands outstretched, pleading for food.

A light burst above Burn's head, making her jump. The others around her kept walking, ignoring the loud noise and sudden darkness. Burn composed herself and followed suit, stuffing her hands into her pockets and focusing on the road.

After a few minutes she checked her tab and changed course, heading off the main walkway and through a maze of smaller streets and alleys. Instead of shops, the area was now covered with small houses and shared units, broken up every so often by a rickety bar or derelict food stall.

Burn stopped around the corner from her target: a peeling green house with broken shutters. Once upon a time someone had tried to make it look nice, putting flowers out front and a small canopy over the door. But time had not been kind to it. The flowers had long since died, and the rusted awning beams barely managed to hold up the ripped cloth that fluttered in the breeze.

Down here, the houses were almost on top of one another. (In fact, many of them actually were, stacked in precarious ways until they were touching the platform above.) That would make this harder – but still well within Burn's capabilities.

She glanced around to make sure she was alone before closing her eyes and letting down her guards. The onslaught was immediate. The sheer number of people talking at once made Burn's head throb. She narrowed her concentration to the homes in front of her, directing particular attention to the sad green house.

Her mind suitably focused, she opened her eyes. Next door to the green house, a man and a woman ate dinner while a child cried. Above them, an older lady sat talking to her cat.

But the green house was silent. Burn pushed her mind farther into the building, checking for any sounds of movement – like writing or typing or cooking. She heard none. All she could discern was a subtle creaking sound, like an old-fashioned swing swaying in the breeze.

The house was empty. That would make things easier.

Burn walked quietly to the door. She dug in her pocket, coming out with another one of Scar's gadgets – a small blue tube that was useful for bypassing biometric security.

Slipping it over her finger, she moved her hand to the scan pad and froze.

Something wasn't right. The door was already open – just a sliver, as if someone had tried to close it in a hurry and it hadn't latched properly. A chill went up Auburn's spine.

She sent her senses out again but still heard nothing from inside. She told herself she was being paranoid. There was nothing in there.

She pocketed the finger sensor, then eased the door open. The interior was cramped and dark and eerily quiet – except for the strange creaking.

Burn gathered her courage and tiptoed farther into the house, flinching when a board groaned under her feet. She could now tell that the noise she had detected was coming from behind a closed door at the end of the hall. She paused to arm herself with her taser pen before turning the handle and gently pushing the door open.

She let out a terrified shriek before clasping both hands over her mouth. She had been wrong. Amblys was home after all. And, judging from his stiff body, which was hanging from one of the rafters, he was very, very dead.

# CHAPTER 5

Auburn stood in shock, staring at the body. She couldn't seem to move or even look away from the horrific sight.

Amblys had clearly been dead for some time. Rigor mortis had set in and his limbs were rigid and gray, swaying eerily back and forth in the breeze from a nearby window. The creaking sounds accompanied the body's movements, adding a chilling soundtrack to the scene.

Burn tried to keep her eyes from glancing up, but she couldn't seem to stop herself. His eyes were open and cloudy, staring down at her in a terrified panic, and his mouth was parted in a silent scream.

This hadn't been suicide. This was murder. Burn was sure of it. The look on his face, paired with the obvious defensive abrasions on his arms, painted a gruesome picture. There wasn't even a stool or chair around with which he could have hoisted himself up. They hadn't even tried to make it look real. Of course, no one would question it when the Peace

Force ruled this a suicide, unless they wanted to end up like Amblys.

The breeze wafted in Burn's direction, and the scent of death made her stomach lurch. She clasped her hand tighter to her mouth and willed her stomach to settle. Her mind reeled, trying and failing to process the sight.

Amblys was dead. His information had led to a pointless raid and he'd paid the price. It was the Peace Force's signature brand of justice, no doubt courtesy of General Illex Cross.

Burn's mind felt sluggish, but she knew that she had to tell the others. They were no doubt already on their way, but their presence would only complicate things further. She grabbed her tab from her pocket and, hands shaking, started to type.

"Abort. Target terminated. Abort."

Her heart pounded in her ears and she tried to breathe, but the overpowering scent made her gag.

And then she heard it: footsteps, headed her way. At least eight pairs. She had been so focused on Amblys that she'd completely blocked out all other stimuli. She immediately sharpened her hearing to focus on the surrounding area, her body prepared for flight.

They were a few blocks away but rapidly closing in. They were clearly military, judging by the coordinated movements and the clacking of their hard-soled boots against the pavement.

Shit, Burn thought. She must have tripped some sort of alarm. Or they'd been watching the building the entire time. Either way, she had to get out of there. Quickly. But she obviously couldn't leave through the front, as that would put her right into their hands. She cast her eyes around frantically, looking for another way out.

Then it struck her: the window. It was high on the opposite wall, but it was just large enough for someone of her size to squeeze through. And it was open. She had no idea where it led, but right now it was her only option.

She sprinted to the wall, swerving to avoid the body in her path. But the window was too high. She could just reach it with the tips of her fingers, but she would never be able to pull herself up. Her vision momentarily dimmed with panic but brightened again when her eyes alighted on a small wooden table near the bed.

Burn rushed to grab it, narrowly missing Amblys' swaying form on the way back. She placed it under the window and silently prayed that it would be strong enough to hold her weight.

The footsteps were nearing the house now, and she had no time for another plan. If this didn't work, she'd be cornered – and maybe even killed onsite. And Meera would pay, as well, once they realized that her house had only been a front for Burn to hide behind. She couldn't let that happen.

Burn hoisted herself onto the small table and grabbed the window ledge with both hands, pulling herself up. It was a tight fit, but she just managed to squeeze her body through. She tumbled ungracefully out of the window, twisting to land on her side instead of her head. Her shoulder jarred as it hit the pavement, but she scrambled to her feet and began to run.

Her shoes hit the ground with loud slaps as she took

corner after corner, winding her way through unfamiliar alleys. The footsteps behind her grew louder, following her every move. She risked a glance back and saw at least two black-clad forms trailing her.

She put on a burst of speed and rounded a bend, gashing her shin on an exposed metal gutter as she changed direction in the narrow lane. She ignored the sudden hot surge of pain and kept moving, her breathing heavy.

Burn moved up a level, then another, hoping to lose her shadows in the labyrinth of corridors. But luck was not on her side. They were relentless, like armor-clad hounds on the trail of their prey. And Burn was tiring fast, her side aching from the prolonged sprint and her leg beginning to throb in earnest. The grime of the city clung to her nose and throat, threatening to choke her as she drew in short, shallow gasps.

She had to do something. She knew she couldn't outrun them. What they lacked in stealth they more than made up for in endurance. Soon they'd overtake her – or they'd start shooting.

Burn fumbled in her pocket, searching for anything that could help. Her taser pen wouldn't do much good against so many assailants – especially ones that were so heavily armed. And her tab would be no help, as she had no time to stop and type out a message. Besides, she didn't want to get anyone else mixed up in this. If she had to go down, she'd go down alone.

Her fingers closed around the biometric bypass device, and she wrenched it out of her pocket. She'd only have one chance at this, she thought, so she'd have to do it right. Burn slipped the tube onto her finger, then made three consecutive turns so she was out of view of her pursuers. She hurriedly scanned the street, zoning in on a dark gray home with no lights on. If she was lucky, nobody would be home.

Burn made a beeline for the door, swiftly sticking her finger in the scanner. The few seconds it took to override the system seemed like an eternity, but it finally accepted her print and she dashed inside, wrenching the door shut and locking it.

She slid down until she was crouched beneath the handle, her breath coming out in short, uneven bursts. Her side was burning and the gash on her leg began to throb painfully, but she kept quiet and still, listening to the street for any hint of noise.

A moment later, the officers careened around the corner. Burn held her breath as the footsteps neared the door, but the figures kept going, passing her hiding place and continuing on.

She let out a small sigh of relief, but she didn't dare move in case they realized they'd lost her and decided to backtrack. For the time being, however, she was safe. She gently removed her mask, sucking in the cool evening air, and pushed up her goggles so she could wipe the sweat from her face. Her legs started to protest the awkward position, yet she remained perched against the door, mentally tracking the footsteps as they receded into the night.

Burn's mind must have been so thoroughly consumed with the action taking place outside the house that she didn't hear the stirrings within it – at least not until a deep voice emerged from the darkness.

"Can I help you?" the man said evenly.

Shocked at the nearness of the figure, Burn gasped – and promptly tumbled over.

# CHAPTER 6

From her new vantage point on the ground, Burn could see that the man was tall and young, maybe a few years older than she was. By the looks of it, she had woken him up. He wore loose gray pants and a light shirt, clearly pajamas.

He also held a bit of pipe, but kept it at his side, not threatening – merely warning. They stared at each other, neither daring to break the silence that had fallen.

Burn's heart raced, and tingles of shock still lingered in her system. She knew she had to get up, but for some reason she didn't want to break eye contact with the stranger, fearing what would happen if she did.

The man began to approach, but, as if sensing her unease, he moved slowly and purposefully, bending down and offering Burn his hand. After a series of mental calculations, factoring in several worst-case scenarios, Burn took it and he helped her to her feet. In all her scenarios, it was better to be standing.

Hastily dropping his hand, Burn stepped back, attempting to put more space between them. She immediately regretted the movement. The pain in her leg burst to life, making her stumble. She glanced down to find that her pants had ripped open and she was bleeding freely onto the floor.

The man's gaze followed hers, but instead of demanding answers or throwing her out, he merely raised his thick dark eyebrows in question. Not sure how to get herself out of this new scrape, Burn stayed silent. After a beat, his deep voice rumbled to life again.

"Why don't you take a seat. Then, maybe we can discuss why you're here. In my house. Bleeding." He indicated a chair in the kitchen, next to a small table. He still held the pipe, but his grip was promisingly loose. Burn limped over, shuffling sideways so as not to lose sight of him.

He turned around, rooting in a cabinet before producing a rag and bowl, the latter of which he filled with water. She had expected him to hand the items to her, but instead he knelt down at her side and rolled up her tattered pants. Dipping the rag into the cool water, he began to dab at the tear in her leg.

Burn flinched – both from the pain and the unexpected contact. Her instinct was to pull back, but the man held tightly to her leg, continuing his administrations.

Burn knew she needed a story, something believable that explained why – and how – she had burst into his home and why she was out of breath and bleeding. She discarded a few implausible stories before settling on one that might work. She prayed he was the sympathetic sort. Or at least very, very stupid. The last thing she needed tonight was to get turned in to the Peace Force for trespassing.

"I was out shopping," Burn started explaining, a slight wobble to her voice that wasn't completely feigned. "My sister is rebuilding her tab and needed a new part. I was told I could get a cheap one in the Saffron Quarter."

There was a hint of truth to that, as Scar was always in the process of taking apart and updating her tab. She hoped that dropping the name of the nearby market sector – known for its mix of food stalls and secondhand vendors – would lend more credibility to her tale.

The man looked up, silently urging Burn to continue.

"Well, I eventually found the part, but by then it was already dark. I started making my way home, but I got a little turned around. I bet I was an easy target," Burn looked away as if remembering the awful scene.

"These two men cornered me. I thought they wanted my bag so I gave it to them, but they wouldn't back off. I guess that wasn't what they wanted after all." A little damsel in distress element couldn't hurt, especially if this guy had a savior complex, which seemed likely given his behavior.

"I ran. I managed to slip past them, but they started chasing me." A little more truth mixed in with the giant lies. "I'm not sure how long I ran for, but I couldn't shake them. And to make everything worse, I gashed my leg on a piece of old metal. That's when I started trying doors, but everything was locked. Except yours." Burn raised her gaze to his, making her eyes as wide and innocent as possible.

"I don't know why your door was open. But it saved me," Burn finished. She hoped she hadn't gone too far. She still held his gaze, mentally willing him to accept the lies.

Because both of them knew that the door had been locked.

After a beat, he broke eye contact and returned to cleaning up her leg. He wasn't reaching for the pipe, which he'd placed on the counter beside him, so that was a good sign. But if he wanted, he could easily overpower her even without the pipe.

She braced herself for questions, debate, contradiction, but when he finally spoke, he said, "This cut is deep, but it should heal. Stay here." With that, he got up and left the room.

Burn briefly considered making a break for it. But, with the pain in her leg, she knew she wouldn't get far. The adrenaline had faded, taking with it the pain relief she'd felt while fleeing. So she remained seated, putting her life in the stranger's hands.

He returned a minute later, carrying a handful of bandages. He set them down on the table and produced a small white tube, which he opened and began applying to Burn's leg. She winced as the salve came in contact with the cut, creating a sharp, stinging pain.

"Why are you being so nice to me?" Burn couldn't help it. People didn't just help other people for no reason. They always had a motive.

He hesitated, struggling to put his thoughts into words. "It was the way you looked when you burst in here. Like the devil was on your tail." He chuckled. Burn didn't see what was so amusing.

He continued, "I couldn't throw you back out there. It would have been like throwing a puppy to the wolves."

Oh great, Burn thought. He considered her to be a

helpless puppy. She checked herself before making a snide comeback. People protected puppies, she reminded herself. Better to be a puppy than a prisoner in police custody.

"I don't know who was out there," the man went on, "but I'm glad I could help."

So he didn't believe her story. But he was helping her anyway. Burn opened her mouth to speak, then closed it, trying to find the right words.

"Thank you," she finally managed to say.

"Kaz. My name is Kaz." He unwound some of the bandages and began wrapping them around her leg.

It was nice to put a name to the stranger, although she still felt wary about his motives. She wasn't about to return the courtesy and tell him her name. It wasn't worth the risk.

Burn pulled her leg back, out of Kaz's gentle grip. "My... sister will be worried," she said, looking into her lap. "I should be getting home."

"Let me walk you back," he said, picking himself up off the floor. "It's clearly not safe out there. Just give me a second to change." He gestured to his pajamas.

Burn considered it for a moment. She knew she needed to get back, but she couldn't exactly have him walk her to Meera's front door. Damn his chivalry. All of this would be much simpler if she could tase him and leave. She briefly considered that, as well.

"No, no," Burn stammered. "I'll be fine. As long as those men are gone, I don't think I'll have any more trouble."

"Besides," she added, "you should get back to sleep. I'm sorry I woke you." It was a little strange that he'd been asleep so early, but then again many of the factory hands in Kasis

49

started work at dawn. Although he didn't quite look like the factory worker type.

Kaz looked at her dubiously but didn't protest. She got up, dusting herself off, and began hobbling to the door. Her leg still ached, although the pain had subsided a bit thanks to his first aid.

"Wait," Kaz said before she reached the door. He turned back to the kitchen, grabbing the pipe from the counter. Burn stiffened, panic momentarily shocking her system, but she relaxed when he held it out to her. "Take this. Just in case."

Burn reached out warily, taking the pipe from him. It felt heavy and reassuring in her hand. She wasn't sure how much good it would do against an entire squad of military personnel, but it was nice to have something other than a pen to defend herself with.

"Thanks," Burn replied. It seemed inadequate, but it was all she could offer. She turned to go, her ears alert to any sounds on the road outside, but she stopped when she heard his voice instead.

"Hold on. You haven't even told me your name."

Burn glanced back, a wry smile on her face, and gave a slight shake of her head. She turned around and opened the door, stepping out into the night. As she began to walk down the empty street, Kaz's voice floated into the darkness. "Goodbye, mystery girl."

# CHAPTER 7

The next morning, the pain hit Burn before the noise. Everything hurt. Her legs felt like dead weights, and her arms were similarly useless. She moaned, trying to sit up and failing. Instead, she stared at the ceiling, recalling everything that had happened the night before. In detail.

One thing stood out from the others, demanding her attention: Amblys was dead. Murdered.

She hadn't been the man's biggest fan, but nobody deserved that kind of ending. Revulsion churned in her gut. The Peace Force did whatever they wanted, killed whoever they wanted, and paid no price for their actions. It wasn't right. That kind of tyranny needed to be stopped.

The anger in that thought gave Burn the strength to propel herself out of bed and into the hall. She made a bee-line for the bathroom, where she spent a few extra minutes scrubbing off the grime and disgust of the previous night's events. The cold jet of water was bracing, but it helped remove the cobwebs from her mind and focus her thoughts.

Something had to be done. Not small baby steps. Not freeing a prisoner here, exposing bribery there. They needed a plan – a solid plan – to affect real change.

She stalked out into the hall, noticing that Scar had once again taken up residence in the living room, surrounded by metal and wiring. She silently cursed herself as she realized that she'd forgotten to pick up extra batteries as an apology. Her scowl deepened.

It wasn't until Scar spoke that Burn looked up, taking in her sister's manic, energized state. "You were right," Scar said by way of a greeting.

Her thoughts already jumbled, Burn just cocked her head in question.

"The Peace Force stopped by for one of their 'friendly visits' about an hour after you left yesterday. Searched the place from top to bottom. Routine, they said. Just sweeping the entire street. They bandied around words like 'plot' and 'rebels' without going into any detail."

Burn sighed, rubbing her eyes as if it would wipe away the whole situation. "And?" she shot back tersely.

"We're good," Scar countered. She gave a sharp burst of laughter, startling Burn. "They seemed so disappointed. They were apparently hoping to find an entire resistance force concealed in your bedroom. They did take your tab, though."

Confused, Burn fumbled in her pocket and removed her tab. "But I have it right here. How could they have taken it?"

A twinkle sparkled in Scar's eyes as she took in her sister's bewilderment. "Well, it might not have been *your* tab exactly. They did, however, take *a* tab."

"Scar?" Burn queried, drawing out the name like an accusation.

"Let's just say their tech team will be busy. For some reason you seem to keep your shopping lists very well encrypted."

Burn shook her head, turning around. Scar was baiting them. Didn't she have any sense of self-preservation?

"Hey," she shouted from the living room. "At least I resisted the urge to create a fake diary detailing your explicit love for one Illex Cross!"

Without thinking, Burn grabbed the loaf of bread and hurled it in the direction of Scar's head. It missed, hitting a pile of chains and gears in the corner. Scar laughed, taking it as the playful gesture it was intended to be.

"Next time just tell me what you're planning," said Burn with mock exasperation. "Plus, if I'm meant to be in love with that buffoon, I think I've been sending him some mixed signals lately."

After a breakfast of cheese and eggs, Burn retired to her bedroom to work. She shut the door behind her to drown out the sound of Scar's ceaseless banging.

Neither of the sisters had what you'd call a typical job. But their particular sets of skills, paired with the funds they'd received from the Peace Force following their father's untimely demise, made maintaining their way of life manageable. For Scar's part, she used her talents to fix electronics, upgrade old devices, and make new creations to sell and barter with.

Burn's side of things was a little less above board. Her contributions relied on blackmail. Like father, like daughter.

Burn wasn't going to pretend she was perfect. Far from it. But she'd given up on simplistic moral definitions a long time ago. Good, bad, right, wrong, evil, just. The world was shades of gray and so was she.

To her credit, she picked her targets carefully. The rich, the cruel, the corrupt. The ones who owned the city and thought they could get away with anything.

It didn't always work. Some thought they were immune to blackmail, that her threats were mere empty shells with no intention behind them. They were wrong. Those were the ones who'd wake up to find their secrets leaked via a hacked news feed to the whole city. Then, buoyed by a cry of public outrage, they'd be hauled in by the Peace Force or stripped of their position or thrown to the curb by their family. Or they'd disappear. Or, sometimes, they'd pay an inordinately large sum to the right parties and sweep the whole thing under the rug. You couldn't always win.

But most would pay and pay well. Scar had set up an ingenious system to facilitate everything, from personalized messages delivered directly to the person's tab to untraceable bank accounts that changed on a regular basis. No personal contact and no risk of Burn's identity being revealed. All she had to do was keep gathering secrets, something which was now second nature to her.

Things were different when it came to the Peace Force. It wasn't that they lacked secrets. It was that Burn didn't want their money. She wanted their information. So she curated their lies, their thefts, their backhanded dealings, waiting for the sweet little moments when she could strike back.

But this was not one of those times. Despite her rage at Amblys' fate, she knew that without a clear goal in mind she'd only end up wasting the precious ammunition she held. Besides, she reminded herself, she didn't have enough. Sure, she had dirt on low-level officers and bits of mid-level data, but not enough to trade for any real info – or any real action.

So she settled for taking her frustration out on the rich and powerful. It wasn't as cathartic as taking down someone on the force, but it managed to ease some of Burn's irritation, nonetheless.

She was so caught up in tracing the intricate lies of those in power that the sudden beep of her tab made her jump. She glanced down, abandoning her work once she saw the message.

Decoded it read: "We need to meet. 20 at Teak. – Hale"

20 minutes. The Lunaria were gathering in 20 minutes at their safe house in the Teak Sector. Why so soon? Burn racked her brain. It couldn't be about Amblys. That could wait; it wasn't like he could get more dead. She didn't have time to ponder, though. She had to get ready.

Burn jumped up from her desk, the sudden movement sending a wave of pain down her leg. She cringed but re-mained standing. Moving slower, she changed into a clean outfit and cloak, grabbing her mask and backup goggles on her way out of the room.

She made it all the way to the door and was about to exit when she heard a muffled "wait!" from the living room. She turned around, searching for Scar, and ultimately spot-ted her on the ground with her legs splayed on either side of yesterday's robotic head. Not looking up from her work, Scar merely pointed with a screwdriver to a nearby table and muttered something that sounded like "googles."

Glancing in the direction Scar had indicated, Burn saw a brand-new pair of goggles amidst the clutter of scraps and gears on the table. She walked over, picking them up and giving them a closer look.

They were beautiful. Leather straps connected the lenses, with intricate carved details that resembled a meadow glimpsed through a canopy of trees. She slipped them on and was delighted to find they were a perfect fit. As she adjusted them to sit on the bridge of her nose, the world suddenly sprang to life. Everything was a little brighter, a little sharper than before. Glancing at Scar, she could almost make out the individual hairs and wires in her unruly mane.

"These are...amazing," Burn stammered.

"Wait till you see the other features." Scar didn't even try to hide her pride. "Enhanced night sight. Increased transmission range. They even have a built-in camera. Handy for those late-night blackmail missions. And maybe one or two other things, but I'll let you discover those on your own."

"Thank you," Burn said earnestly. These were the nicest goggles she'd ever seen. People would pay a large sum for such a well-crafted piece of tech.

"Don't lose these," Scar said flatly. "I'm not making you another pair." With that, she went back to her robot.

Burn reminded herself of her mission and hastily related the update to Scarlett, who didn't look up from her work but gave a grunt acknowledging that she'd heard. With that done, Burn set off.

She didn't see any Peace Officers outside her house. That didn't mean they weren't there, although Burn had a feeling that after their fruitless stakeout and search yesterday, they had probably been called off. She wasn't about to take any chances, though. Unfortunately, she didn't have enough time to make a stop at Meera's or another such safe house, so she resorted to her tried and true evasion tactics to lose any would-be follower.

She weaved her way in between stalls and shops, taking sharp turns and ducking down dark alleys as she went. She didn't notice anyone on her tail, which was a relief, but she still continued her evasive maneuvers all the way to the Teak Sector.

After a few minutes, she came to a nondescript house and looked around surreptitiously before placing her finger on the biometric scanner. The door swung open and Burn ducked inside the dimly lit room, shutting the door quietly behind her.

She wasn't the first one there. A handful of people stood and sat around the room, whispering their theories as to the reason for the meeting. Hale, a burly Lunaria operative who worked out of the manufacturing sector, stood silently in the corner giving nothing away. He was over a head taller than Auburn, making her feel diminutive, and he gave off an air of silent censure.

It wasn't that she didn't like Hale. He had been part of the organization for far longer than she had and always contributed valuable information and insights. But she found him unpredictable, and his methods often favored violence over diplomatic action. That might have had something to do with his gift.

Hale was strong. Not godlike by any means, but definitely a convenient ally in a fight. His brute force skill set came in handy when breaking locks and gates – and heads. It was a counterpoint to Burn, who prided herself on stealth and secrecy, listening from the shadows. She knew there were times when you had to step out of the shadows and take real action, and people like Hale gave them an advantage. Still, his readiness for violence made Burn uncomfortable, so she had learned to give him a wide berth.

Burn picked a seat across the room and settled herself between two familiar members – Ramus and Symphandra – greeting each with a curt nod. Ramus, on her right, was a lean, gangly man with blond hair so light that it verged on white. Burn knew his gift had something to do with plants. It wasn't a wildly useful contribution in the subtle war they were waging, but it was refreshing, adding a little beauty to the blighted urban landscape of Kasis – and resulting in some delicious produce.

Symphandra, on the other hand, had no gift to speak of, but she was smart and cunning, and she brought forth a wealth of ideas on any proposed initiative. She was also hard to miss. Symphandra was an amazon of a woman, her extraordinary height accentuated by the dramatic leather high-heeled boots she always seemed to wear. They gave her the aura of someone otherworldly and dangerous, especially when paired with the leather corset she was currently sporting.

Burn looked closer at the garment and noticed that the pattern was almost identical to the one on her goggles.

Symphandra must have noticed her curiosity, because she turned and said, "You like? I did it myself."

"It's extraordinary," Burn said honestly. On her goggles, the pattern was small and ornate, resulting in a subtle kind of beauty. But on Symphandra's corset, the flowers and trees burst to life, climbing and growing from her waist up her ribcage until ultimately blooming on her chest.

"Actually, I think you may have had a hand in making these," Burn said, pointing to the goggles currently resting on her head.

"Oh, yeah!" she said excitedly, a smile brightening her face. "Scar drives a hard bargain, doesn't she? I gave her that AND one of my best belts in exchange for an upgrade to my goggles. Although she did throw in this pen," she said, her eyebrows waggling. As Symphandra produced the pen from her pocket, Burn instantly recognized Scar's handiwork.

"Hey, that will come in handy," Burn said, chuckling. "Just don't get it mixed up with your real pens. It comes as a bit of a shock, if you know what I mean." Both of them laughed lightly for a few seconds.

Their mirth was interrupted by a deep voice from the other side of the room. "Everybody, take your seats," Hale said commandingly. The rumble of chatter cut off immediately as the room obeyed, giving him their full attention.

The crowd had increased by a few members since Burn had entered, taking the total up to almost 20. These were the leaders of the Lunaria, the planners and decision-makers. They represented different classes, professions, and skills, and each brought with them their own background and their own reason to fight. But that desire to fight, to deliver a better world than they'd been handed, was what united them.

Hale took the floor in the center of the circular gathering, looking around at the faces of his comrades. He bathed in the silence, enjoying the palpable tension building around the room.

"Friends," he began slowly, "welcome. It's been too long. Too much has happened in our city – is happening in our city – that we must address. And too long have we stood on the sidelines, dipping our toes in the fight only when the waters are high."

He certainly possessed a commanding presence, Burn thought. The rest of the room seemed to feel the same, some staring in rapt attention while others nodded or clapped their hands in agreement.

"But before we act, we must know the terror we're acting against. To that end, I invite Burn to the floor to update us on the unfortunate situation regarding our newest recruit."

All eyes turned to Burn. The budding respect she'd been feeling for Hale turned to ice in her veins the instant he'd said her name.

Damn it, she thought. He was throwing her to the wolves, getting the crowd ready for action then tossing in a sacrificial lamb.

She got to her feet, slowly treading the short distance to the center of the circle. Unlike Hale, Burn was not meant for public speaking. She'd never been one for rousing speeches or debates, opting instead for a comfortable post on the sidelines from which to listen. That was her wheelhouse, and Hale knew it.

The room was silent as Burn scanned the upturned faces

around her. Her nerves fizzled, sending quick shocks of panic up her spine. She tamped them down, clearing her throat to rid it of its cobwebs.

"Thank you, Hale." Good, her voice sounded strong. She just had to keep it that way. "As many of you know, we've been tracking a proposed member to the group, a pickpocket and con artist who went by the name Amblys." A few nods greeted her from around the room, acknowledging her statements and urging her on.

"On the night of his initiation, however, we discovered that he'd betrayed us. The Peace Force appeared in the Corax End en masse, taking anyone and everyone they came across. Luckily, I was able to alert the others to stay away."

She had no doubt that her subsequent arrest was already common knowledge, but she thought better than to go into it. Her relationship with certain members of the force, like Detective Grayland, was polarizing, with many of the Lunaria still harboring their suspicions about her. Letting them know that he had helped her would add nothing to her credibility.

"The following night," Burn continued, jumping ahead in the story, "he was found dead in his home, murdered. It was made to look like suicide but was poorly done. It reeked of Peace Force intervention. The crime scene was itself a trap, with military members guarding the area in hopes of capturing a resistance member. They were once again unsuccessful."

No need to tell them about the chase, she decided on the spot. Or the injury. Or Kaz. Sensing that the crowd wanted some kind of wrap-up, like a heartening lesson or inspiring conclusion, Burn pressed on.

"The Peace Force is on high alert, sniffing out any signs of our existence. Stay safe. Report anything suspicious. Be on your guard."

With that, Burn nodded to Hale and resumed her seat. Her hands were sweaty, with indents where her nails had dug into her palms. She spared a glance over at Symphandra, who gave her a small smile and a nod. Burn relaxed a bit more into her seat, glad the whole thing was over.

Hale once again took his place in the center of the circle. "Thank you, B, for the update. But you're wrong." Burn stiffened in agitation as he continued. "Being on our guard is no longer enough. If we wait for their next move before we take action, it will already be too late."

Burn sighed quietly, bracing herself for yet another call to arms, which was Hale's first recourse in almost any situation.

"I have recently gathered some disquieting intel that, when paired with Burn's recent experiences, paints a grim picture for the future of Kasis. According to my informants, factories on the edge of the city have been steadily increasing their production of weapons components." He looked around, ensuring all eyes were on him for his next declaration. "The Peace Force is arming itself for war."

Murmurs danced across the room as people took in his words. Kasis wasn't close enough to any other planet for all-out warfare. If it had been, the military would have already sent out their troops to conquer more land in hopes of sending their "undesirables" off-planet. No, if the Peace Force was preparing for war, it would be against its own citizens.

Hale raised a hand for silence. "You know what we need

to do. We need to attack first. We need to infiltrate the factories, arm ourselves, and destroy the rest of the ammunitions. With the weapons in our hands we would finally have an advantage."

Burn couldn't stop herself. Standing up, she bit back, "We don't even know what they're planning. Shouldn't we learn as much as we can before blindly attacking? The armories are heavily guarded, highly fortified. Going in blind could decimate us."

Hearing whispered affirmations from the crowd, she continued, emboldened. "Besides, we don't have an army." Burn gestured at the handful of shopkeepers, tradespeople, and professionals around her. "Even if we were armed, the Peace Force would still have the advantage – in both numbers and tactical skills. And you know they would take any act of sabotage against their armories as high treason, putting the entire city on lockdown and killing anyone they saw fit, Lunaria or not. You wouldn't just be putting us in danger. You'd be putting all of Kasis at risk." More murmurs of assent from the crowd.

Before she even knew what she was saying, she continued, "I can find out what they're planning. Just give me time to listen in, to discover why the Peace Force is arming themselves. Then we can determine if an attack is even necessary."

Hale stared at her, wrath in his eyes. "Of course you would stand with *them*," he spat out. "They're coming for us. Why can't you see that? This is the only way we'll stand a chance."

"We can't protect the city if we're already dead." They stared at each other, the world dimming until it was just them, one against the other.

A new voice broke through the commotion, shaking Burn out of her stupor. "It's clear we have to do something," said Symphandra, coming to stand between Burn and Hale. "But it doesn't have to be one or the other. Burn's right that we need more information before we act. But, like Hale says, we do need to act."

Both Hale and Burn looked at her warily, unsure of where she was going.

Symphandra continued, unabated. "I say we give B time to discover their plans. Meanwhile, Hale returns to his contacts to get any additional information he can. We reconvene back here in three days to review the intel and plan a course of action."

"And if they make a move in the meantime?" Hale asked gruffly.

"We act," Symphandra said simply. Hale smirked. "Everyone in favor?" she asked. Hands shot up around the room, clearly favoring her compromise. "Then it's settled. Three days."

She turned to Burn, lowering her voice. "Good luck," she said before returning to her seat.

Burn stood there, lost in thought and unable to reply. Three days. She had three days to discover an entire secret plot and come up with a way to foil it that didn't include mass casualties. She would need more than luck on this one.

# CHAPTER 8

Burn paced down the hall for the hundredth time, going over her options. Or, to be more precise, her option. She'd been racking her brain for the better part of an hour but could only think of one way she could get the information she needed.

She had to go down to the station. She really didn't want to do that.

If only she could use blackmail to find out what they were planning, but she had nothing of that magnitude to leverage. If an officer were found to have tipped off someone to a plan like this, they would die, as would their family, friends, and possibly even their entire squad. General Cross made an example of traitors. Even with the best blackmail, no one would risk it.

So she would have to go to the source – literally. If she got within the Peace Station walls, she could listen in to conversations throughout the building. It was her best chance to overhear something of value.

The only problem was Cross. He wasn't exactly her biggest fan. If he saw her lurking around, there was no telling what he would do. The thought made Burn grimace.

But it was up to her. The Lunaria were depending on *her.* Cross be damned. If she got the information they needed, it would all be worth it in the end.

Buoyed by that thought, Burn grabbed her cloak and set off, throwing a quick farewell to Scar as she shot out the door. This was going to work, she told herself. She'd learn what they were planning, figure out a clever way to stop it, and avoid any bloodshed. It was all going to be fine.

By the time she arrived at the station, she'd nearly convinced herself, but the imposing structure, paired with the swarms of officers flowing in and out, put a dent in her confidence. She was on their turf now, and if anything went wrong she would be at their mercy.

She'd been coming to the station since she was a child, but somehow it still managed to amaze her. Polished white floors connected to double-height walls with arched ceilings, evoking the feel of a chapel rather than a prison. The space was lit with hundreds of incandescent lights, banishing the dim haze and replacing it with pristine radiance. The sudden brightness made Burn blink.

It was all a façade, of course, with beauty and light masking the true darkness within. It was the palace where Peace Officers played while Kasis burned. It was a lie. And she'd come to expose the truth.

But first, she needed an excuse to be there. Standing in the entry, she'd already gotten occasional looks from passing officers. She couldn't afford to be conspicuous, so she moved farther into the building, stationing herself at the end of a short queue.

In no time, she was at the front. She didn't recognize the officer behind the desk, but he was young and green, likely a new recruit forced to serve his time here before graduating to actual duty. Without glancing up, the man repeated the same line he'd presented to each previous citizen. "Please state your full name and your reason for coming here today."

"Auburn Alendra. I'm here to talk to Detective Grayland." The boy looked up, paying a bit more attention. Her name had struck a chord – hopefully because of her father and not because she'd been added to some sort of watch list.

"What's this regarding?" he asked, skeptical. It wasn't typical for commoners to walk in and demand a chat. "If it's a police matter, we have paperwork you can fill out..." his voice trailed off.

"No, nothing like that," Burn said, smiling sweetly. "He's an old friend of the family. In fact, he worked with my father, Arvense Alendra. You may have heard of him."

The boy nodded. Burn noticed that he kept glancing to her lips – and other parts of her – as she talked. She could work with that.

Burn inched closer to the desk, leaning in as she spoke. "I wanted to stop by and talk to him, to thank him for helping me out the other day." She placed her hand on top of his on the counter, then looked into his eyes, making hers as wide and sincere as possible. "It would mean so much to me to see him."

The boy swallowed, then stammered that he'd be more

than happy to assist. He indicated a bench along the wall and told her that if she'd care to wait, it would be his pleasure to personally find Grayland.

Burn took a seat. She felt guilty for manipulating the boy's emotions and hoped he wouldn't face any repercussions for leaving his post. But the sooner she got the information she'd come for, the sooner she could leave – and the less chance she'd have of running into Cross.

She scanned the lobby yet again to make sure he wasn't in the vicinity. Once she was sure of his absence, she closed her eyes and sharpened her hearing, searching for a clue. The building was abuzz with activity, each conversation merging with the next to create a constant hum. She focused in closer, scanning each group as she went. Typing, laughing, crying. Reports of pickpockets. Cracking down on ManniK dealers. Gossip about some opulent Peace Force party.

Nothing about ammunition or weapons or rebels. Nothing she could take back to the Lunaria. She needed to go deeper. This was merely the gateway, where the public and low-ranking officers mingled. What she needed was to get behind enemy lines, into the belly of the beast.

As if on cue, the eager officer returned with Grayland trailing in his wake. The detective smiled when he saw her, and she couldn't help but return it.

"Back so soon, Burn?" he asked lightheartedly.

"I couldn't stay away." They chuckled with the ease of old friends.

Noticing the officer was still stationed at his side, Grayland turned. "You can go now, Officer Straad."

The boy nodded and turned to leave but couldn't resist

another glance back at Burn, nearly colliding with another officer before finding his way safely back behind his desk.

"What did you do to that poor boy, Burn?" Grayland asked, his voice low and friendly.

She looked up at him, feigning innocence. "I have no idea what you mean."

He shook his head, not believing her for a second. "Don't go making trouble, Burn. I won't always be here to help you get out of it." He took a deep breath, changing the subject. "So, what can I do for you?"

"Do you think we could talk in your office?" she asked plainly. "It's just so loud out here." It was the truth, after all, although it wasn't exactly silence she was seeking.

Grayland didn't question her. Gesturing for her to follow, he snaked through the maze of desks and people until they reached a door at the end of the room. He pressed his thumb to the pad to grant them access to the inner sanctum. Weaving through yet more halls and doors, they inched closer and closer to the heart of the building.

Reaching Grayland's office, Burn situated herself in the low chair across from his desk. But instead of sitting behind it, Grayland perched on the corner, looking at her expectantly.

"I wanted to thank you for helping me out yesterday," Burn said truthfully. "My dad would have been grateful. It's the kind of thing he would have done."

"I was glad to help. You didn't belong down there," he replied gently. "But you didn't need to come to my office to tell me that."

"I know," Burn sighed. "I actually need one more small favor," she said, looking up at him sheepishly.

"Ahh, of course," he said, nodding. "Now we're getting somewhere. And what else do you need from me?"

"Well, I'm not sure if you heard, but our whole street had a routine search yesterday." Grayland shook his head. "They took my tab. There wasn't anything on it. Well, nothing important. Just...personal." If you could call a fake encrypted shopping list personal.

"I was hoping you could check on it? See if they're done processing it yet? It would be nice to have it back."

Grayland nodded knowingly. "You'd be surprised how often this happens. I can't promise anything, but I'll see what I can do. I'll be right back."

"Thank you," Burn said sincerely. His willingness to help her yet again, even with something so trivial, was a testament to his character.

Grayland nodded and departed, leaving Burn alone. This was her chance. She took a deep breath and closed her eyes, focusing on the sounds around her. Office chatter, typing, papers being pushed around. Not what she needed.

She shifted her attention to another part of the building, alighting on a spirited conversation. Apparently they'd recently brought in a dozen more dangerous "freaks" and stashed them in the cells. Interesting, but unhelpful. She scanned some more before another conversation piqued her interest.

"Did you hear they sent out a team to the Saffron Quarter?" said a male voice conspiratorially. Without waiting for a reply he continued, "Apparently some guy's gone insane. Started smashing anything he could find. Even took out a patrol officer who tried to stop him. Flung him across the street and into a wall."

Burn heard an intake of breath before another male voice replied, "Tough break, man. I bet it's more of that damn tainted ManniK that's been hitting the streets. The same thing happened last week. The cases are ramping up."

Again, interesting but not what Burn was searching for. She was getting frustrated and knew she only had a few minutes before Grayland returned. She took a deep breath, centering herself, and went deeper into the building.

Then she heard it – a familiar sneering voice that instantly made her blood boil: Illex Cross. Bingo, she thought, smiling.

"That's not enough," Cross said, low and insistent. "When the time comes, we'll need more officers on site."

"But sir," a smaller voice broke in, "we don't have enough protective gear. It won't be safe."

"As long as we have the weapons, we'll be fine," Cross cut back. "Just hand out the gear to the higher officers. The rest are disposable."

"What then?" the little voice asked. "What's the plan when we get there?"

This was it. Burn shut out all other stimuli, immersing herself in their words.

"When the men are assembled in the streets," Cross said casually, as if he'd gone over this a hundred times, "we're going to…"

But Cross' words were abruptly cut off by a third voice. "Sir, I'm glad I found you. Do you have a minute?"

No! Burn had been so close. Maybe Cross would send the man away and they'd pick up where they'd left off. Maybe the conversation could still be salvaged. Yet fate was not on her side.

"What do you want, Officer...?" Cross spat, searching for the man's name.

"It's Officer Petala, sir. Kaz Petala."

# CHAPTER 9

Burn froze, her head swimming. Kaz. The same Kaz whose house she had broken into. The same Kaz who had saved her from the Peace Force. He was one of them.

She had no doubt it was the same Kaz. The deep voice matched that of the man who had so gently taken her leg and dressed her wound. She listened with rapt attention as he continued.

"It's the prisoners, sir," he said. "A few of them are acting very strangely."

"How so?" Cross said flatly, with no hint of curiosity in his voice.

Once again, Burn wasn't destined to discover the answer. The door to the office suddenly swung open, startling Burn back to the present. She tried to slow down her pounding heart as Grayland entered.

"Well, Burn, I'm sad to say that I can't help you."

Burn stared at him, lost. She'd been so wrapped up in

the conversation with Cross and Kaz that she'd momentarily forgotten why she was there in the first place.

Grayland continued, not seeming to notice her confusion. "Apparently your tab has been misplaced. No one in evidence seems to know where it went. It's simply vanished."

Right, her tab. She was there to see about getting her tab back. She put on a disappointed face, hoping Grayland couldn't see past it to the turmoil within. Why did she even care that Kaz was on the Peace Force? He wasn't anything to her. Just a stranger she'd passed in the night.

Then it hit her. If he saw her there and asked around about her, he could easily learn about the tail that Cross had on her the night before. He'd figure out that she hadn't been where she was supposed to be. He could piece it together. The chase, the blood, the body. He could turn her in. She needed to get out of there.

"Well, thank you for checking. I'm sure it will turn up." Burn didn't even know what she was saying. She got up and moved toward the door, hoping Grayland would take it as a sign to show her out.

He seemed surprised at her sudden change of tone, but merely replied, "I'll let you know if we find it."

He opened the door and led her back out into the hall. Burn's concentration was shattered, and she could no longer locate Kaz or Cross in the building. She kept checking over her shoulder, expecting to see them appear behind her at any second.

Grayland guided her back the way they had come, the journey seeming to take 10 times longer than it had on the way in. Finally they reached the building's lobby.

"Say hi to Scar for me, will you?" asked Grayland.

Burn assured him she would and promised to keep in touch. With that, he left her and she turned to leave, relief peeking through the stress of the last few minutes. But she wasn't out of the woods yet.

"Well, well, well," said a cold voice behind her. "Who do we have here?" Burn stopped, not daring to turn around. Or speak. She merely stood there like a statue, her eyes trained on the exit.

Cross walked around her languidly, coming to stand between her and the doors as if blocking her escape. "Auburn Alendra. Back already?"

Shock and panic still fought in Burn's mind, making her feel stupid and slow. She knew she had to say something, but no words came to mind.

"I'm just here to see an old friend," she eventually managed to say, her voice tight and clipped. "Now, if you don't mind, I'll be on my way." She started to walk around him but stopped when a large hand latched onto her arm.

Cross' warm mouth dropped to her ear, whispering, "You have no friends here. Remember that." With that, he dropped her arm and sauntered off into the bowels of the station. Burn stood still, locked to the spot.

After a few beats, she risked a glance behind her to make sure he was gone. She could still feel his breath on her face and his hand digging into her arm. She tried to shake off the feeling, but it persisted, like a ghost of his presence.

Burn willed her feet to move, walking slowly through the doors, out, and down the front steps. She secured her goggles and mask, forcing herself to breathe. It was over. He was gone. She was fine.

A shout came from behind her, muffled by the crowd, but she didn't turn. Keep walking, she told herself. Get as far from this place as you can. The shout came again, this time louder, and she could now make out the words. "Auburn! Auburn Alendra!"

Not again, Burn cringed. She turned around slowly, coming face to face with Kaz.

He was smiling, the expression lighting up his face and making his green eyes twinkle. She hadn't noticed his eyes the night before. They were captivating. And dangerous, Burn reminded herself. He was a Peace Officer. And even though he didn't know it, he had the power to ruin her.

"How did you know my name?" Burn asked, keeping her voice low and glancing around. The last thing she needed was Cross to come out and see them together. Yet they seemed to be alone in the crowd.

"Officer Straad, the boy at the front desk," Kaz confessed sheepishly. "I saw you walking out and asked if he knew who you were. He seemed more than happy to tell me about you."

Burn cocked her head and shrugged. So Kaz didn't know more than the basics, she thought. Good. She wasn't in any immediate danger, although she would be if he kept asking questions or bringing her name up around the station.

"I didn't think I'd ever see you again," he continued. "You disappeared without even so much as a name. But now you're here. It's like fate."

Yup, Burn thought, it was fate alright. Fate's idea of a cruel joke.

She weighed her options. She could brush him off, say

"thanks but no thanks" and leave. Maybe then he'd forget about her and go on with his life. Or he'd start telling his coworkers – including Cross – the story of the odd girl who broke into his house, used him for a hideout, then ditched him the first chance she got.

On the other hand, she could play along and see where this whole thing went. He obviously liked her. He had chased her out into the street, for god's sake. Maybe she could use that.

She smiled, the latter option winning out. "I didn't think I'd see you again either."

"Are you sure?" he asked. "I mean, you did just turn up at my place of work. A day after breaking into my house. How do I know you're not stalking me?"

Burn was taken aback. When he put it that way, she did sound a little insane. Then she noticed the smirk playing at the corner of his lips.

"You caught me," she said, throwing her hands up. "I have a thing for Peace Officers. Must be some sort of daddy issue."

"Wait, your dad was an officer?" Kaz asked with surprise.

"Oh," Burn said, thrown. "I thought the esteemed Officer Straad would have mentioned that."

"No, I definitely would have remembered that. It was more like 'Hey, do you know who that girl is talking to General Cross?' 'Oh, her? That's Auburn Alendra. Isn't she perfect? I think I'm going to marry her.'"

"I really did make an impression, didn't I?" Burn said, her cheeks flushing. She had just needed his help. She hadn't intended to make the poor boy fall in love with her.

"Well...?" Kaz asked expectantly.

"Well, he's a nice boy, but not really my type."

Kaz let out a loud, booming laugh. "No, I meant 'well, your father was on the force?'"

"Oh, of course," Burn said, her face going redder. "Yeah, he was on the force for over 20 years. He went missing a few years ago. Presumed dead." Her voice took on a flat quality, the same way it always did when she discussed her father. Presumed dead? More like presumed murdered. Or presumed set up by that conniving boss of yours and tossed out like yesterday's garbage.

"Oh, I'm sorry," he said, faltering.

"It was a long time ago," was all Burn said in response. She was about to make up an excuse to leave when Kaz spoke again.

"Look, can I walk you home?"

"Won't you be missed?" Burn asked, glancing toward the towering Peace Station.

He perked up. "My shift just ended. I work the early shift." That would explain why he'd been asleep when she'd burst into his house. "Besides," he continued, "they can survive without me. It's not like the city is in imminent danger of collapse." He laughed.

Burn started. Was he being facetious – or did he know something? She studied his face but couldn't find any signs of seriousness. Instead, he just gazed back, as if studying her, as well.

"So, how about it?" he asked again, holding out his arm like some sort of old-fashioned gentleman.

Burn turned, ignoring the arm, and walked a few paces

78

before looking back over her shoulder. "Well? Are you coming?" Kaz sprang to life, closing the gap between them in a few long strides. "You better not slow me down," she warned him jokingly before setting off.

In the hazy daylight, Kaz looked different than he had in the darkness. She had thought his hair was black, but it now appeared a deep, rich brown. He had a straight nose and strong jaw, offset by a full mouth that seemed to be in a permanent smirk. It wasn't a look of superiority or derision – more a playfulness that made his eyes twinkle.

She watched as he pulled up his mask and dug his goggles out of his pocket, lowering them over his shaggy mane. In his full black uniform, he looked every bit the soldier. Tall and strong, walking like he owned the world.

Kaz caught her staring at him and she hastily looked away, focusing on the street in front of her.

"So," he said, breaking the silence. "Auburn. What really brought you to the station today? I mean, if you weren't there to see me – which I still think is a possibility."

Burn was silent for a time, debating how much to tell him. Letting him know about the search on her house would lead to questions that she didn't want to answer. Like why had she been the target of a search the same night she'd been on the run from some unknown thugs? The two things couldn't possibly be a coincidence. Anyone could see that.

So she told him simply, "I was there to see Detective Grayland. He was a friend of my father's – well, a friend of the family. I was hoping he could help me track down something that I'd lost. But no luck."

Kaz nodded, seeming to accept the story.

"Oh, and it's Burn, by the way," she threw in.

"Burn? What's burn?" Kaz asked, confused.

She chuckled. "I am. Auburn was my dad's idea. He thought it was cute, naming his daughters Scarlett and Auburn. He said he always wanted a colorful family."

"Hmm, Burn." Kaz considered the name, rolling it over on his tongue. "Nope, I don't like it," he finally declared.

Burn scoffed. "You don't like my name? What' wrong with it?"

He thought for a moment, choosing his words carefully. "It's too harsh, too...serious. Almost like a threat." Burn glared at him, but he continued on, purposefully ignoring her expression. "Auburn, on the other hand, now that's a good name. Pretty. You just seem like an Auburn to me."

If he only knew how well Burn suited her, he'd never call her Auburn again, she thought. But she let it drop. If he wanted to call her Auburn, let him.

The pair walked up a level, their pace slow. They passed shops and stalls and people haggling loudly for goods. Every once in a while, Burn would sneak a look at Kaz, measuring him up. And every once in a while, Burn could feel his gaze on her, no doubt doing the same. It felt strange and tentative, unsure but hopeful.

Burn couldn't help but smile slightly. It was nice to have someone notice her. Well, notice her as a woman and not just as a tool for subverting the military regime. It felt...unusual, and Burn didn't know what to say.

Thankfully, she was spared the trouble by Kaz, who took it upon himself to direct the conversation. "So, Auburn, tell me about yourself. What do you do for fun?"

Fun? The question stumped Burn. What *did* she do for fun? Sure, her life was full and rewarding. She had a mission, a purpose. But she didn't have fun, per se. Blackmail wasn't exactly a joy ride of a time. Neither was working for the Lunaria.

"Well, I guess I do what everyone else does," she said, trying to think on her feet. "I spend time with friends." The Lunaria. Not quite friends, but definitely a group of people with whom she spent a lot of time. "We talk about the world." And how corrupt it is. "We go out." And try to undermine the Peace Force and everything they do.

Kaz didn't seem satisfied with her answer. "Right..." he said.

"What do you want?" Burn bristled, getting defensive. "I don't have 'hobbies.' I can't sew or cook or do anything useful. Most of my time is spent figuring out how to get through the day. Buy the food, pay the bills, make sure the house doesn't fall down around me."

Instead of lashing out, like she had expected, Kaz chuckled. That seemed to be a habit of his.

"I don't really have hobbies either," he confessed. "I think that's just something people ask to be polite."

Burn felt her cheeks go red. She had overreacted big time. He was trying to make polite conversation and she had jumped down his throat. Well, this was going smoothly, she thought sarcastically.

"But I agree with you," Kaz went on. "Just getting through the day is enough of a battle without having to worry about 'fun' on top of it. Come to think of it, I don't think I've had fun since before I joined the force."

His mention of the force brought Burn back to herself. He was an officer, a part of the problem, not someone she should be getting close to. Instead of revealing anything else about herself, she should be using this opportunity to discover more about him.

"Why did you join the force?" she asked, trying not to sound too curious. She was curious, though. Was he one of those men who craved power? Did he aspire to climb the ranks and establish himself as a ruler among men? Was he just as corrupt as the rest of them? Burn found herself hoping he was different.

He considered her question, mulling over what to say. "I don't know," he finally said. "I was good at it. They said I was a natural. And I wanted so badly to be good at something."

"Right..." Burn said, mimicking Kaz's earlier response. She wanted more from the man, a real reason why he had joined up with that corrupt organization.

"You got me," he said, raising his hands in mock surrender. "I guess it was more than that."

His face went darker and he looked away, silent for a long beat. Then, without warning, he stopped walking. The sea of people around him parted, moving around this new obstacle. He didn't seem to notice.

Burn pulled him out of the main thoroughfare, dragging him into a nearby alley. The noise of the street was still audible there, but it was muted, dimmed to a background hum. Kaz looked at Burn, weighing whether or not to continue his story. She gave him an encouraging nod, hoping he'd go on.

"I was 7," he began timidly. "We didn't have much money. It was only the four of us – my parents, my older sister, and me. But we were happy. We lived…down there," he said, pointing toward the lower tiers.

"God, it's been so long since I thought about this." He looked into her eyes. "I'm not even sure why I'm telling you. I guess you just seem like the kind of person who would understand – what with your dad and all." Burn nodded, judging that it was better not to speak.

Kaz looked down the alley, as if watching the story play out in the distance. "My mother took us shopping, my sister and me. We did it all the time. Nothing was different or special. We needed bread or meat or something mundane. It was just an average day. Until it wasn't."

He lifted up his goggles, rubbing at his eyes. He looked different in that instant, weary and older somehow. For the first time, the twinkle was gone.

"We were on our way home," he said, replacing his goggles. "It was getting dark and my mom wanted us to hurry. But I wanted to look in the window of every single shop – at the gadgets and the treats and the people buying them. I think I was purposely dawdling, slowing us down so I didn't have to go home to chores and homework and all the other banes of childhood." He paused briefly before continuing.

"The man came out of nowhere. He wanted our shopping, our money, anything we had. My mom gave it to him, but he wasn't satisfied. He was sure that she was holding out on him. It was my sister who pushed me out of the way. I must have crawled behind a bench or something because he didn't notice me.

"He struck my mom first. He had a knife and he was so strong. My sister tried to help. She picked up a piece of metal and started for him, but he was faster. I watched it all. It didn't take very long. In a minute they were both down. And I just sat there, unable to move, unable to help. He ran. They never caught him. I don't think they even tried. Just another crime in the ghetto."

So it had been a desire for power that made him join the force after all – but not the type of power Burn had assumed. It was power as an antidote to powerlessness, power as a salve for injustice.

Kaz looked up at her, his gaze boring into hers. "That's the real reason why I helped you." His voice didn't waver. Neither did his eyes. "Because I couldn't then. Because I wished somebody had done that for them, protected them and given them a place to hide, no questions asked. Because it was a way to make up for what I didn't do then."

Something dawned on Burn. "The pipe?" she asked gently.

He let out a humorless laugh. "I've kept it by my bed ever since. It's the same one Fen had that day. That was her name, Fen. It's both protection and a reminder. Or it was, until I gave it to you."

The full force of his gesture struck her. That he had given her, a complete stranger, something so precious stunned her.

"Thank you," Burn said, genuinely touched. "I still have it. I'll get it for you when I get home."

"No, I have a feeling you need it more than I do," he said. His voice once again held the humor she'd gotten used to. "Come on," he said, holding out his hand. This time, Burn took it.

# CHAPTER 10

Kaz and Burn finished their walk in easy conversation. No more passed between them about Kaz's past, but something had shifted.

With Kaz's confession, his vulnerability, he'd unknowingly unlocked something. They no longer felt like strangers who had been forced together in a moment of crisis. They had lowered their guards and now felt more like friends getting reacquainted after a long absence.

Burn told him about Scarlett and her crazy projects and that one time she had almost set the house on fire. And he told her about the force and his friends and that one time that he, too, had almost set his house on fire.

For the first time in a very long time, Burn forgot about the Lunaria and her orders. She let go – and she discovered that she liked it. And sooner than either of them had hoped, they arrived at Burn's front door.

Neither of them wanted the conversation to end, but

Burn wasn't about to invite Kaz inside. Who knew what kind of thing Scarlett was currently concocting – what kind of anti-Peace Force thing? Or what kind of mood she was in. Whatever mood it was, it wouldn't be improved by the sudden appearance of a Peace Officer in their home.

Burn turned to face Kaz, her back to the door. "Thank you for walking me home," she said, smiling. "It was…nice." That wasn't quite the right word for it, but it worked. "I guess I'll see you around?"

"Yeah," Kaz said hesitantly. "Unless…" he trailed off, unsure.

"Unless what?" Burn asked, her curiosity piqued. She knew she shouldn't want to see him again, but she did.

Kaz worked up his nerve and looked her in the eye. "Unless you might want to go with me to the annual Peace Force ball tomorrow?"

"What?" Burn blurted out, despite the fact that she had heard him perfectly fine. She was just so shocked that her brain momentarily stopped working.

After the initial hiccup, though, it whirled into overdrive. She couldn't be seen at a police party. If Cross saw her, she had no idea what he would do, but it wouldn't be pleasant. Plus, she had just met this man. Despite their easy rapport, he wasn't yet someone she trusted – or even knew that much about.

Then again, she thought as her brain changed tracks, this could be exactly what she needed. In a room full of Peace Officers, drinking and letting their guards down, she could learn more than she ever could in the station. Her mind spun with the possibilities.

"I know it's probably stupid to ask," Kaz said, taking her silence as uncertainty. "I wasn't even planning on going. But it could be fun – if we went together, that is." He glanced up at Burn, his eyes hopeful.

Burn's stomach did a little flip. She told herself it was excitement about this new avenue of secret gathering, but it was more than that. It was the way he looked at her. And his nervous smile. She shook her head, trying to collect herself, but found her mind wandering down a different road entirely.

"My parents used to go to that, before my mother passed," she said, her voice low. "I remember them both looking so beautiful. My mother would put on her best dress and a pair of earrings, and suddenly some of the life would come back into her eyes. She looked younger, somehow, and more alive than I'd ever seen her. And when my dad saw her…he looked so proud. Like he held the jewel of Kasis in his arms."

Reality came rushing back as she remembered who she was talking to. Kaz. Peace Officer Kaz. She instructed herself to focus on the task at hand.

"But, Kaz, I don't know if I can go with you." She wanted him to protest, wanted him to ask why. She wasn't disappointed.

"What's wrong?" he asked, suddenly self-conscious. "Is there someone else? Did I misread this?"

Burn chuckled. "No, there's no one else," she said quickly. She faltered, unsure of how to explain.

Kaz jumped in, supplying another possibility. "Then you have plans? Another evening with your various friends talking about the world and going out to vague places in

87

search of fun?"

Now he was mocking her. It wasn't going to rile her. "Nope," she responded. "No plans."

"Then I fail to see the problem," Kaz said resolutely, as if making a point.

"It's General Cross," Burn finally blurted out. "I can't go because of Cross."

Kaz thought for a second. "Ah," he began sagely, as if he finally understood the situation. "I get it. You're in love with my boss. That is a problem."

At that, Burn let out a loud guffaw. That was not what she had expected and was, in fact, so far from the truth that it was absolutely absurd. She laughed freely, letting herself ride the waves as the humorous thought kept popping back into her head.

After her mirth subsided and she was able to catch her breath, she shook her head and stated, "No, not in love. Definitely not in love. Rather the opposite, I'm afraid."

"Phew," Kaz said, miming the motion of wiping his brow. "Well that's a relief. Because you're right; that would have been a problem. But you hating him? Now that's completely fine. It's understandable, actually." He leaned closer to Burn, whispering loudly in her ear. "In fact, most people who have met him secretly hate him. We're thinking of forming a club."

Burn smirked but didn't let his levity sidetrack her. She needed to make her point. He needed to know what he would be walking into if she was at his side tomorrow.

"I'm afraid it's a bit more than that. The feeling is mutual. He detests me. Just like he detested my father. Showing up with me might not be the smartest idea, especially if you intend to further your career on the force."

Kaz considered her for a beat, weighing her words. Burn was briefly afraid that he would heed her warning, that he would decide she was not worth the trouble and uninvite her. But her worries were for nothing.

"I think, dear lady, that you might be worth the risk," he declared gallantly. "So, will you come?"

So much could go wrong. It could all end up in fire and bloodshed. But there was a chance – a very small chance – that she could pull it off, that she could avoid Cross' detection, learn what they were planning, and get out of there alive. It would be risky, perhaps the riskiest thing she'd ever done. But it could also be wonderful. Wonderful for the cause, that is, not for herself.

Burn bobbed her head in a small nod of consent, and Kaz's face lit up. "But don't say I didn't warn you," she said, employing the old cliché. "If this all goes pear-shaped, you only have yourself to blame." Maybe adding on more clichés would drive the point home.

Kaz was too ecstatic to notice. She had said yes and that was all that mattered to him. Burn shook her head, an unusual feeling creeping into her stomach. She couldn't put a name to it, but it was something between excitement and pure dread.

"I'll pick you up here tomorrow night at about 7?" Kaz asked, his mind already captivated by the upcoming festivities.

"Fine," Burn said, mesmerized by his enthusiasm. It was contagious, like a single drop of brilliant color released in a colorless pool. You couldn't help but be affected, changed.

"Then, dear lady, I bid you adieu." He bowed, continuing his exaggerated gentility, and turned back the way they had come. Burn watched him weave his way through the crowd until he disappeared out of sight.

What had she gotten herself into?

Sometime later, Burn let herself inside. She still couldn't believe what she'd agreed to, and her head was swimming with visions of how the night could progress.

Lost in thought as she was, it was a bit of surprise when Scar popped up from behind a pile of clutter and demanded to know where she'd been.

Fifteen minutes later, with Scar caught up on the events of the day, the two sisters sat on the living room floor, pondering the situation. Burn was focused on the specifics of the event – how she would avoid Cross, how she would sneak away, how she would discover what the Peace Force was up to. But Scar's thoughts had gone in a different direction entirely.

"You know you're going to need a dress," Scar stated matter-of-factly. Burn stared at her, open-mouthed. She hadn't even thought of that – and was frankly surprised that Scar had.

"But I don't even own a dress," said Burn, mentally going through the few items in her closet. All of them were older, mostly patched, and not at all what anyone would call high fashion. And, of course, not one of them was a dress. Dresses weren't practical, and Burn had imbued practicality into every aspect of her life.

She looked to Scar, hoping she had a suggestion. "Well, I don't have a dress either," Scar responded, shrugging her shoulders. "I just know that you need one – and fast. Especially since the ball is tomorrow."

Burn tilted her head back, leaning it against Scar's robot for support, and stared at the ceiling. This whole spy thing was a lot more work than she had anticipated. And it hadn't even started yet. As adept as she was at gathering secrets, she had rarely gone undercover in order to gather them.

Instead of a life or death mission to infiltrate a military compound, she thought, what if she regarded the whole thing as a play? She would need to find a costume, get into character, and naturally slot herself into the story like she belonged, like she had always been there. She would need to adopt not only new clothes, but a new version of herself, one who felt at home in the top tiers, among the decision-makers and the elite. Among the people she had targeted and hated and plotted to bring down. That was going to require one hell of a dress.

While Burn contemplated her new role, Scarlett's mind was apparently on a separate track. "You take care of the dress, and I'll handle the accessories," she stated, scribbling furiously in one of her many notebooks.

Burn scoffed, a knee-jerk reaction. Scarlett had never accessorized anything in her life. The thought of her picking out jewelry and purses verged on the ridiculous. Then again, Burn had learned long ago not to question her older sister. So she shut her mouth and nodded. This was going to be interesting.

Half an hour later, as Burn tended to her affairs – or, rather, blackmailed other people for theirs – Scar silently entered her room, dropped a list on the table, and walked out.

This was a common habit of her sister's. She would get an idea into her head for a new project, set to work meticulously listing everything she would need down to the smallest screw, then send Burn out to gather it all.

The contents of this particular note did make Burn raise an eyebrow, though. Unlike Scar's typical demands, which usually read like a parts inventory of a small vehicle, this one seemed more like the shopping list of a typical Kasis housewife. Fabric, thread, needles, a pair of stockings, a plain silver chain. These were things normal women bought, women who cooked casseroles and patched up holey socks and made sure the children had new school clothes. Scar and Burn were not such women.

The last few things on the list, however, were more Scar's style. Computerized chips, sensors, switches, and gages, paired with scrap metal and casing components. It was everything Scar needed to build her own brand of microelectronic masterpieces. She was creating an accessory artillery, Burn realized as she reread the list, a wearable set of devices and gadgets perfectly suited to the undercover role she was undertaking. She was simultaneously anxious and elated.

Now the only problem would be finding it all. Scar had long since trained her on where to find the best chips and parts, showing her how to recognize fakes on peddler carts and dig through scrap heaps for buried treasure. That part of the list was simple, just a matter of getting the best deal or finding her way through the detritus mills without cutting herself too badly on the sharp metal waste.

It was the rest of the list that was giving Burn trouble. Jewelry? Fabric? Burn racked her brain trying to remember the location of shops and stalls that sold such domestic wares. She was at a loss. She needed help.

As the evening wore on, Burn made her way down an unfamiliar street. Her arms were already laden with several bags of electrical components and spare parts, everything Scar had listed apart from the actual accessories. She'd had great luck at the scrap heaps — although not so much luck with the haggling peddlers. But, after some terse negotiations, she had managed to check off all the items without too much financial strain.

Burn stopped outside of a colorful red door, decorated with flowers and vines in a familiar pattern. She checked her tab to make sure she was in the right place, despite the fact that she knew she was. She had never been here before, but it felt cheery and welcoming, like a beckoning oasis on the otherwise dim lane.

She knocked on the door in three successive raps, then waited. After a moment, she heard a click that sounded like a peep hole opening before the red door swung open. Symphandra stood in the soft yellow light, a smile beaming from her unmasked face.

"Come in, come in," she beckoned, stepping aside to let her through. Burn did as she was told, crossing the threshold into the warm interior.

The inside of Symphandra's house was unlike any home she had previously been in. It was a riot of color — hanging on the walls, covering every surface, even resting on the floor under her feet. There were soft blankets, half-finished leather projects, clothes draped on bright couches, and walls drenched in the brightest hues.

It wasn't neat or organized, but it was a festival for the senses. The home even smelled like it looked: bright and exotic, with wafts of citrus and spice.

The house itself was narrow, with a small living space on the right and a dining area on the left that led off into the kitchen. Beyond the living room lay a single closed door, likely the home's only bedroom. But instead of feeling cramped, the space felt enveloping, like a pair of soft arms welcoming you into its embrace. It felt like Symphandra and exuded the same vivid liveliness.

As Burn took in her surroundings, Symphandra offered her some tea, which she gladly accepted. She settled herself on one of the soft living room sofas, this one a bright red color verging on orange. Burn wondered to herself where Symphandra had found such eccentric furnishings. Kasis wasn't ablaze with colorful goods or accessories, although Burn supposed she just didn't know where to look. Maybe somewhere there was a different kind of scrap heap where, instead of wires and gears, you could dig through drapery and cushions. The thought made her smile.

After a few minutes, Symphandra returned with the tea. It was a sweet-smelling brew that mimicked the scent of the house, with spicy notes that bit at her nose and tickled her taste buds as she sipped.

"Thanks for helping me," Burn said in between sips of her tea. "My sister and I aren't...well, we've never put much thought into what we wear." She looked down into her cup, as if it held the words she was looking for. "I guess that's kind of something a mother teaches her daughters. But ours was…she didn't get the chance. So Scar and I ended up dressing like our father instead." Burn laughed and Symphandra laughed along with her.

"So, tell me what you need," Symphandra said, inviting Burn to explain more. All Burn had told her so far was that she needed a dress, something glamorous. It was unquestionably out of character for her, so Symphandra was naturally curious.

But before explaining further, Burn paused and asked, "Can you keep a secret? Because I need this to stay between us and not reach the Lunaria."

Symphandra nodded, even more curious than before. "Of course," she replied. "Whatever you need."

Burn hoped she was telling the truth. "I have a plan. A very risky plan. One that Hale would shut down in a heartbeat. But it's the only way to find out more about what the Peace Force is up to." She took a breath, preparing herself. "I'm attending the Peace Force ball."

Symphandra was suitably stunned. Whatever she had expected Burn to say, it clearly wasn't that. "But how?" she asked, confused. "Are you planning to sneak in? I mean, you're not really on friendly terms with most of the force. Especially Cross." She spat the general's name out like a curse.

"Not exactly." She wasn't sure how to explain this part, but she started in anyway. "I do have one friend on the inside. He's a new friend. A very new friend. And yesterday he asked me to the ball. Which was kind of perfect since my first plan crashed and burned."

Symphandra didn't comment on the way Burn smiled when she talked about her "friend," although she clearly noticed. "Hale wouldn't approve of that, either," was all she said on the matter.

"Right," she continued, getting down to business. "Well, we have our work cut out for us." She eyed Burn and her shabby clothes. Burn would have taken offence if the statement wasn't, in fact, completely warranted.

Symphandra led Burn back into her bedroom, which was also adorned in colorful fabrics and soft cushions, with a small, fluffy bed situated along the wall. Burn took a seat as Symphandra began rifling through her closet.

Burn was more than a little doubtful that anything in there would fit her. Symphandra was taller than she was, as well as more…heavily endowed. Burn glanced at her own flat chest, suddenly self-conscious and afraid she would look like a little girl playing dress-up in her mother's clothes.

Symphandra clearly harbored none of the same fears because she emerged from the closet with an armful of garments, each as colorful as the next. She handed the top few to Burn, then directed her to the attached bathroom to change.

The first dress was green and gauzy, a flowing thing that felt soft and feminine going over her head. Once on, however, she appeared to be drowning in the fabric. Symphandra no doubt looked like a goddess in it, but she looked like she had stumbled into a tent and had walked out with it around her neck.

The next dress was equally unsuccessful. A tight red number, she couldn't even figure out how to get the complicated dress over her head, so she gave up. A lacey purple gown, an orange backless dress, and a pink thing covered in tulle all met with similar fates. Soon, Burn felt like every color in the rainbow had betrayed her. But Symphandra was tireless, pulling dress after dress from a seemingly bottomless closet for Burn to try on and discard.

Eventually, near the bottom of the pile, Symphandra pulled out a midnight blue gown bordering on black, handing it over for Burn to try. The material felt like water in her hands, a slippery cool fabric that felt wonderful against her skin. She pulled it over her head, hoping that this was the one, but she was once again disappointed. It was too big, made for someone with more chest and more leg. But it was beautiful.

She went out and showed Symphandra anyway, then turned back to try on another dress, but Symphandra stopped her. She turned Burn to face her, then considered the dress for a moment before going to work. She tugged at the laces crisscrossing the sides of the dress, tightening the fabric to a silhouette more similar to Burn's. Then she started in on the hem, pinning it along the ground so it sat even with her feet. Next she turned her attention to Burn's hair, twisting the short mane at the base of her neck and pinning it in place.

Symphandra stepped back, admiring her handiwork. "I think that might just work," she mused thoughtfully. With a light hand, she turned Burn to face the mirror on the opposite wall.

What Burn saw made her gasp. The gown had gone from too big to fitted, hugging the small curves of her body and dropping elegantly down. At first glance she had assumed that the dress was a solid blue, but she'd been wrong. Within the blue there were twists and twirls of a deeper blue that shimmered when she moved, like the night sky had transposed itself onto her body.

Along the sides were elegant laces, pulled tight, but through the gaps you could see hints of a soft black fabric, adding another level of darkness to the night sky. Small strips of fabric that were not quite sleeves attached at the bust and rested on the tops of her arms, just below her shoulders. The pulling and pinning had done its job and the dress now accentuated Burn's delicate figure, pushing up her small breasts and emphasizing her narrow hips. The whole dress cascaded down to the floor, with a delicate knee-height slit on the right side that added a sensual element to the graceful gown.

"It's beautiful," Burn said, feeling that the word was inadequate but unable to come up with something better. Even her hair looked elegant, twisted back in a style she'd never worn before with loose wisps encircling her face. She twirled back and forth slightly, feeling the dress waft softly across her legs and watching as the fabric shimmered.

"It's perfect," Symphandra replied, pleased with herself. "Just give me a few minutes to hem it."

Burn reluctantly took the dress off, careful not to stick herself on the pinned hem. Once again back in her normal clothes, she felt too plain somehow, like she was hiding behind the neutral colors and baggy fabric. She shook off the feeling and returned to the living room, where Symphandra was already at work shortening the garment to Burn's measurements.

"Did you make all of those clothes?" Burn asked, watching her friend's skilled fingers glide over the fabric as the sewing machine did its job.

"Yeah," she replied nonchalantly. "I got tired of blending in. I wanted to stand out."

"Well, you certainly do. Stand out, that is," Burn clarified. Symphandra smiled as she worked, pleased.

"Most Kasians like to blend in," Symphandra mused. "There's nothing wrong with that. I make clothes and masks that help them do that. But I always try to add a little beauty to everything I make, something that goes beyond functionality. It makes me feel like I'm covering the city in small works of art, at least for a time."

It was a beautiful way to look at the world. Burn's mind couldn't help returning to the flowers and vines covering her goggles and the matching ones on Symphandra's corset. They were little bits of life in a dead city.

It must be nice to be able to add beauty where there was none, Burn pondered. She felt a stab of jealousy, but it promptly passed. She might not be adding beauty to the city, but she was fighting for justice. There was beauty of a sort in that, she reminded herself.

Within no time, Symphandra was done hemming the dress and held it up to Burn for inspection. The length was now perfect, and Burn felt a hum of excitement when she thought about putting the garment back on for the ball. With her costume now secured, Burn's spy mission felt simultaneously more real and more feasible than it had before.

As Symphandra put the dress in a garment bag for transport, Burn's mind returned to the list Scarlett had given her. She pulled it out of her pocket and examined the items again. Fabric, thread, needles, a pair of stockings, a plain silver chain.

She handed the list to Symphandra, asking if she might know where to get such things. Symphandra considered the list for a moment before ducking back into her room. She returned with her hands full of items, placing them delicately on the table in front of Burn.

"I don't have a silver chain, but I know a local merchant who can help with that. He always gives me a good price," Symphandra said.

Burn glanced down at the items in front of her. There was a piece of dark blue fabric with shimmering swirls, the exact same material that had been used to construct her dress. Next to it was a little pocket sewing kit, containing a needle, thread, a thimble, and a few other small instruments Burn couldn't place. There was also a nearly sheer pair of stockings that looked almost as silky as her gown. She automatically reached out to caress them, feeling the soft fabric slip through her fingers.

"Thank you," said Burn sincerely. She was struck by Symphandra's generosity and her eagerness to help. She hadn't known a lot of that in her life, so it always caught her by surprise.

Symphandra just nodded and helped Burn pack the things carefully into the garment bag with her dress. Then she wrote down the name and location of the jewelry vendor who sold the silver chains and handed it to Burn.

As Burn turned to go, Symphandra spoke, stopping her. "Be careful tomorrow," she said, nervous for the first time. "If they even suspect that you're up to something, they'll make sure you never get out of there."

Burn's nerves fizzled as if waking up. Symphandra's tension was contagious, and she felt her own heartbeat quicken. Still facing the door, her body turned away from Symphandra, Burn replied, "If something happens…if I don't make it back, tell them what happened. Tell them I tried."

"Of course," Symphandra stated like a general, her voice no longer betraying any emotion.

Collecting herself, Burn continued, "I'll send word back as soon as I learn anything. With luck, I could know their whole plan by midnight tomorrow."

"Good luck," she heard as she opened the door. She didn't look back.

# CHAPTER 11

Burn lay in bed that night, going over her plan and mentally listing all of the ways it could go wrong. There were a lot of them.

They could scan her and refuse her entrance to the party. They could discover one of Scar's gadgets while searching for weapons and arrest her. Or she could gain access to the ball only to find herself trapped inside, caught red-handed in her espionage and surrounded by teams upon teams of enemy soldiers.

Somehow, analyzing all of these dire possibilities made Burn feel better, as if she were preparing herself for the worst-case scenario – and coming to terms with her own fate.

As Burn contemplated the myriad ways she could be discovered and punished, Scar toiled away in the living room, creating Burn's secret arsenal of accessories. Burn could hear the intermittent sounds of a welding gun, a small saw biting its way through metal, and a hammer crashing down on whatever was in its path. She found the familiar sounds of her sister's tools comforting, and the hum and whine and banging eased some of her tension.

Her thoughts drifted to Scar, and Burn wondered what would happen to her sister if she never returned home. Scar was amazing in so many ways, but she wasn't built for a solitary life. No, Burn thought, she had to get through this. She had to come home for Scar. And for the Lunaria. They were counting on her.

The next day dawned bright and warm – or at least as bright and warm as it could get on Kasis. As Burn woke, the sound of her sister's tools once again greeted her ears. Scar had worked through the night getting everything ready for her. Burn smiled sleepily at the gesture as her brain steadily came back to life.

She closed her eyes and let the sounds of the city filter through her, listening for anything out of place. For some reason, it felt like the world should be different today, but the sounds that met her ears were normal and mundane, the sounds of everyday life going on just as it had before. Maybe it was Burn that was different.

She felt different. No, that wasn't it. She felt…nervous. Or excited. Or scared. Or some other mess of emotions that marked the day as significant. Her body seemed to tingle in anticipation, its nerve endings alight and her muscles prepared for action.

Burn had to remind herself that she still had half a day

to go before the ball. She felt both annoyed and relieved, two more warring emotions to add to the confusing jumble in her brain.

That also meant she had 12 hours to kill. She immediately regretted her brain's choice of words. No killing. Killing bad. Twelve hours to mildly assault? Or 12 hours to inflict minor wounds that would heal with little to no surgical intervention? Maybe she hadn't gotten enough sleep after all.

Burn shook the last of the fog from her brain and decided some sort of caffeinated beverage was in order. She dragged herself up from the bed, her body painfully reminding her that it had only been a few days since she had been chased through the streets by officers and accosted by a sharp metal gutter. The wound on her leg was still far from healed, but the pain had gone from insistent to mildly annoying.

She plodded to the bathroom, taking a few extra minutes to unwrap her leg and inspect the injury. It wasn't infected, which was a relief. It still looked angry and red, though, and would definitely leave a jagged scar along her shin. Burn carefully dabbed ointment on it before wrapping it back up in a protective bandage.

She hoped that the evening's festivities wouldn't involve dancing, as she didn't know how well her leg would hold up to such an assault. Plus, she didn't know how to dance. It wasn't precisely part of the standard curriculum on Kasis, and her father had never considered it an important skill to teach his daughters. No, evading police tails and eavesdropping on unsuspecting targets had been much more important lessons.

Her wound properly tended to and her morning routine complete, Burn changed into a loose-fitting gray tunic and black pants, throwing on a light black cloak for good measure. She passed Scar on her way out, yelling "I'm getting breakfast" over the clanging. Scar didn't respond, meaning she either hadn't heard or she didn't consider a response to be socially necessary.

Donning her mask and goggles, Burn merged with the clusters of people making their way through the city streets. She listened as she walked amongst them, absorbing their murmured pleasantries and heated conversations.

"Can't talk. I'm late." "I saw you flirting with her! You bastard." "But mom! I want it!"

So many lives, so many stories. Their words mingled with the sounds of the city – engines purring and metal grinding and thousands upon thousands of footsteps climbing and descending the city's many levels.

Burn was so wrapped up in the sounds of the city that she didn't notice the large man in the alley until he grabbed her arm and dragged her off the street. She gave a shout of surprise, but a beefy hand abruptly clapped over her mouth. Then a familiar voice whispered from behind her.

"I've been looking for you," Hale said, his mouth to her ear. "You've been a hard person to track down." He let his hand drop from her mouth and loosened his grip on her arm, allowing her to turn and face him in the narrow lane.

"What do you want, H? I still have two more days to figure out what's going on, in case you've forgotten." Her quick burst of fear had mellowed into simmering anger.

"I know," said Hale coolly. "I wanted to check in, see what progress you've made."

"If I'd learned anything you would know." Burn's voice

was clipped.

"Would we? Sometimes I'm not sure whose side you're on." He was bating her, Burn thought, hoping to get a rise out of her. It wouldn't work.

"I've never done anything to make you or anyone else question my allegiance," she responded evenly.

"Except hang around with Peace Officers," he said accusingly. Her mind flashed to Kaz. How did Hale know about him? Had he been following her? Or had Symphandra betrayed her?

"You're too close with your father's *associates*," Hale continued, unconcerned by Burn's sudden silence. She felt her body relax in response. He didn't know about Kaz after all.

He kept talking, glaring at her through his goggles. "The Peace Force has been one step ahead of us this entire time. How do we know you're not playing us, stalling so they can get their plan in motion? It would be so easy for you to take us down."

So Hale thought she was a spy for the other side. She knew that he had never trusted her, but this was something else entirely. The accusation felt like fire in her blood.

"I've never done *anything* to endanger our cause," she spat out, careful not to mention the Lunaria. You never knew who was listening. "I have a plan. I'm going to get the information tonight. And as soon as I have it, I'll let you know."

Hale was still glaring at her, his mouth set in a hard line. She continued, "And if you ever question my loyalty again, you will come to regret it." With that, she tore herself out of his grasp and stepped back onto the crowded street, weaving between people and carts in an attempt to lose herself in the maze of bodies.

How dare he question her allegiance, Burn thought, fuming. She had been instrumental in countless Lunaria operations. She had gathered scores of new information, recruited operatives, and discovered fresh avenues through which to target the Peace Force. The idea of her being some sort of double agent was, frankly, absurd.

Hale was probably just jealous, she reasoned, trying to find a motive for his outburst. Her plan had been chosen while his sat on the back burner. Still, she didn't need an enemy on her own team, working against her from the inside. She silently prayed that he wasn't already sewing doubt among the other members.

She needed that night's mission to be a success. If she returned to the Lunaria with a full account of the Peace Force's plans, no one would be able to question her fealty, not even Hale. She imagined the look on his face if she were to succeed, and it calmed her. She stopped weaving in and out of the crowd and slowed to a more moderate walk.

Burn had been so focused on getting away from Hale that she hadn't even been paying attention to where she was going. She looked around, trying to regain her bearings.

Carts and stalls lined the road, just like in every other part of the city. But instead of selling electronics or supplies, the vendors here were holding out flowers and sweet treats and books. She had apparently wandered into the Collina Quarter, an area of Kasis known for its "luxury" goods. It was typically frequented by those of a higher status level than Burn, and her family had never spent much time in the area.

Instead of backtracking, Burn slowed, enjoying the

colorful products and sweet smells wafting from the various carts. She stopped beside one selling flowers and bent her head to sniff at the intoxicating scent.

The harsh atmosphere and high levels of pollution made it hard to grow flowers on Kasis, so they weren't a common sight. Once in a while, a house with a window box or a planter pot might manage to make a flower or two sprout from their secondhand soil, but the blooms were often small and delicate. These, on the other hand, were strong and vibrant, with colors and shapes Burn had never seen.

She wandered around the cart, her attention caught by a brilliant red flower. The sight brought back a half-forgotten memory of her mother pinning a similar flower to her father's suit. It must have been right before the Peace Force ball. She smiled and fingered the silky petals.

The vendor noticed her attention and asked if she was interested in purchasing a bouquet. Burn started to protest but changed her mind mid-sentence and ended up ordering a single stem of the bright red flower. She imagined pinning it to Kaz's suit, just like her mother had. It somehow made her feel more connected to the mother she had hardly known and the father she missed so dearly.

She spent a while longer browsing the wares of the Collina Quarter. Most of the products and goods were out of her price range, but she did splurge on a coffee and a buttery pastry that melted in her mouth. She imagined what it would be like to have such luxury at her fingertips every day. Would she get used to it? Would she take it for granted?

She watched the people around her, the people who could afford to have such things delivered to them on a daily basis, and frowned. They lived in a world of their own, barely aware of the grit and poverty that existed only a few zones away. Here they were, reveling in their good fortune, while the rest of Kasis struggled to survive.

The sweet scent of the quarter suddenly soured and Burn turned, now eager to leave. She did, however, pick up another coffee and pastry for Scar on her way out. Luxury was nothing if you couldn't share it with someone, she decided.

Scar was sewing when Burn arrived home. It was a strange sight: Scar, a girl made of metal, with her legs crossed and her head bent low over a needle and thread. Burn hadn't even known she could sew. She wondered briefly what other skills her sister was hiding.

"I brought you something," Burn said, holding up the pastry and coffee. Scar looked up, but instead of answering just cocked her head in question before returning to her work.

"Long story," Burn continued. "Just enjoy it." She placed the items next to Scar before taking a seat on the small armchair opposite her. She let out a long sigh as she sank into the sagging cushions and put her head back.

With her eyes closed, she relayed a general overview of the morning's events as Scar continued her sewing, pausing every so often to sip the coffee or nibble the pastry. "Hale still doesn't trust me. He thinks I'm going to double cross him the first chance I get. You'd think that years of loyalty would count for something." Another sigh.

"Well, there might be a reason for that," Scar said

cryptically.

"What – something other than his desire to control everything and everyone?" Burn asked tartly. Scar just looked at her with a knowing smile.

"What have you done?" Burn queried, suddenly suspicious. "Scar?"

"I needed to find out if Hale was a threat. So I took certain steps to ensure that I could keep tabs on him."

An uneasy feeling began churning in the pit of Burn's stomach. "What did you do?" she repeated, emphasizing each word in an attempt to draw out the truth.

Scar's smile grew. "I hacked his tab," she said simply, like it was something people did every day. Although, to be fair, it *was* something she did every day.

"Scar!" Burn declared. "You can't go around invading people's privacy like that."

"Why not?" she countered. "We do it all the time to the people you're blackmailing."

Scar had a point. Although this felt different somehow, underhanded in a way that put Burn on edge.

"If Hale ever found out, there's no telling what he would do. He'd certainly have us kicked out of the Lunaria – if not worse."

"Good thing my hacks are untraceable, then," Scar said proudly.

Burn sighed, rubbing her eyes. Sometimes there was no use reasoning with her sister. She just had to go with it.

"So, what did you learn?" Burn asked, giving in. "Why is he so dead set against me?"

"Well, I've only managed to gather snippets so far, but

it's enough to piece together a picture. Apparently, he lost someone to the Peace Force, a woman. I don't know the particulars, only that he's never forgiven them – or himself."

"He's never mentioned anything like that," Burn mused, processing this new information. "But what does that have to do with me?"

"Ever since then, he's dedicated himself to bringing them down, whatever the cost," Scar continued. "I think in his mind, you're either completely against them or you're not worth his time."

"So that's why he doesn't tolerate anything – or anyone – associated with the Peace Force? That's ludicrous."

Scar shrugged. "When dad went missing, you wanted the Peace Force to pay. You saw them as the enemy – and still do. How is that any different?"

"Because I know that there are exceptions to the rule, good people who are trying to make a difference. Like dad. Like Grayland. Why can't he see that?"

"I think some people are just scared to trust those with different ideas," Scar said quietly. Burn lifted her head to look at her sister. "Hate is what he knows. It makes sense to him. It's comfortable," Scar continued. "Then you come along and disrupt his status quo. You shoot down his ideas, bring your own way of doing things, and involve people he's always considered to be enemies. Of course he's going to lash out."

"When did you become such an expert on people?" For someone who didn't get out much, Burn thought, she sure did notice a lot.

Scar ignored her sister's question and continued. "Don't be so quick to judge him. You're on the same side, remember that. Someday you're going to need him."

Burn groaned. She hated the thought of needing Hale – or needing anyone, for that matter. She would rather go it alone. Other people just tended to complicate matters.

"Done," Scar said, putting down her needle and cutting a final thread. She held up her handiwork proudly. Burn crouched forward in her chair to get a better look.

"It's a purse," Burn said, stating the obvious. Scar had used the extra fabric from Symphandra to make a small reticule that matched her gown. The pouch was about the size of a small picture frame, and it cinched at the top with a blue cord that doubled as a handle.

Scar smiled a wicked little grin. She held up a finger, indicating that Burn should wait, and she scampered around the room placing objects in the bag. After a minute, she returned to her seat and handed the bag to Burn.

It was heavier than it looked. Burn put the bag over her wrist, testing its weight on her arm, and deemed it comfortable enough to carry for an evening. She looked closer at the bag's exterior, but nothing seemed out of the ordinary. The stitching was small and neat, and the handbag itself looked just like any other.

She turned her attention to the bag's interior, dumping its contents out onto her lap. Once again, very ordinary. A tube of lipstick, a pair of eyeglasses, a tin of mint candies, a cash card. Burn also pulled out a pair of earrings adorned with sparkling black stones and a necklace comprised of a simple silver chain with another solitary black stone affixed at its center.

Burn turned the items around in her hands, but all of

them appeared completely normal, just the average contents of a woman's purse. But that wasn't Scar's style. No, there was something else to these items that she wasn't seeing. She looked to Scar, knowing she must be bursting to explain her ingenious arsenal.

Just as she had expected, Scar was beaming. "OK, I give up," Burn said, yielding to her sister. "What are they?"

Scar jumped up to demonstrate her genius, picking up the lipstick first. "On one side, it's a normal women's lipstick." She opened the cap to show Burn the bright red wax. "But on the other..." Scar twisted the bottom of the container to reveal a secret compartment from which she withdrew Burn's small fingerprint bypass tube. "This will get you through most normal doors. However, I assume there will be added security, which is why I also gave you these." Scar picked up the glasses.

Burn didn't need corrective lenses, so the glasses obviously had a different purpose. "Let me guess," said Burn, "they'll bypass any retinal scan?"

Scar looked a little crestfallen that Burn had beaten her to the explanation, but she kept going, nonetheless. "Yes, but there's more. They're also equipped with telescopic lenses, night vision, and a beta version of a lip-reading program. And just like your goggles, they'll only work for you."

Burn was impressed. Those would definitely come in handy, she thought. Scar continued, picking up the cash card.

"If you encounter a computerized tab or system, put this on top of it and signal me. It will give me remote access to the system, and I can find a back way into the device, overriding its security measures."

"Signal you?" Burn asked. She wouldn't have her goggles on, since the party was taking place indoors, and Scar hadn't mentioned a messaging feature on the glasses.

Scar's self-satisfaction leveled up a notch and she grinned wickedly. "The necklace is a comms unit. Hold down the center stone and I'll be able to hear anything you say. And the earrings will relay my response. They're tuned to an ultra-low volume so only you will be able to hear me. Even if someone else put them on, unless they had your gift they wouldn't be able to hear a thing."

"Genius," Burn murmured, admiring Scar's handiwork. Even on closer inspection, Burn could see nothing of the jewelry's true nature.

A little of her tension abated. With Scar there, on the other side of her comms, she wouldn't be alone in this. They would be going in together, with her as the eyes and ears and Scar as the mad genius in charge of everything else. Together, they could handle this.

Burn ran her eyes over the equipment again, this time stopping on the tin of mints. "Wait, you didn't tell me about these." She picked up the tin and moved to shake it, but Scar's hand darted out and grasped her arm. The look in her eyes was deadly.

"Don't do that. At least not unless you want your arm blown off." Scar took the tin of mints from her hand and carefully placed it back in the handbag. "They're explosives," she explained, a little belatedly. "They're sort of a last resort. If you're backed into a corner and have no way to get out, throw one of these. The ensuing chaos should give you enough time to escape."

Burn's eyes widened in understanding. "Good to know," was all she could think to say. She hoped she wouldn't run into a situation where those were necessary. Exploding a bomb – no matter how small – inside a Peace Force party would certainly raise some questions.

Burn's gaze swept over the objects in front of her, taking in the new equipment. She could now get through any door, crack any computer, and even blow up small targets, all while in constant contact with Scar. It was a Peace Officer's wet dream. Plus, it was all packaged in an utterly unassuming handbag.

Curious, Burn picked up the bag itself, turning it over in her hands before reaching inside to feel around. No secret pockets that she could find. No obvious weapons components or hidden function. It seemed to be an ordinary bag. Scar looked on as Burn carried out her inspection. Giving up, Burn held it out to Scar for an explanation.

"Technically, it's an ordinary handbag," Scar started. Burn doubted that. Nothing Scar created was ordinary. There was definitely something else to it. She raised an eyebrow to coax more from her sister.

"OK, OK," Scar gave in. "It's a normal handbag in that it doesn't have any weapons built into it. But it does have a secret. I put in an extra layer to shield its contents from any scans. Meaning it can pass through security checkpoints without issues."

"Damn," Burn said, shaking her head. "You thought of everything. Is there anything else you were planning to add?" she asked sarcastically. "Perhaps a belt that's secretly an armored vehicle or a ring that allows me to fly?" She chuckled as she glanced up at Scar, who seemed to be considering those as feasible options for future missions.

"I'm kidding, Scar. These are great," she said, trying to tear her sister away from her far-fetched technical schemes. "I swear you're going to singlehandedly save this godforsaken city. You know you're smarter than most of the Peace Force put together, right?"

If Scar could blush, she would have. Instead, she gave a small smile of appreciation. "Thanks. But you know that's not true. You're the one risking her neck to make this world a better place. I would rather be like you."

Burn opened her mouth to reply, but closed it again, at a loss for words. Scar had never voiced such a thought before, and she didn't know how to respond. She had the urge to get up and embrace Scar, but she knew that her sister wasn't big on physical contact.

Instead, she smiled and said, "Well, together we might just have a fighting chance."

# CHAPTER 12

The light was rapidly fading as Scar helped Burn into her dress. Tying up the laces on the sides was a two-person job, and she was glad she had her sister there to help. Together, the pair also figured out how to twist Burn's hair in a passable imitation of the style Symphandra had done, albeit with a few more unintentional tendrils framing her face.

Symphandra had also loaned her some makeup for the evening, although Burn was less than familiar with how to apply it. Scar helped with that, too, smudging kohl around her eyes and along her lashes, and dabbing rouge along her cheekbones and lips. Burn wondered again how her sister had learned all these life skills which she had apparently missed. Maybe a few extra years with their mother had instilled in her more feminine expertise than Burn had previously noticed.

Standing in front of the bathroom mirror, Burn hardly recognized the person staring back at her. Her face looked foreign to her, with its too-big eyes and brightly tinted lips. She cocked her head and watched as the figure in the mirror did the same.

Her sister had done a good job. She looked like a woman, elegant and coy. Definitely not like a spy. Although, come to think of it, she didn't really know what a spy looked like. She supposed that was the point.

Her dress was tight along the chest and ribs, accentuating her figure without impeding her breathing – or her ability to flee, if necessary. The knee-height slit in the gown ensured she could always make a quick getaway if the situation turned ugly. Burn had, of course, tested it out, just to make sure.

She admired the way the dress moved and how it looked in the dim light – like a clear night's sky just coming to life. Equipped with her handbag arsenal, she felt ready to take on the world – or at least a party full of crooked cops.

"Burn!" she heard Scar shout from the living room, her voice taunting. "I think your date is here."

Suddenly, Burn's nerves returned, and she felt just as unprepared as she had when Kaz had first asked her. Breathe, she told herself, trying to calm her racing heart. It's only stage fright. The costumes are on, the stage is set, and the first act is about to begin. All it needs is its leading lady. With that thought, she left the relative safety of the bathroom and strode out into the living room and up to the front door.

Stopping with her hand on the doorknob, she turned to Scar. "Thank you," she said simply. Her sister smiled and nodded. "Don't wait up," she added as she gathered her shawl, mask, and goggles and stepped out into the night.

In the dim evening light, Kaz looked almost like a specter. Burn could see his figure approaching, but the details were hazy and muddled. After a few seconds, a man appeared from the mist, resolving into the tall, broad-chested Kaz.

"Hi," came his deep voice. The familiar sound made Burn's stomach do a little flip.

"Hi," she parroted, her voice sounding small in the dark night. The two stared at one another, each taking the other in.

The shadows and haze of the city obscured some of the detail, but Burn could see that Kaz wore an old-fashioned black suit, with his rank insignia and corresponding stripes pinned to his left breast above his heart. Her eyes roamed upward, and she noticed that his face was clean-shaven and his hair slicked back in a style that accentuated the hard lines of his face and jaw.

She knew it was silly, but she missed the shaggy mane and the way it had fallen over his eyes. This Kaz looked more serious, more official. More than ever, he looked like one of "them." Until he smiled. Then his whole face changed, softening into a look of utter delight.

"You look wonderful," he said, breaking the silence. Burn, who, unlike Scar, was capable of blushing, proceeded to do so. She was glad the darkness obscured her features.

"You do, too," Burn replied, meaning it. "Oh, I almost forgot," she added after a second. She dug around in her purse and returned with the single red flower. Taking a step closer, she reached up and pinned it to his lapel.

She took a step back, admiring her work. "There," she said proudly, "now you're ready."

Kaz stood taller, as if preening. "Why thank you, my dear." The mock gentlemanly voice was back, playful and inviting.

"Of course, darling," Burn responded, playing along with her best ladylike lilt.

With that, Kaz nodded and held out his arm. She took it and the pair walked off into the night.

Burn didn't know where they were going, but Kaz walked confidently through the streets, over bridges, and up stairs, leading them gradually upward and away from the familiar.

Their conversation was light and easy, focusing on no particular topic for long. They discussed the evening, which was mild, the haze, which was strong but gradually lifting as they ascended, and their mutual difficulties in finding something to wear for the occasion.

"It was my father's," Kaz said, pointing to the suit. "I did look for something more modern, but there are surprisingly few secondhand suit shops around." His voice had adopted a hint of sarcasm as he spoke. "I was hoping it would come across as classic, but I'm afraid I just appear out of touch with fashion." He shook his head in mild disdain.

"Unlike you, my dear," he added gallantly. "You will no doubt be the best-dressed person there. With you on my arm, I will be the envy of the entire party."

Burn raised an eyebrow. His sentiment was a tad cliché, she thought, but effective, nonetheless. "Well, you should try taking advantage of the generosity of friends," she replied, indicating her own attire. "You're at least guaranteed a more modern ensemble. Although major height differences do pose somewhat of a risk."

"I'll have to keep that in mind for the next ball," Kaz said, chuckling.

While the pair had been talking, they had passed beyond Burn's zone of familiarity and started to climb into the upper echelons of the city. Burn was beginning to wonder how far they would have to climb when they suddenly stopped in front of an iron door.

She looked around, confused. While it was a nice area, it wasn't what she had imagined. There were still some shops here, interspersed with houses that were larger than her own, but not disproportionately so. The strangest thing, though, was the iron door, which didn't seem to lead to a house at all. In fact, Burn couldn't tell what it led to.

Kaz, who seemed to know what he was doing, approached the door and pushed a button she hadn't previously seen. The button lit up and a gentle whirring noise sprang to life above them. Burn glanced up, into the dark night, but could only make out the floor of the next level above them, nothing else.

Still, she waited patiently. Or at least she tried to look patient. Inside her chest, her heart was hammering. What if this was a trap? What if the Peace Force had realized what she was up to and this was an elaborate way of ambushing her? Instinctively, her hand reached into her bag and gripped the tin of mints. If she was going down, she was going down fighting.

But, as it turned out, she wasn't going down at all. In fact, she was going up. The iron door dinged and opened before them, revealing the interior of an elegant elevator. Kaz led her inside and pressed a button on the wall, and the doors closed behind them.

Burn had never been inside an elevator. She had only ever seen a few in her life, and never one as intricately fashioned as this one. The walls were covered in a soft, velvety fabric, which Burn couldn't help but touch. It felt smooth and cool under her fingers and seemed to give off a scent of flowers and honey.

The metal accents in the space, like the panel that held the collection of buttons, were similarly intricate, with graceful swirls that beamed golden in the elevator's bright light. Coming from the hazy darkness outside, the light was painful, and Burn blinked as her eyes adjusted to the space, with more details gradually coming into focus.

The interior itself was small, with room for maybe six or seven at the most, but for the moment Kaz and Burn were its only occupants. As she studied the space, imprinting the details on her memory so she could share the whole experience with Scar later, the doors to the elevator closed and the room started to ascend.

The movement was slow and even, but the unfamiliar sensation caused Burn's stomach to turn uncomfortably. She grasped Kaz's arm tighter as they rose, and he brought his other hand to stroke hers in a comforting gesture.

A short time later, just as Burn was starting to get acclimated to the new space, the contraption stopped and the doors opened once again, revealing a completely different world than the one they had left.

Gone were the haze and the darkness of the lower levels. In their place were clean, crisp air and bright lights that lit up the tier as if it were day. If her eyes hadn't already become accustomed to the light in the elevator, Burn was sure this new brightness would have blinded her. Instead, she stepped out into the new world with her eyes wide open.

She had never been this high in the city before. She wasn't even sure citizens like her were allowed to be up here under normal circumstances. Looking at it all now, Burn felt a pang of anger that they should have so much while others had so little.

Glancing at Kaz, Burn could see he was similarly stunned. She felt better, somehow, knowing that she was not alone in her awe. Hand in hand, they ambled farther into the alien world, where more grand and extravagant details gradually resolved themselves.

There were no shops here, only houses – if you could call them houses. Maybe mansions was a better term. Mansions made of glass and iron and starlight. Because from here you could actually glimpse the twinkling light of the stars, although their brilliance was dimmed in competition with the glaring streetlights overhead. Her gaze held skyward, Burn thought she could almost make out the edges of the dome itself, although it could just as easily have been her imagination painting boundaries where she knew they ought to exist.

As a child, Burn had steadfastly believed that the people up here existed amongst the clouds and the stars. She thought that they could simply open their windows and gather up armfuls of fluff and stardust, then use their special powers to turn them into magic, which she had believed fueled the city. But looking at the place now, Burn knew that they had no need for magic.

Magic is the dream of those who are left wanting, those

123

to whom life has not been kind or generous. But these people, the people who had everything and watched the rest of mankind from a lofty perch above, they didn't need magic. They already owned the world.

Maybe that's why there were no gifted amongst the elite. They didn't need extra abilities to get ahead. They were born to privilege and comfort. Perhaps that power dichotomy, paired with the massive amounts of pollution pumped down into the lower levels, was what had led to the existence of people like Burn and her sister. Maybe it was nature's way of rebalancing the equation.

That was what she was there for, after all. If she got the information she was searching for, she would tip the scales in favor of the Lunaria, taking power from the powerful and redistributing it in hopes of fostering change.

Her mission clear in her mind, Burn lowered her gaze and trained it on their destination. It was difficult to miss, with its array of glass rooms lit up like a beacon in the night and hordes of finely dressed people making their way to its entrance.

Kaz and Burn joined the crowd filtering into the building, queuing behind a stout man with a blue sash and sharp woman with a long feather stretching from her hat. From this vantage point, Burn could make out even more details about the house and its adjoining estate.

The residence itself appeared to be three stories tall. With the exception of the Peace Station, it was the largest building Burn had ever seen. She wondered how one family could possibly make use of all that space. The crowded lane obscured her view into the ground floor windows, but she could make out an extravagant living room and kitchen on the second story, with more rooms branching off behind them. The third floor was dark, but Burn surmised that it likely housed bedrooms and personal spaces for each of the family's members.

To the left of the house was a sprawling terrace with a garden, although not in the traditional sense of flowers and trees and riotous color. This was a stone garden, a dead place full of cold sculptures and sharp metal art. In the flimsy light cast on it from the house, it looked menacing, like a threatening field that had been drained of color and left as a warning.

Burn looked away, a chill creeping up her spine. Kaz eyed her inquisitively, as if sensing her unease, but she reassured him with a small nod. The pair hadn't spoken since stepping into this strange new world, as if a single word might break its spell. Or maybe, like Burn, Kaz didn't know how to put into words the awe and revulsion and unease he felt warring inside. Or, more likely, Burn thought enviously, he was just taking it all in, enjoying the moment and the crisp air and the pretty girl on his arm.

The woman in front of them, the one with the pointed features and quivering feather, glanced back at Burn and frowned, audibly tsk-ing in disapproval. Burn, confused, looked down at herself then up at Kaz, who wore a similarly bewildered expression.

A sudden fit of laughter bubbled up inside of Burn, due to some combination of his look and her nerves and the utter absurdity of the whole evening, and she had to clutch her hands to her mouth to contain it. Kaz caught her eye and silently mimicked the woman's disapproving sneer, and the pair dissolved into an audible fit of giggles that had several heads turning in their direction.

The spell – or curse – that had held the pair in thrall lifted, and some of Burn's tension eased. Feeling lighter than she had since the evening began, Burn returned her arm to Kaz's and the pair made their way forward.

The crowd converged at the home's grand front entrance. Several armed officers manned the doors, assisted in their endeavors by revolving portals that scanned each guest before allowing entry. Burn was familiar with the portals, which had made a prominent appearance in her anxious worries. They not only scanned your body and belongings, but also your face and fingerprints, almost instantaneously comparing them against the entire Peace Force database of criminals and suspected terrorists.

Even though Burn knew that the portals would not be able to see into her handbag or detect her hidden comms unit, she was still worried as she approached the whirring machines. It was entirely possible that Cross had marked her as a suspected terrorist in their system and that her presence would be flagged immediately. If that happened, she was done for. In this crowd, there was no easy means of escape. The best she could hope for was getting thrown out – although she doubted they would be that kind.

Kaz breezed through the machine with no trouble. He waited on the other side as Burn crossed through, her nerves fizzing under her skin. But the machine made no noise, no alert that she had been flagged as suspicious. She breathed a sigh of relief and began making her way to Kaz.

"Excuse me, ma'am," came a deep voice behind Burn,

startling her. Gulping, she turned around to find a burly man with curly dark hair whose muscles bulged menacingly through his dark suit. Unable to speak, all she could do was gaze up at him questioningly.

"Could I please see your bag?" he asked, his tone unreadable. Mutely, Burn handed over her reticule.

She cursed her stupidity. She never should have come. This was far too dangerous a mission to undertake, especially alone. Maybe Hale had been right from the beginning. Maybe violence was the answer.

As her head spun with worry, the man stuck his beefy fingers into the bag, drawing out her lipstick, her cash card, and her glasses. He fished around some more and found the tin of mints, opening the container to examine them. With interest, he grabbed one of the "mints" and was about to place it into his mouth when Burn spoke up.

"Be careful!" she shouted. The guard glanced at her, his hand halfway to his mouth and confusion contorting his troll-like features.

Scrambling for a suitable explanation for her outburst, Burn continued, "They're cinnamon." She prayed to any god who would listen that this man hated cinnamon. She didn't think it would go over well if his head randomly exploded in front of the city's most powerful – and most well-armed – inhabitants.

Frowning, the man returned the mint to the tin and closed it, clumsily stuffing the items back into the bag and handing it to Burn. She forced a smile and threw him a curt "thank you" before joining Kaz.

That was a close one, she thought as two servants held

the doors open and ushered them inside. She would have to talk to Scar about that particular product design. Maybe exploding coins would be more practical. Or an exploding key. Something people didn't automatically want to put in their mouths.

Her thoughts continued in that vein as another pair of servants took their goggles, masks, and cloaks and steered them through a set of massive doors into the main hall. Once she saw the ballroom, however, all thoughts of exploding trinkets vanished from her mind.

Kaz and Burn stood at the top of a grand staircase, which swept downward into a cavernous space. Sizing it up, Burn guessed it was at least twice as tall as her own humble abode and at least three times as wide.

Her gaze was automatically drawn to the ceiling, which was dominated by an enormous glass chandelier that broke the light into rainbows and showered them back onto the partygoers. The room was clad in windows along two of the walls, with the remaining two blanketed in intricate wallpaper depicting a shimmering silver-gray forest that danced in the light. Even the smell of the room was enchanting, a wafting sweetness that reminded Burn of honey and oranges and a spice she couldn't place.

It was enough to make Burn's head spin, even without the throngs of people dancing and eating and talking all around her. The presence of so many people added a buzz to the room, a noise that vibrated in the space like a long, unending note.

Burn could have stood at the top of those steps all night, absorbing the grandeur and the energy of the room and its inhabitants. But people continued to enter behind them, pushing Kaz and Burn forward like leaves in a swirling stream. Once again arm in arm, the couple descended together into the chaos.

# CHAPTER 13

As they reached the bottom of the stairs, Burn took stock of her surroundings. She needed to get her bearings and discover everything that this place – and these people – were hiding. She couldn't do that if she was frozen in place, awestruck by the beauty and excess.

"Let's explore," she suggested, guiding Kaz to one side of the room. "I want to see this place. And maybe you can point out your colleagues while we go." It would be nice to put names to the faces – and determine who to listen in on as the night progressed.

"Sure," Kaz responded, smiling down at her.

They started off on a lap around the room, pausing almost immediately as Kaz grabbed two drinks off a passing tray, handing one to Burn. She sniffed at the unfamiliar fizzy liquid before taking a tentative sip. An explosion of flavor hit her tongue, melding a sweetness like nectar with an unfamiliar tartness and a shallow burn of alcohol as it went down.

Liquor wasn't common in Kasis. Well, good liquor wasn't common. Back alley swill, concocted in bathtubs and basements, could easily be acquired if you knew the right people, but it wasn't a pleasant beverage. It did the trick, though, if you were looking to forget your problems for an evening.

But Burn had never tasted anything like this. It left the flavor of honey on her tongue and made her want another sip as soon as she'd swallowed the last. This was more dangerous than any back-alley spirit, she decided, resisting the temptation to down the glass in one gulp.

She scanned the room, noting that most of the guests held similar drinks – plenty of which were already empty. If they kept drinking like this, getting information on the Peace Force's plans would be a breeze. She just had to keep a clear head until then.

Drinks in hand, the pair started walking again, ambling around the edges of the room while Kaz pointed out his fellow officers and superiors.

"That's Sergeant Radix," Kaz said, pointing at a gangly man whose too-long limbs stretched out from his too-small suit. "And that's Corporal Brika," he continued, indicating a brunette woman in a tight green dress.

Women weren't as common on the force as men, although there were no rules banning them from serving. The type of woman attracted to the job, however, was typically the same as the type of man who found his way onto the force: brash, arrogant, and in search of power. They held no more compassion for the people of Kasis than their male counterparts, and believing otherwise was the downfall of many.

Kaz pointed out a few more officers and superiors as they finished their lap around the room. There were many people he didn't know, or only knew by sight and not by name, so Burn was left with a good number of gaps in her knowledge. Still, she knew more than she had upon entering the room, which was a start.

She hadn't seen Detective Grayland around, although she hadn't really expected to. This wasn't exactly his type of event, and his rank wasn't high enough to make his presence required. It would have been nice, though, Burn thought, to see his familiar face in the crowd.

She was thankful that she hadn't yet spotted Cross amongst the guests. Burn knew he had to be around somewhere, but she was hoping she could stealthily avoid him for the duration of the party – or at least avoid being spotted by him. She knew, no matter how much she wished it otherwise, that listening to him and his conversations would be the best way to learn more about whatever the Peace Force was planning.

"Do you think they'd mind if we explored the house?" Burn asked, hoping to scout out more of the building and its secrets.

"Bored of the party already?" Kaz asked, finishing off his drink and placing it on a nearby table.

"No," Burn said truthfully. She didn't think she could ever get bored of such splendor. "I'm simply curious to see what else this place holds."

Kaz considered this. "Hmm," he said, rubbing his chin in thought. Then he held up a finger. "Give me a minute," he said before turning and disappearing into the crowd.

Burn didn't follow him, trusting he'd return and explain. Instead, she took the opportunity to survey the room as only she could. She closed her eyes and focused her thoughts, centering herself before opening them again. Homing in on small groups at a time, she scanned the room in search of useful conversations.

Most of the party's guests were discussing the event itself – the house, the food, the people. Others were flirting or joking or complementing each other's appearance. Two were swiftly getting to know one another behind a large curtain, out of sight of the rest of the party. Burn didn't linger on that particular interaction for long.

The party was just beginning, and it seemed nobody was yet discussing business. Right now, people were getting acclimated to the space and the crowd. Time, plus the addition of more drinks, would change that, freeing tongues and inhibitions alike. Burn just had to be patient.

She sifted through a few more conversations, this time focusing on the people Kaz had pointed out as his superiors. She was just zeroing in on Sergeant Radix when a cold voice came from behind her, making her muscles tense.

"Ms. Alendra, how nice to see you," the voice stated, sounding anything but pleased. "I don't remember seeing you on the guest list."

Burn turned, coming face to face with Illex Cross. He looked her up and down, as if appraising her value, and Burn instinctively crossed her arms over her chest.

"I'd heard how fun your parties were," she said, her tone sickly sweet, "and I couldn't stay away."

Cross moved closer, his posture stiff as he towered over

her. "You're not welcome here, *Burn*." He spat out her name as if it were a swear word.

"I was invited," she said simply. She kept her face blank and her expression neutral, stemming the tide of her anger so it wouldn't come crashing out. The last thing she needed was to be chucked out of the ball before she'd even had a chance to discover anything.

He scoffed, not even trying to hide his scorn. "You mean you tricked someone into bringing you? Who's the poor soul you're using now? Does he know what you're really after?"

"And what am I after, Mr. Cross?" she bit back, purposely omitting his title. As he glared at her, she took a step back, folding her hands in front of her in a gesture of innocence. "I think you have me wrong, sir. All I want is to enjoy a nice evening with you and your fine officers. Nothing more." Her eyes didn't leave his as she spoke, and Cross returned her glare mutely.

Kaz chose that instant to suddenly reappear behind her. "There you are!" he said, relieved and a touch out of breath. "I thought I'd lost you. This place is…" He trailed off as he caught sight of General Cross. "Sir," Kaz greeted him, bobbing his head respectfully.

Burn broke her eye contact with Cross and turned to face Kaz, noticing that he held two plates piled with food. Seeing her gaze, Kaz said, "I didn't know what you liked, so I got a bit of everything." Smiling, he held out a plate. She took it, giving him a small smile in return.

"Officer Petala," Cross said by way of a greeting. "I didn't know you and Ms. Alendra were acquainted." He sounded genuinely intrigued, and Burn had to dig her nails into her palm to keep from spitting back that their relationship was none of his business. Instead, she remained silent, letting Kaz do the talking.

"We're…new friends," he responded delicately. "I've always wanted to attend the ball, and Burn did me the enormous favor of accompanying me." He beamed down at Burn as he spoke.

Cross' face was unreadable as he processed the new information. "How nice," he said after a brief pause. "Well, I wish you two the best tonight. I must go and mingle." He turned to go but paused as a thought struck him. "Ms. Alendra, would you do me the honor of saving me a dance? I would love to continue our fascinating conversation."

Burn wanted to slap him. Or spit in his face. Or hand him a mint and watch his head explode into a thousand little pieces. But instead, she smiled and said, "Of course." With that, Cross turned on his heel and strode back into the crowd.

"What was that about?" Kaz asked, his face betraying mild concern.

"Nothing," Burn said, picking at her food. "He wanted to know what I was doing here. Can we get out of here?" she asked, indicating the ballroom.

"Sure," he replied, although he sounded as if he wanted to ask more.

The two made their way out of the crowded room and into an adjoining hallway. Burn kept walking, passing portraits and doorways and sculptures, until she found a semi-secluded set of chairs set into an alcove in the wall. The location was perfect for a private conversation – and an equally good place to watch passersby without being noticed.

She positioned herself on one of the low chairs, fanning out her dress on either side of her.

Kaz sat down tentatively, something clearly on his mind. Finally, gathering up his nerve, he spoke. "Is something going on between you and General Cross?"

Burn let out an unladylike snort, a knee-jerk reaction to such an absurd question. "No," she replied promptly, almost laughing at the suggestion. "Very much no."

Kaz kept his gaze down, not entirely convinced. "It's just that…the times I've seen you together, it seems like there's something between you. Something intense."

Burn looked him over and sighed. "You're right. There is something between us." She watched as Kaz's face fell slightly, then reached over and took his hand in hers. "It's called hatred. Utter hatred. He wishes I didn't exist, and I feel the same way about him. I did warn you about this when you asked me to the ball," she reminded him.

"Yeah, you did," he said, shaking his head. The smile was coming back slowly but surely. "Sorry. I guess I got jealous when I saw the way he was looking at you. It sounds so stupid now."

Burn shook her head, resisting the urge to roll her eyes. "He was looking at me like he wanted to throw me out of the party. And if you hadn't come along when you did, I'm sure he would have. So thank you." She paused, but he didn't seem inclined to respond. "So…what is all of this?" she asked, gesturing to the plate of food in front of her.

Kaz perked up at the mention of food, turning his attention to the piles he had scavenged for them. "I don't even know," he admitted, his eyes roaming over it all. "It all smelled so good. I think there are a few types of meat on sticks. Some exotic fruits. And a bunch of desserts."

It turned out that the food tasted even more wonderful than it smelled. The contents of her plate put her plain pastry that morning to shame. The roast meats were delicious, dripping juices that she sopped up with wonderfully soft herbed bread. And there were types of cheeses she had never even heard of.

But it was the desserts that made her mouth water. Soft, sponge-like cakes drizzled with honey that tasted like flowers, chocolates filled with sticky sweet caramel and clusters of nuts, and perfectly rounded cookies that hid bursts of lemon and orange that tickled her tongue.

They chatted as they ate, sharing bites and stories and sweet smiles. For a moment, Burn forgot her mission, swept up in the elegance and abundance of this world. But as she pushed the final crumbs around her plate, her reason for being there resurfaced, and she knew that she needed to get to work.

"Do you think you could give me a few minutes?" she asked as sweetly as she could. "I need to find the ladies' room," she lied, getting up from her seat and looking around. "I'll join you back in the ballroom when I'm done."

He agreed, giving her a bright smile before walking back the way they had come. Glancing around to make sure she was alone, she moved her hand to her necklace and pressed down the button.

"Scar, are you there?" Burn was half afraid that the pendant unit wouldn't work or that her sister wouldn't be there, but her worries were for nothing. The reply came within seconds.

"I'm here. What took you so long?"

Burn sighed in relief. "I had to mingle," she said in place of an excuse. "Cross says hi, by the way."

"Shit, you've been busy. Find out anything good yet?"

"Nothing," Burn said quietly as she began testing out various doors in the hallway.

One opened into a small kitchen area, and she glimpsed a few servants plating trays of food before quickly shutting the door again. Another opened into an elegant bathroom with shiny fixtures and deep red wallpaper. She closed that door, too, venturing farther down the hall.

The next door she tried was locked, and she slipped out her lipstick and unscrewed the bottom to free her biometric key, which opened the door in seconds. She glanced inside, but it was dark, and she couldn't make out the shapes. Burn dug through her bag again, this time coming out with the glasses. Turning on night sight, she glanced around the room again, but saw only piles of old furniture and rolled-up carpets leaning against the wall. A storage cupboard.

Burn narrated her movements for Scar, giving her brief updates with each new room she discovered. Eventually, she reached the end of the hall and turned left, following a new hallway into the back of the house.

This hallway was dark, obviously not intended for guests, and Burn was grateful for the night sight feature Scar had installed on the lenses. There were fewer doors here, and each led to a larger space than before – a spare bedroom, a fitness area, a library with plush chairs.

Soon, she had reached the end of the hallway, with only

one more unexplored door left. Burn was running out of time and knew if she was gone much longer that Kaz would start to worry. But she couldn't leave empty-handed.

She approached the final door and placed her finger on the scanner. But instead of allowing her entry, the door beeped and another panel slid open above the first. Curious, Burn looked closer – and was surprised when a red light shot out and swept over her eyes. It was a retinal scanner, she realized after a beat, glad that she had Scar's glasses on.

The machine thought for a few seconds, taking its time to process her scan. The extra wait made Burn nervous, and she wondered if some sort of silent alarm would be triggered if the glasses didn't work. She listened for footsteps coming in her direction, but all was quiet.

Eventually, she heard a small click and the door swung open before her. She let out a quiet sigh of relief and slipped inside.

The room was almost completely dark, save for the light coming in through a large window on the opposite wall. The window looked out into the night sky, like a framed picture of the stars and moon and nearby planets. For a heartbeat, before her eyes and her glasses adjusted to the space, the window and its contents were all she could see.

Gradually, the rest of the room came into focus. The walls were dark, covered in a wallpaper design Burn couldn't quite make out, and dotted with canvases in golden frames. Inching closer, Burn realized the framed pictures weren't paintings, like she had presumed, but maps. She walked slowly around the space, mentally cataloging the places depicted on them – the Saffron Quarter, the Peace Sector, the

Collina Quarter, and on and on.

This was Kasis, reduced to flat, two-dimensional space and repurposed as art. Burn found it strange to see her city like that – lifeless and displayed like a prize on the walls of the powerful. The sight made her uncomfortable, and she turned her attention away from the maps, surveying the rest of the room.

Along the far edge, just in front of the window, was a large desk bathed in moonlight. It looked solid and heavy, the kind of desk specifically crafted for important people to sit in while they made decisions about other people's lives. Burn turned to make her way to the desk, hoping it might hold some key piece of information, but her progress was almost instantly impeded by another piece of furniture in her path. Outside of the reach of the window's light was another surface, this one a circular table, and Burn had walked right into it, sending the small figures on top of it clattering in various directions.

Burn swore under her breath as she tried to replace the small toys in their previous locations. Her mind, confused as to why an office would house a collection of children's toys, froze when she looked down at the statuettes she held in her hands. Soldiers. Little toy soldiers. Cautiously she bent down to the table, looking more closely at the scene. Then she understood. This wasn't an office at all. It was a war room.

# CHAPTER 14

Little toy soldiers were set against little helpless citizens who were fleeing in terror. Burn couldn't tell where in the city this gruesome diorama was depicting, but she could tell it was going to be a massacre. Little barricades had been constructed at the end of tiny alleyways and miniature streets, trapping the people within the nightmare. Many had already perished, lying facedown on the table, and Burn was unsure how much of that was her doing and how much had already been staged.

She felt a sudden pain in her hand and looked down, seeing one of the toy soldiers still clasped in her angry grasp, his gun broken and his legs twisted at an unnatural angle. She had been clutching it so hard that its gun had pierced her palm, covering the soldier in small drops of blood that appeared black in the darkness.

"Burn? Burn, what's happening?" came Scar's voice in her ear, soft but insistent.

"They're planning a slaughter," was all she could get out.

"What? What do you mean a slaughter? Slaughtering who?"

Burn came to, pulling herself up from the table and back into the real world. "I don't know." Then she spotted the desk again, her brain ticking. "But maybe I can find out."

Careful to avoid colliding with the table – or any other furniture in the dim room – she made her way purposefully to the desk. Pushing back the large leather chair, she set herself down in its cool embrace and got to work examining the wooden monolith.

The surface of the desk was annoyingly tidy, holding only a pen, a paperweight, and blank pad of paper. Burn flipped through the pad, hoping to find an absentminded note or code word, but discovered nothing among its pages.

Disheartened, she turned her attention to the drawers. Her heart dropped deeper. Instead of biometric scanners or retinal readers, they were secured by large old-fashioned locks with perfectly crafted keyholes.

"Damn it," she muttered, both to herself and her sister. "They've gone old-school, Scar. I need an actual key to open this."

A few seconds of silence greeted her, but then Scar's voice returned, bright and eager. "Unscrew the earpieces of your glasses," she advised without further explanation.

Confused, but not wanting to argue, Burn removed the glasses, casting the room back into complete darkness. After a few moments of fidgeting with one of the ends, however, something gave, and a long thin utensil dropped into her hand. Doing the same with the other side, she released the second half of the antiquated lock-picks and stared down at them.

"You're a genius," she muttered to Scar through the comms. "A mad genius." Her sister didn't reply, but Burn knew she was proud of herself for this one. She put the glasses back on, now lighter, and looked down at the small metal tools in her hands.

It had been years since she'd used tools like these – maybe even a decade. In his training lessons, her father had instructed her on how to open even the most difficult of locks, but she'd never put the skill to use in the real world. Despite her doubts, though, her fingers seemed to remember the familiar objects, and she hastily got to work on the top drawer.

A minute went by. Then two. Burn was getting frustrated with herself and knew that she didn't have much time before Kaz came looking for her. She had to do this and do it now.

A small click sounded from inside the lock and Burn sighed in relief, pulling the drawer open. Bingo. Sitting atop a stack of documents was a tab, the screen black and lifeless. She pressed the button on the side to boot it up and watched as the screen came to life.

"Enter Password," the screen read. Burn dove back into her bag, coming up with the cash card Scar had made for her.

"You're up," she told her sister, placing the card on top of the tab.

Her sister didn't respond, but she heard the clattering of a keyboard as Scar began breaking down the device's security. As she worked, Burn leafed through the papers in the drawer. Most were unimportant – departmental finance statements, memos on rising crime rates, dossiers on assorted inmates and their crimes. Burn glanced over these briefly but couldn't find a connection between them and the tabletop battle the Peace Force was planning.

Then her eyes alighted on a report at the bottom of the drawer. She held it up, adjusting her glasses to focus in on the text. "New strain of ManniK found to be particularly potent when administered to mutants," said the headline. Intrigued, Burn read on.

"According to this," she told her sister after scanning a few more lines, "the tainted ManniK that's been hitting the streets affects those with gifts differently than it does everyone else. Listen to this: 'Symptoms for the *freaks* go beyond the blind rage typically seen in normal citizens. When dosed, these mutants demonstrate increased strength, loss of inhibitions and memory, and monstrous violence, even to their friends and loved ones.'"

"Wait," Burn said as she looked closer at the page. "Some notes have been inscribed in the margin. It looks like it says, 'Good start. More testing needed to extend duration.' Testing? They're testing it on us?!"

A ball of fire rose in Burn's chest, threatening to blind her. What were they doing testing drugs on citizens? What right did they have? Her head pounded as she rooted through the rest of the files, looking for more.

"Burn. Burn!" Scar almost had to scream to get her attention. She'd been so focused on her rage that she hadn't even heard her sister speak. "I'm in," Scar continued, drawing Burn's attention back to the tab. "But it looks like most of the files have been wiped. I've copied what I can and am downloading it now, but there doesn't seem to be much there."

Burn picked up the tab to examine it, but instantly stiffened, her eyes on the door. Footsteps. She had heard footsteps coming down the hall in her direction. Multiple people were approaching – and quickly. Her heart sped up in panic. She grabbed the cash card and threw the tab and papers back into the drawer, slamming it shut.

"Someone's coming," she relayed to Scar as she scanned the room for an adequate hiding spot. Her eyes came to rest on the flowing floor-to-ceiling curtains flanking the window, and she darted behind one. She had just enough time to cover her feet and nestle herself into the corner of the window before the door opened and light flooded the room.

Burn heard several figures enter before closing the door behind them. Her heart raced, and she could hear the blood pumping through her veins. She tried to quiet her breathing, taking long sips of air instead of shallow gasps, but it still sounded far too loud to her highly attuned ears.

The footsteps moved farther into the room, coming to a halt somewhere between the desk and the tabletop war. Someone sat. Others stood. Burn willed herself to stay still, but it felt like her body was vibrating with anxious energy. She grasped her hands in front of her, each hand trying to stop the other from shaking. She knew that any hint of movement would cause the thin piece of fabric to flutter, revealing her presence.

Someone cleared their throat – a man, judging by the deep sound. The rest of the room hushed, turning their attention to him. Burn, too, focused in on him, holding her breath as she waited.

"Thank you for joining us," the unfamiliar voice began. Judging by its cadence and timbre, Burn imagined the speaker as older and distinguished, probably a senior officer and a member of the rule-making elite. Their identities were kept secret, supposedly to guarantee their safety and to "ensure impartiality" – or so no one could bribe or blackmail them to create laws in their favor. But they were corrupt enough on their own, without external influence, and had been ruling in their own favor for decades.

Burn briefly considered taking out the mint bombs in her bag and chucking the entire container in their direction. With any luck, she'd be able to take out a few of them before she was apprehended or shot down. But, the voice of reason in her head chimed in, they would simply be replaced by equally crooked figures, and life would go on as it always had. Besides, she was more use to the Lunaria alive than as martyr. So she remained where she was, listening from the shadows.

"You all know why we're here." Burn didn't know and was silently hoping that he would explain anyway, in the typical fashion of egotistical rulers everywhere who stated the obvious for the sole purpose of sounding superior. But, once again that evening, she was disappointed.

He continued, "We're standing on the precipice of something exciting, a history-defining moment, if you will. The next few days are crucial to our success – and to the continued success of our great city. I don't want to keep you long from the festivities, but I thought it was important to keep you all apprised of the evolving situation. I'll now turn the floor over to General Cross for an update."

Cross. Burn's blood froze. She had known he was at the center of this, whatever this was. Anger and disdain roiled within her as Cross rose, drawing the room's attention.

"Thank you, sir," came his deep voice, silky and cold. The hairs on Burn's arms prickled. "We stand at a crossroads, one which has the power to change the fate of this city. On one side stand the barbarians, the violent, the mutants who seek to wrench away our control and plunge this city into a sea of blood and chaos. We stand on the other, a barrier between them and the anarchy they so desperately crave."

Cross began to move, coming closer and closer to where Burn stood. She looked down, out the window and into the darkness of a sheer drop-off, which offered no promise of escape. If she were forced to flee, it would have to be through a mess of bodies and fire.

"We only have a few days left to change the tide of this war," Cross continued. She could sense his presence a few short strides away, his body pointed in her direction. "And we're nearly ready to strike." He punctuated his speech with pregnant pauses, reinforcing the importance of his words.

He came even closer to the window where Burn stood, speaking to the group with his back to them. "In a few days, we'll have everything we need to make our move. Production of our assault weapons has been increased, and our operatives are armed and trained to kill. Increased recruitment over the last year means we have more than enough bodies to wield those weapons, with more to spare." A chuckle went around the room at that.

Fury rose up in Burn's throat. They were talking about

people, about sacrificing human lives. Well, officers' lives, but still. He was talking about them as if they were disposable, like pawns in his deadly little game. She thought about Kaz and Grayland, about her father and the men like him still serving on the force. Their lives didn't matter to these people. They were just the currency of war, a commodity to trade for more and more power.

Burn felt her fists tighten into a ball in front of her, as if ready for a fight. But the rest of her body remained still behind the curtain, waiting for more.

"Our research has been promising," Cross finally continued, drawing out his time in the spotlight. "We're testing a few more subjects as we speak to fine-tune the formula. But when it's done, it will be the perfect catalyst."

He sounded so confident, so smug about his plan, like there was no chance of failure. Pride cometh before the fall, thought Burn. She couldn't wait to bring him down and pull that easy confidence out from under him. She just needed a little more information, a few more details to fill in the gaps.

"When will it be ready?" came another male voice from farther away.

Cross remained where he was, dangerously close to the window. Looking out from her hiding spot, she could already see the tips of his shoes. Another step or two and he'd be fully visible – as would she. Burn held her breath, afraid to exhale for fear of alerting him to her presence.

"Three days, maybe four," he said lazily. "I'll send out the signal once everything's in place. Don't worry – you'll have enough time to prepare before it happens. Just make sure you keep your distance." Another round of sniggers rippled through the room.

One man whispered under his breath, "Like we'd ever set foot *there*," but it was too quiet to catch Cross' attention. He merely stood, gazing out the window.

"Gentleman," said the initial speaker once more. "I think that's enough business for tonight. Let us return to the party and our wives – or our mistresses, in some cases." More chuckles.

Such a cheerful bunch, thought Burn in derision. Who would have thought that planning a war was such light-hearted work? Meetings of the Lunaria certainly weren't as entertaining. Maybe if they adopted a similarly laissez-faire attitude toward human life, they'd find more to laugh about.

The men began to make their way out of the room, but Cross didn't budge, his gaze fixed on the window. Burn began to panic. Did he know she was there? Was he waiting until everyone was out of the room to grab her or push her through the thin window and into the night? Enough time had passed that Kaz had no doubt started to worry. She had to get out of there – and soon – but Cross was barring her only way out.

The rest of the crowd filtered out of the office, save for one other figure, who closed the door and turned to face Cross.

"Well, I think that went well," said an old male voice, the same one that had introduced him during the meeting.

Cross didn't reply. Instead, he remained motionless, standing as still as one of the statues in the house's eerie stone garden. Unperturbed by his silence, the old man made his way over, taking a seat on the other side of the desk.

"You know, if this goes according to plan, they may finally consider adding you to the ranks. You could be one of us. You could rule this city."

That got Cross' attention. And Burn's. As he turned to face his superior, her mind raced. Cross wasn't just waging war for pleasure; he was vying for power. He wanted to climb the ladder to its very top, until he stood amongst the most powerful figures in the city.

The idea of Cross wielding that much authority was truly terrifying. With limitless control, he could decimate Kasis. He had to be stopped. Burn's mission seemed more crucial than ever.

"Thank you, sir. It would be an honor to serve alongside you and the rest of the board," Cross said humbly. Burn had never heard him act subservient to anyone, so the change in tone was unnerving.

"Come, come. There's no need to be so formal. I know you've been angling for this for years. You have an impeccable record. But this could be the feather in your cap. It's truly an impressive plan."

"Thank you," Cross said again, taking a seat in the chair behind the desk. "But it would never have come together without your support and encouragement."

"Think nothing of it," the old man said regally, as if he had just bestowed the highest honor upon Cross. "You know, this could be an amazing opportunity for you. Look around. With a position on the board, your family could have all of this and more. Imagine how happy they would be to live in a place like this."

That caught Burn off guard. She'd never pictured Cross

as having a family. He'd always seemed too detached, too void of sympathy to ever find comfort in the presence of others. She tried to imagine a wife who waited up for him at night and children who greeted him at the door, but the images felt wrong somehow, like a lie.

The older man rose, placing his hands on the desk in front of him. "But I must warn you," he continued gravely. "If you fail them, they will have your head for this. The board doesn't take disappointment lightly. You have one chance to prove yourself, and if anything goes wrong, they'll replace you in an instant."

"I understand," Cross said gravely.

The old man turned to go, and Burn risked a glimpse beyond the curtains at Cross. He remained seated in the large office chair, his attention turned downward. An instant later, she heard the top drawer of the desk slide open. Burn's heart stopped in her chest. He hadn't used a key. Meaning she hadn't closed it properly. She'd been in such a rush that she'd just shoved it shut, hoping it would relatch itself. It hadn't.

Cross was no idiot. An utter bastard, yes, but not an incompetent officer. He would know that an open drawer was suspicious. He would know that someone had opened it. The chair creaked as Cross turned, surveying the room. Looking for her. It was only a matter of time before he spotted her, what with Burn having chosen a highly unoriginal hiding spot. She silently cursed her lack of imagination.

He stood slowly, facing the window. This was it, Burn thought, resigning herself to the inevitable. This was the end. She readied herself to pounce.

But the preparation proved unnecessary, as the old man

spoke once more. "Are you coming?" he asked, paused in the open doorway.

"Of course," said Cross, like that had always been his plan. He made his way to the door. "You know, one of the ladies here has promised me a dance. I think it's time to collect." With that, he closed the door behind him and the two began their walk back to the ballroom.

Burn listened for a few seconds as they traveled farther down the hallway, then turned the corner. Once she was sure they were gone, she dashed from her hiding spot and out the door, closing it softly behind her.

Cross suspected her. She was certain of it. And now he was on his way to the ballroom to find her. Unless, of course, he had meant some other lady whom he had intimidated into promising him a dance, but she highly doubted that. No, he was coming for her – except she wouldn't be there.

Burn was out of clever ideas – if any of her ideas that night could actually be construed as clever, which she also doubted. She had been lucky so far, but her luck was rapidly running out. Her heart pounded as she raced down the halls, following the sounds of music and laughter back to the party. Once she neared it, she slowed to a walk, then stopped, trying to get her breathing back under control.

The sudden appearance of a hand on her arm came as quite the shock. Burn reacted abruptly, jumping back and shrieking in an utterly unladylike manner. She flailed, putting her hands up to protect herself, but instead of the violence she was expecting, she was met with an uncontrollable bout of laughter. Kaz was laughing at her.

# CHAPTER 15

"You scared me," Burn said defensively, dropping her hands. Her heartbeat had ticked back up again, and she took slow, controlled breaths to try to lessen its speed.

"The look...on your face..." Kaz said between peals of laughter. "Priceless." The laughter subsided and he wiped at his eyes. He looked over at Burn, his gaze still filled with mirth, but she glared back stony-faced.

"Oh, come on, Auburn," he pleaded. "That was funny. You looked like you'd seen a ghost!" Burn didn't respond, so he continued, "You know, I've been looking for you for at least a quarter of an hour. The least you could do is give me a smile," he teased.

Despite the fact that part of her brain was still obsessing about Cross and what he might know, another part was glad to be back with Kaz. The corners of her lips rose in a small smile.

"Sorry I took so long," she said, willing sincerity into her tone. "That drink hit me harder than I expected. I needed a few minutes to get my bearings, away from all the people."

In reality, the buzz from the spirit had already subsided, leaving only a slight tiredness in its wake – although that also could have been because of the adrenaline leaving her system. She made a mental note to avoid combining the two in the future.

Kaz looked at her as if considering her response, weighing her truthfulness.

"I'm sorry," he finally said, his tone sweet. "I know what that's like. The drinks and the people and the music – it's a lot. Do you want to take a walk?" Kaz indicated a side door that she hadn't noticed, which led to an outdoor balcony that wrapped around the back of the house.

She nodded in agreement, silently noting that it was an ingenious way to avoid Cross while also taking her farther away from the scene of the crime. She followed Kaz to the door, which he held open for her before following her into the night.

The air outside was brisk, but not unpleasantly so. After Burn's exertion, the breeze felt refreshing on her skin. She walked to the railing and closed her eyes, inhaling the sharp, cool air. Kaz joined her, looking out at the city around them.

The patio was a large one, stretching the length of the ballroom and connecting to the statue garden on the house's far side. A few other couples had also felt the call of the outdoors and were currently enjoying the night, although each kept their distance from the next, as if adhering to an unspoken understanding.

The two stood there for a moment, lost in thought. Burn

went over everything she had heard, trying to make sense of it. The Peace Force was planning a massacre. They had the guns. They had the officers. They had a catalyst, whatever that meant. Were they referring to ManniK? That's what they had been testing on people – mainly *mutants* like her. But how would that spark a war?

She had so much information – more than enough to report back to the Lunaria on – but she still felt like she was missing a critical piece of the puzzle. Like who were they targeting? And how were they going to justify a war on their own people?

Burn must have been deep in thought, because Kaz had to repeat his statement twice before she heard him. "I didn't know you wore glasses," he said, his voice light but inquisitive.

"Oh," Burn let out before she knew what she was doing. She took off the glasses, staring down at them in her hands. "I don't, usually. But my head started to hurt – probably because of the drink – and I thought they might help. They didn't."

"Right…" Kaz said, apparently unconvinced by her half-hearted lie.

"Thank you for bringing me tonight," Burn blurted, attempting to change the subject. She began strolling down the length of the balcony and, to her relief, Kaz followed.

She was honestly glad she had come. The information she had gained was invaluable. And, although she wouldn't admit it to herself, she had been having a nice time with Kaz. There was something easy about being with him. He felt comfortable and safe, and some of her anxiety melted as they wandered on.

"You don't have to thank me," Kaz responded, suitably distracted from the subject of her glasses. "You're the one doing me the favor. I never would have come on my own. This," he motioned to the party, "this is something you have to share with someone."

Burn was struck by the similarity of his words to her own thoughts earlier that day. *Luxury was nothing unless you could share it with someone.* She glanced up at him and smiled. He met her gaze and held it for a beat before she looked away, blushing.

They continued walking, leaving the confines of the balcony and entering into the statue garden beyond it. The light streaming outside from the party hit the statues at odd angles, casting unnatural and elongated shadows throughout the space. Compared to the life and vibrancy inside, the garden seemed cold and dead, like a moment frozen in time and sentenced to an eternity of stillness.

Neither spoke at first, both preferring to absorb the eerie scene. They passed a statue of two lovers caught forever in each other's embrace, staring longingly at one another in a passion that would never be satisfied. Crossing farther into the garden, Kaz situated himself on a stone bench at the base of yet another statue. This one depicted a man holding an old-fashioned bow and pointing it up at the stars as if he wanted to pierce one and pull it down from the sky.

Burn joined him on the bench. Her veins were still buzzing from the night's excitement and all that she'd learned. Her goal now should be to find a way to gracefully retreat, without raising suspicion, and update the Lunaria on everything she'd discovered.

So why wasn't she leaving? Burn told herself it would look strange if they left so early – and she almost believed it. But, like a drug addict, she just wanted a little bit more – more time with Kaz and more time being this person, this version of herself who smiled and laughed and made someone smile and laugh in return.

"Kaz, I…" she started then stopped, hating herself for what she was about to say. Kaz, I have to go. Kaz, I'm a spy who could be apprehended at any moment. Kaz, I can't do this – no matter how much I might want to.

Instead, she merely said, "Kaz, I'm having a really nice time." The words felt hollow, a placeholder that should have held real emotions but instead contained mere pleasantries. Kaz simply nodded.

"It's times like this that I miss them," he started, and Burn knew immediately that he meant his mother and sister. He stared off into the distance and continued, "It seems so unfair, somehow, that I get to experience all of this and they can't."

Burn nodded in understanding but didn't know what to say. She opened her mouth, then closed it again, not sure if anything would soothe his loss.

Finally she said, "We can't stop living because they can't. Live, I mean. I think I'm still coming to terms with that. All I can do is live a life that would make them proud. That's all any of us can do."

Burn considered the Lunaria and her mission. She had always thought that it would have made her father proud, her fighting for equality and justice. But how did you really know, in the end, what someone would have wanted?

"Do you think they would be proud of you?" she suddenly asked him, spurred by the thought of her father.

"I don't know," he said, pondering the question. "I was so young. Sometimes I feel like I hardly even remember them. Maybe I just do the things I want, then tell myself in retrospect that it's what they would have wanted to make myself feel better about it."

Tentatively, Burn reached out her hand and placed it on top of his. He sat there for a beat, then removed his hand. Burn's cheeks flared in embarrassment, and she thought she'd misread the signals entirely, but Kaz quickly put his hand on top of hers, intertwining their fingers. She gave him a sheepish smile.

"Burn? Can I tell you something?" He looked at the ground, as if not daring to make eye contact with her.

"Sure. I mean, of course."

"I…" he trailed off, then looked up, meeting her gaze. "I really like you. I know I haven't known you that long, but there it is."

Caught off guard, Burn said the first thing that popped into her head. "That's a very dangerous thing to say." Kaz looked confused, not comprehending in the slightest. Burn sighed and pulled her hand away, preparing herself.

"There's no future for us. I'm…" she paused, searching for the right word, "a pariah, at least in the eyes of the Peace Force. If you plan to have a future with them, I can't be in it."

She stood up and walked a few paces, as if trying to leave her words – and the whole situation – behind her. But Kaz wouldn't let that happen. He followed her, gently putting his hand on her arm to urge her to turn around. She reluctantly did, but she resisted the urge to meet his eyes.

"I don't care." He sounded sincere. But his life was not in danger. His world was intact – and would remain that way as long as she stayed out of it. Burn shook her head.

"I mean it. Screw them. Screw Cross. You matter to me. They…well, it's just a job, isn't it?"

But it wasn't just a job. They both knew that. It was a way of life, a set path for your future. People didn't just quit the Peace Force. It wasn't done. You served until you died. It was the way of things.

"I can't give you what you want." Burn tried to put all of herself into the statement, from the blackmail and the Lunaria to her utter inability to lead a "normal" life.

"And how do you know what I want? You don't." Kaz was getting worked up now, throwing his hands into the air and pacing through the garden. Burn watched him ruefully, her mind set.

"I want you!" he continued, turning around to face her. Then, without warning, he strode up to her, took her head in his hands, and kissed her deeply. His fingers tangled into her hair as she melted into his body.

After a long moment, they broke apart, both breathing deeply. Kaz kept hold of her head and she didn't pull away, enjoying the feel of his body against hers. She knew she should be going. She knew she should break away and leave all of this behind. But for some reason her body would no longer obey her commands.

It felt good to be held by someone, to be clutched in an embrace that made the world around her melt away. She just wanted one more moment. Then another. Maybe this could work, her brain piped in. Maybe they could really be together.

But the world was not that kind.

A frosty voice emerged from beside them, piercing the tranquil night. "What a pretty picture," Cross drawled, striding leisurely over to them and placing himself between them and the party – between Burn and any chance of escape.

# CHAPTER 16

Kaz turned around swiftly, greeting his superior with a nod, but Burn took her time, wiping her face of every emotion before moving to look at him.

Cross glared at her, his expression screaming contempt. "I wondered where you had run off to," he continued, speaking directly to her.

Kaz answered anyway, not seeming to notice his intense interest in her. "We needed some air. And it was such a lovely night. We couldn't resist." His voice was gentle, but there was a hint of something else behind it. Was it defensiveness? Or possessiveness?

"Of course," Cross said, his tone light and artificial. "It's so romantic out here, isn't it? I do hate to cut your tête-à-tête short, but Ms. Alendra did promise me a dance. And I couldn't let the night end without having the pleasure of her company."

Kaz glanced at Burn, his hand tightening around hers in

a silent question. She steeled herself, then gave him a reassuring nod before removing her hand from his.

"I'd be delighted, General," she responded, meeting his gaze. "Although I do have to warn you, I'm not a very good dancer."

"Oh, don't worry on that account. I'm a very strong leader." The fiery way he said that made Burn certain he was no longer talking about dancing. The statement made her shiver.

Still, she approached him, taking his outstretched arm and allowing him to lead her back into the ballroom. The room and its inhabitants had only become louder since she'd left, and the onslaught of noises hit her like a wall of sound. To her sensitive ears, the din was deafening, and she had to mentally calibrate her senses to adjust to it.

Cross, who was paying close attention to her, regarded her curiously, but she just smiled in return, an innocent look plastered on her face.

"Have you been enjoying your evening?" she asked, her voice light and airy.

"Oh, yes. Very much. It's been…educational." Somehow he made that word sound like a threat. He looked to Burn, hoping for a reaction, but she kept her face blank except for a small smile. Her mind, however, was far less composed, with fear and anger and curiosity warring for top billing.

"And you, Ms. Alendra?" he asked, his interest on full display. "How has your evening been so far? I must admit that your disappearing act made me more than a little curious. Tell me, what was so interesting that it drew you away from all of this?" He waved his hand around the ballroom, indicating all the raucous officers and their dates for the evening.

"As you must be aware," Burn started, a hint of steel creeping into her tone, "I'm unaccustomed to such luxury. I've been enjoying myself immensely, but I do need to pace myself. Delicate constitutions and all that." She batted her eyelashes up at him to emphasize her point.

"Oh, come now, Auburn. Let's be honest with each other, shall we?" The use of her first name felt intrusive and far too intimate, and Burn had a sudden urge to pull away, but Cross held her tight. They were now on the dance floor, and he moved his hands to her waist, drawing her close. Instinctively, she put her hands on his shoulders, feeling the hard muscles underneath.

"Every time I turn around, there you are," he continued, his face close to her ear. If anyone saw them, they would just look like two more lovers on the dance floor, holding each other close and swaying in time to the music. "You're in the Corax End the night of an anarchist meeting, you show up at the Peace Station, and now you're here. I sincerely doubt any of this is a coincidence."

"You caught me, Illex." He twitched satisfyingly at the use of his Christian name. But if he could use hers, she would be doing the same. "I can't stay away from you. Such power, such masculinity. How could a girl resist?" Sarcasm to the fullest degree. She knew she shouldn't poke the bear, especially a bear that was clearly hot on her trail, but her fuse was getting dangerously short.

Cross grimaced, his mouth flattening into a thin line before he spoke. "Don't you get it? Whatever you're up to, you'll fail. You're no one. And you have nothing. And if you keep getting in my way, I'll make sure you lose everything you hold dear. Got it?"

The fire in Burn's chest erupted, sweeping up her throat and into her mouth, but she clamped her teeth, trying to contain the words. You already took my father, she wanted to say – no, she wanted to scream. She kept her mouth shut for several heartbeats, trying to keep the anger at bay.

When she finally opened her mouth again it was to say, "I don't think I understand what you mean. I was invited here on a date by a friend. Nothing more. If you're on the hunt for hardened criminals, I'm afraid you'll have to look elsewhere."

Cross let out a long, exaggerated sigh before glancing back down at her. "Oh, Auburn. I must admit that I'm disappointed. I thought we'd agreed to be honest with each other."

"I don't make deals with people incapable of keeping them." The words were out before Burn could stop herself, and she immediately regretted them. But Cross just looked amused, like a small, weak puppy had tried to attack him but had merely managed to nip at his ankle.

Cross lapsed into silence, enjoying the moment and his control over it – and over her. Burn, on the other hand, struggled to retain her composure. That feat doubled in difficulty when Scar's voice crackled through her earrings. Burn was so startled that she missed a beat and stepped on one of Cross' feet, producing a barely contained grunt of pain.

"Burn!" Scar cried. True to her word, only Burn could hear her sister's voice through the comms. Cross remained blissfully unaware.

After a few seconds of waiting for Burn's reply, Scar

continued, "Something's happened. Something bad. You need to come home now."

Burn plastered a blank look on her face, but her insides were churning. Had someone been hurt? Was something wrong with Scar? Had Cross done something to her? Although she desperately wanted to ask, she couldn't risk it – not in front of Cross.

Undaunted, Scar went on. "Hale sent a message to the Lunaria – a message about you. I told you that hack would come in handy." Even in moments of crisis, Scar still found time to bask in her own genius.

"Apparently he was following you tonight. He saw you with Kaz. He tracked you to the party. He thinks you're working with them. Burn, he told the Lunaria that you're a traitor."

Shocked, Burn missed another beat and collided with Cross, sending a shock of pain through her injured leg. She gasped and stopped the dance, clutching at the spot in a futile attempt to soothe the pain.

"Why, Ms. Alendra, I am so sorry," he said without a hint of feeling behind the words. "Here, let me escort you off the dance floor so you can sit down." Burn limped away, refusing Cross' assistance.

Her mind whirled, coursing with pain and anger and fear. Hale thought she was a traitor. And right now he could be convincing every member of the Lunaria that she was not to be trusted. If that happened, all of the information she had gained would be for nothing.

On top of all of that, Cross knew about her leg. If the officers who had chased her had reported back about the intruder's injury, he'd be able to place her at the scene of the crime. He'd connect her to Amblys and to the Lunaria, and he'd make sure she paid.

"I'm so sorry to have to cut our dance short," she finally said. "I did warn you that I wasn't a good dancer. I guess you're not as good of a leader as you thought." She didn't know what she was saying. She wanted to say something – anything – to deflect his unwavering attention.

Focus, Burn, she told herself. Get out of here. Get out now. Figure out the rest later. But right now, GET OUT.

"It was…nice to see you again, General Cross," she said haltingly. "But I think I should be getting home. I hope you enjoy the rest of your night." With that, she turned and fled, all but running up the stairs and into the entrance hall. After hastily collecting her mask and goggles, she tumbled out of the house and into the night.

She'd just stepped into the elevator when a voice echoed behind her in the darkness, calling her name. Spinning around, she saw Kaz rushing toward her, a look of confusion and desperation painting his features.

Burn knew she had a choice. She could forget the Lunaria, turn her back on them like they'd done to her. Maybe Kaz could keep her safe – or maybe they could go into hiding, taking Scar with them and building a new life somewhere Cross would never find them. Or she could fight. She could take on Hale and force the Lunaria to listen. It was love versus duty. Happiness or justice. She made her choice in an instant.

"Kaz, this was a mistake. I can't do this," she said as he reached her, panting.

"Wait! Just tell me what's going on," he pleaded, trying to make her stay.

"I don't belong here. Just leave me alone. Forget I ever existed." With that, she let the elevator doors close between them, sealing them in their separate worlds.

The anger and frustration inside of her were threatening to tear her apart, and she slammed her hand against the upholstered wall with a thud. How had everything fallen apart so fast? How had she allowed this to happen? She cursed her own stupidity for ever accepting Kaz's invitation, for ever thinking she could do this.

The elevator bell dinged and the doors opened, ushering her out into the smog-filled evening that she'd left behind only a few hours before. Was it only a few hours, Burn thought? It felt like a lifetime ago. So much had happened. So much was going to happen.

She hurried out, her pace quickening into a run as she made her way downward. She needed to get home, needed to get to Scar. Together, they would find a way through this.

She scrambled over a walkway, then down a set of stairs, not even sure if she was heading in the right direction. She took a turn, then another, pausing for a minute to get her bearings before backtracking in the opposite direction. All she knew was that she needed to keep running, needed to go farther, faster, and maybe everything would be fine. But that's not how the world works.

Without warning, a shadow stepped out in front of her, blocking her path. Burn had to grab onto the cold brick wall beside her to slow her momentum, slicing her palm in the process. She panted heavily, the filth of the city making it impossible to draw a clean breath.

Burn backed up slowly as the figure moved toward her, his measured pace menacing. In an instant she found herself with her back against a cold stone wall. The man, however, kept inching closer, emerging from the fog and resolving into the all too familiar form of General Illex Cross.

"What a coincidence, running into you here," came his cold, cruel voice. But, despite his words, Burn knew this was no coincidence.

"What do you want?" Burn asked. She knew it wasn't the most pertinent question. In fact, she would have bet anything that she already knew the answer to it. But her mind had suddenly gone blank, emptying of anything and everything until only his voice was left, echoing dangerously through her thoughts.

"You, my dear. I want you."

By this time he was in front of her, and he leaned in, putting his hand on the wall behind her. She couldn't think of anything to say – or anything to do to get herself out – so she merely stood there, like an animal hoping against hope that a predator will pass them by after catching their scent.

"You are such a little nuisance, aren't you? Always turning up where you're not wanted. Always sticking your nose where it doesn't belong. You think you're so clever. But in reality, you're just a sad little girl who wants something she can't have."

He leaned closer, pressing against her much the same as Kaz had earlier that night. Except it was nothing like his touch. This was basic, primal, and savage, a move fueled by a desire for power rather than any kind of sexual intent. It made Burn's skin crawl and she writhed, trying to find a weak spot. But her movement only seemed to provoke him further, and he pinned her to the wall tightly, his hands trapping her arms at her sides. She moved her face to get as far away from his as she could, but she could still feel his warm breath against her cheek.

"You're pathetic," he whispered into her ear. "Just like your father was."

She spat in his face, the only recourse she could think of. He twisted his head to the side to dislodge the saliva, but he didn't loosen his hold on her.

"Don't you DARE mention my father. He was more of a man – more of an officer – than you'll ever be."

At that, Cross let out a small chuckle, shaking his head in disdain. "You only idolize the man because he's gone. Why, I could tell you stories that would make your skin crawl – of the things he did, the people he hurt. He wasn't better than me. In fact, he was just like me. Only I'm better at staying alive."

"If I'm so pathetic," Burn spat back, "then why are *you* here? Why not send more of your cronies to bring me in?"

"If you want something done right, blah, blah, blah." He sounded almost bored at having to explain it to her. "Besides, who knows how many of my officers you've corrupted with your lies? You clearly have your claws into more than one. So sneaky of you, by the way. Kudos on your devious plan."

Burn wanted to protest, wanted to say that Kaz and Grayland had nothing to do with any of this, but she kept her mouth shut. Bringing their names into it would only cause more trouble, and she didn't want them to have to pay for her ill-fated choices.

Burn's legs were trapped beneath his considerable bulk. She tried to move one out from under him so she could strike, but the move only made him press into her more deeply. So instead, she used the only part of her body not currently imprisoned by his – her head. She gathered her courage and swung it forward, attempting to headbutt him with all the strength she could muster.

But he was quicker, moving his head out of the way with such speed that her neck snapped and her head bounced back into the hard wall behind her, momentarily stunning her.

"You're so plucky," Cross said from a safe distance, smiling wickedly. "It's such a shame that I can't keep you around. But I can't have you getting in my way." He didn't sound sad at all. Actually, Burn thought through the pounding in her head, he sounded quite giddy about it.

"If you're going to kill me, just do it already," she bit back, the sharpness in her voice a match for his own. "I'd rather be dead than listen to you prattle on any longer."

"Ouch, you hurt me," he retorted. "But seriously, you've got me wrong. I don't want to kill you. No, death would be too good for someone like you, too quick."

Burn almost wished for death then. The alternatives flashing through her head were more vile than just ceasing to exist. Torture. Or worse, Cross forcing himself on her. He was already pressed so close against her, and he was clearly enjoying it.

"So what do you intend to do with me, then?" she asked after an inordinately long pause.

The all-knowing look was back as he leeringly looked

her over. "Oh, I have something much better planned for you. But I don't want to spoil the surprise. What fun would that be?"

"Oh, come now," Burn said, panic bubbling up in her chest. She squirmed, trying to get free, and felt one of her legs start to loosen from his hold. All she had to do was keep him talking. Then maybe, just maybe she could work her way out of this. "Give me a hint? We are old friends, after all."

Another bemused chuckle. Just start talking, Burn thought. I know how you like to listen to yourself talk. "Well, let's just say that you're going to come in handy. I have this experiment going, you see, and I think I've just found my next test subject."

Burn wriggled her leg, finding more give beneath his heavy body. She saw her chance – and she took it. She wrenched her leg free of him and kicked in the direction of his kneecap. She heard a satisfying crunch as she made contact, and Cross' hands loosened their grasp on her.

She didn't hesitate, pulling her arms free of him and pushing his body off hers. The refreshing night air met her free limbs, cooling the places where Cross' skin had burned against hers.

She was free. She started moving blindly, her only goal to get away – as far away as she could and as fast as she could. Her legs felt too heavy, but she kept moving, putting more space between her and Cross. Or so she thought.

Suddenly a sharp pain blossomed on the back of her head, accompanied by a dull metallic thud and an unnatural ringing in her ears. She collapsed to the ground, stunned. Without wasting a moment, Cross grabbed her hands, tying them tightly behind her back. Darkness descended as he secured a blindfold over her eyes. Burn used her last ounce of energy to muster a scream, but that, too, was cut off as Cross stuffed a gag into her throat, silencing her calls for help.

# CHAPTER 17

The pain in Burn's head was what finally woke her. She'd been having some sort of dream – well, more of a nightmare. Something about a decadent party and a hero and a villain. But something had gone wrong. The hero had left. And no matter how fast she ran, she couldn't escape the evil force that was trying to trap her.

She awoke in a cold sweat, gripping her head. She should have drunk less last night, she thought groggily. Last night. Something important was nagging at the back of her mind, trying to find its way out. What had happened last night?

Burn sat up abruptly, the full force of the night's events coming back to her. She tried to open her eyes, but for some reason her goggles were missing and the haze in this place made her eyes sting. The best she could do was squint into the misty light around her.

As her memories of the night before came crashing into place, a sense of panic tightened in her chest. That, combined with the poor air quality and her lack of a mask, led to a coughing fit, and she knelt down on all fours to brace herself against the cool floor.

Once the attack had subsided, she tried to open her eyes again to get a sense of her surroundings. She could only make out bits and pieces of the room around her, but she got the sense that it was small and dim and seemed to be crowded with discarded pieces of furniture. The only source of light was a single bulb on the ceiling, which cast fuzzy shadows on the walls and floors.

There were no windows to give her a sense of where she was or even what time of day it was. Burn had no idea how long she had been out.

Her head pounded, and she vaguely remembered being hit with something large and hard before Cross had seized her. The ensuing journey had been a blur of sounds. At one point, she had been dragged along the ground before being placed (not too gently) on some sort of cart that had transported her here. At least they'd been kind enough to remove her restraints.

She tried to stand up, but a sudden overwhelming dizziness brought her crashing back down, and she collided with a wooden table on her way to the floor. Another bruise to add to the collection.

Burn crawled over to a chair in the corner and gently hoisted herself onto the seat. It was old and full of holes, and the springs were poking through in more than one place, but it felt good to sit on something other than the cold ground. She let her head rest on the high back, relishing the temporary relief. Because it was just that: temporary.

This was a holding cell of sorts, a place to store people and things until their owners found a proper way to dispose of them. Burn had no misconceptions on that account. She was here to be "taken care of," and whatever Cross had in store for her it was going to hurt.

Burn looked around the room slowly, eyes closed into slits, scanning for a weapon. Sure, she could barely move without falling down and she could hardly see a thing through the haze, but that was no reason not to be prepared. However, nothing useful jumped out of the rubbish as an obvious weapon. Each piece of furniture in the room seemed to be large and cumbersome, not anything she could easily break or fashion into a makeshift bat, especially in her weakened state.

She closed her eyes again, breathing through the panic and the pain. She took stock of her situation, trying to think calmly and rationally about her options and her prospects. How could she get out of this? Was there anyone out there who could help her?

Scar didn't know where she was. She remembered belatedly that she hadn't even told her sister all of what she'd learned. Burn could have kicked herself for her stupidity. But then she remembered Scar's amazing spy gadgets, and a glimmer of hope fluttered to life inside her chest. It was promptly extinguished, however, when she realized that she'd been stripped of her necklace and earrings, and her bag was nowhere to be found.

Burn slumped deeper into the chair, the eradicated hope leaving an even deeper despair within her. If only she'd had one thing – one solitary thing – from her bag, then she

175

might have been able to find a way out. What she wouldn't give right now for an exploding mint or a set of lock-picking glasses!

But no, that would have been too simple. The most Burn could hope for was that her bag had made it here with her and that Scar could somehow track it and find her. But what then? Scar couldn't rescue her on her own. She could barely venture out of the house to buy food on her own.

Scar would have to recruit others to help save her – and that would only lead to disaster. It wasn't as if Burn had many people on her side right now. Hale assumed she was a traitor – and had convinced the Lunaria of it, as well. And Kaz thought she wanted nothing to do with him. Besides, he was one of the very people who had put her in this place.

What if Kaz had been in on this plot all along? A brief flash of pain flickered through Burn as the thought crept into her mind. Had he purposely put her in a compromising situation so Cross would have an excuse to take her in? Had it been Cross' idea all along, and Kaz was just his obedient lapdog?

She didn't want to believe it. Kaz had seemed so sweet, so sincere. Burn didn't have that much experience with men, but she had at least believed that she could sense a liar in her midst. But what did she really know? Everywhere she had turned last night, Cross had been there, as if he had known where she was going to be and what she was going to do. It would have been so simple for Kaz to feed her whereabouts back to his superior. She could just about imagine him doing it, too, laughing at how easy it was to con her.

Burn closed her eyes harder, forcing the images out of

her head. Even if it were true, lingering on it now wouldn't help. She needed a plan, not a broken heart.

She opened her eyes again, willing herself to see past the small room, to pick up some trace of life beyond. Burn breathed deeply, choking on the polluted air. Something felt strange about this room, oppressive, like the whole world was on top of her, weighing her down.

It was obvious she wasn't in the Peace Station. Those cold gray walls and too-bright cells were familiar to her. This place was entirely different, almost foreign with its smell of dirt and its too-thick smog. Then the pieces clicked into place. She was underground. Or at least at the extreme bottom of Kasis, farther down than she'd ever ventured before, even below the Corax End.

But why would Cross have brought her here? The only people that lived down here were the poorest of the poor, the ones whom life passed by and the world forgot about. She'd heard stories that they didn't even live in houses, but merely camped out in tents and shacks built of anything they could find. They lived on – and with – rats and mice and insects.

Looking around, though, Burn could tell that she wasn't in a shack. So what kind of person would take the time and money to build a house here, in the depths of the city, amongst the garbage and refuse?

Think, Burn, she commanded herself. Her brain felt slow and foggy, a lingering effect of the nice little blow Cross had dealt to the back of her skull. She found her fingers instinctively traveling up to investigate the wound. They came away flaked with the rusty brown of dried blood. Well, at least she wasn't still bleeding, she thought giddily.

Focus. Concentrate. Where was she? Whose house had Cross brought her to? Then something Cross said came drifting back into Burn's mind, and she tried to grasp at its fuzzy edges. *Death would be too good for someone like you.*

No, that wasn't it. That was almost it. But he'd said something else, something after that. Burn remembered that she'd found it odd, whatever he'd said, but she hadn't had time to pick it apart, to parse it for deeper meanings.

All of a sudden, a word appeared in her head, followed by another and another. *Experiment. Test. Subject.* Burn's body went numb with the realization. She was going to be a test subject in one of Cross' inhumane experiments. The panic returned with a passion.

There was no one coming to rescue her. She was trapped. And it was up to her to get out of it. That was a sobering realization. The panic abated – or, more accurately, the panic was overshadowed by something else. A determination. Or a steely resolve. She was not going to die here – or anywhere that Cross dictated. Her life was hers and hers alone.

With that, she closed her eyes and opened up her mind to the world around her. If she was going to get out of this, she would have to use everything she had.

It took longer than usual to tune in to the world outside, and when she did the sounds were muted and fuzzy. Burn concentrated harder, willing her mind farther outside of itself, past the walls and the pain and her own addled state. She reminded herself of her daily exercises and breathed gently, trying to find clarity amidst the chaos.

The first thing she picked up on was the noise from the street – or at least she assumed it was a street. Footsteps falling on dirt paths, coughing, people greeting each other in low, murmured voices. Everything seemed subdued, not just the sounds but also the people themselves. It was as if everything and everyone was struggling to get through – get through the haze, get through this place, get through the present and on to something, anything different.

The limited sounds from the outside world made it difficult for Burn to form a complete picture of her surroundings. But she did come to the conclusion that the pollution was just as bad in the rest of the tier as it was in her little corner of it. That, paired with the sporadic coughing and choking she heard, reinforced her conclusion that she was somewhere deep in the bowels of Kasis.

With that theory confirmed, she turned her attention to the inside of the building. Burn stood up, carefully this time, and made her way to the far wall on which stood a large wooden door. She closed her eyes and leaned her head against its rough surface, willing herself to hear beyond it into the rest of the building.

Her first impression was silence, heavy and oppressive, like the house itself had been scared into muting all that took place within its walls. But the more she listened, the more Burn heard hints of life. Pots and pans clanked lightly somewhere above and to the left, which she took to be the kitchen, while someone strode gently down a carpeted hall even higher above her.

As she stood there, her head to the door, Burn could almost make out the outlines of the house itself. It was tall, at least three stories, and wide, with a couple of rooms stretching out across from her. It was shallow, though, with more dwellings crammed against its back and sides, enhancing the feeling of claustrophobia.

Burn turned around and slid down the door, her body already tired from the mild exertion. She landed on the hard floor and sat there, knees to chest, continuing to explore the house with her senses.

There was someone else in the place, someone on the topmost floor whose limited movements made them difficult to track. She cocked her head, straining to hear more. Scribbling. Tapping. Intermittent pacing. Someone in an office, perhaps? Maybe the person who was holding her hostage in this place, one of Cross' minions? Or maybe Cross himself, pacing in his secret lair while deciding what to do with her? Without the benefit of dialogue, it was difficult to say for sure.

A sudden coughing fit broke Burn out of her contemplation. In the quiet space, with so little noise to compete with it, the sounds of her cough bounced off the furniture and walls, coming back to her in staggered echoes. Compared to the oppressive silence of her surroundings, the sounds were jarring. She covered her mouth with her elbow in an attempt to suppress the noise. There was no need to draw attention to herself.

Above her, a chime rang suddenly, sending small, tinny waves of sound floating through the house. Someone was at the door. The figure in the upstairs room rallied, brought to attention by the noise. They made their way down the stairs to what Burn supposed was the front door, opening it to allow entrance.

"Ah, it's you," came a high male voice. Not Cross, then.

"Come in, come in," the man drawled with lofty superiority.

"Any issues?" asked the newcomer, nearly whispering. Even in a whisper, though, Burn knew that voice, knew its malice and cruelty. Cross. So this wasn't his house, after all, but he was clearly involved in whatever was going to become of her.

Burn instinctively dashed to the other side of the room, putting as much space between her and the villains as possible, since it was only a matter of time before they came for her. She resumed her search for a weapon while paying close attention to the conversation above her, praying for something – anything – she could use to aid her in her escape.

"No, nothing," the higher voice answered happily, sounding more like a faithful lapdog than an equal. "Not a sound, in fact. Hope she's still alive down there. But if not, well, it's not a great loss."

"She better be alive," Cross growled menacingly. "I have plans for her." The way he said it made a shiver of pure terror crawl down Burn's spine. She clutched at herself tightly to keep from shaking.

You're brave, she told herself as the footsteps began to draw closer. You're resourceful. This isn't the end. She repeated those three phrases again and again, willing herself to accept them.

Cross and his lackey descended a set of stairs, pausing down the hall from her cell.

"I don't get it," said the high-voiced man questioningly. "I mean, she's not like the others. She's…just a girl. Why her?"

Cross chuckled quietly. "You underestimate her, which is

your first mistake. There's more to her than you think. I'd bet you that she's just like the rest of them – a *freak*. I don't know what it is yet, but she's hiding something. Don't worry, she'll make an excellent guinea pig."

So Cross did suspect that she had an ability after all – but he didn't know what it was. That worked in her favor, Burn thought as she mentally cataloged Cross' words, saving them to dissect later. If there was a later.

The pair started to move again, rapidly approaching her location. A beep sounded as the biometric lock disengaged and the door to her room swung open, revealing the towering figure of Cross. He was flanked by a rotund little man who barely fit in the doorway, his girth blocking out most of the light from the hall.

Burn made no move toward them, choosing instead to remain still and motionless in the corner. Cross strode farther into the room, stopping a few feet away from where she stood. They eyed each other slowly, each taking stock of the other.

"Well, well, she's not dead after all," Cross said to the squat man, his eyes never leaving her. "We were afraid your little blow to the head was too much for you." He addressed her directly now, his voice dripping with sarcasm and disdain. "Delicate constitutions and all that. But I'm glad to see you're doing so well. This wouldn't have been half as much fun without you."

Burn kept her mouth shut, biting the inside of her lip to keep from spitting out a sarcastic retort – or just plain spitting at him. Both were viable options. Cross reveled in her silence, taking her lack of response as submission. He came closer, towering over Burn, and her thoughts flashed back to the events of the night before.

"We could have been friends, you know. Even allies. You could have gone far had you joined us. But, no, you had to join *them* and their petty little cause. Oh, yes, I know all about your little Lunaria. So powerless, so futile. They're never going to accomplish anything, poor creatures."

He licked his lips before continuing, and Burn shuddered in disgust. "I guess it runs in the blood, though, this rebellious attitude, this distaste for authority. I mean, your father was the same, just as much of a dirty, spineless rat. But I took care of him. And now I'm going to take care of you."

"What did you do to him?" Burn whispered between clenched teeth, straining against her instincts in an attempt to stay still.

He laughed that evil little laugh, his eyes twinkling in the darkness. "I threw him in the Pit. I dragged him there with my own two hands and dropped him in. You should have heard him beg. So pathetic. Oh, but the way he screamed as he fell – it was such a satisfying sound. A traitor getting what he deserved."

Burn couldn't hold back the fire any longer. "You're a sadist, a sad little man who has to resort to violence because he has no real idea how to lead. You deserve to rot in hell along with everyone else on your fucking *Peace* Force."

Before she could prepare herself, Cross backhanded her across the face, sending her head flying back. As she tried to regain her balance, Cross grabbed her by the hair and pulled her head up in front of his.

"You're worthless. Remember that," he said as his eyes

scanned every inch of her face. "No one will miss you when you're gone. You're just a pitiful little girl who tried to play with fire and got burned. You're out of your depth, and it will be my pleasure to make sure you pay."

With that, he threw her toward the door. Burn landed hard on her knees, hearing them thud grotesquely against the cold stone floor. "Take this *garbage* out of my sight. Put her in something more suitable, then dose her and send her out. The sooner she's gone, the better."

Still reeling from her fall, Burn flinched when two warm hands grasped her arm and pulled, yanking her roughly to her feet. Once she was standing again, the hands let go of her, and the fat little man clamped a smooth metal collar around her neck.

Burn's hands instinctively reached up to the collar to pull it away from her neck, but she was stopped by a small tsk-ing sound from her rotund jailer.

"I wouldn't do that if I were you. You see, this little beauty is a marvel of modern technology. If you try to remove it, it explodes – along with your head." He sounded so gleeful, as if he wanted her to try to escape just so he could watch the aftermath.

"I'm the only one who can get it off," he continued, smiling. "And that won't be happening until we have you right where we want you."

He turned on his heel, sprightly in his excitement, and grabbed a chain that Burn hadn't noticed before. He attached the chain to her collar and pulled, propelling her along the hall behind him. He almost skipped up the stairs, Burn following in his wake and Cross bringing up the rear.

It was difficult to see where she was going, but the chain attached to her neck tugged her along in the right direction. Both Cross and her captor wore goggles, allowing them to see through the fog, but apparently sight wasn't something they wanted to grant her.

Burn almost tripped when they reached another staircase but steadied herself on the banister. The heavy man tugged harder on her leash, pulling her up the stairs and onto the landing. Once they were on the same level, he turned, leading her into another small room at the end of the hall.

He stopped at the doorway, and Burn felt a prod from behind her as Cross pushed her into the room.

"Be a good little girl and get changed," said the fat man, indicating a pair of rags on top of a rickety wooden table. "And if you don't, we'll do it for you." With that, he shut the door in her face.

# CHAPTER 18

$\mathrm{B}$urn took stock of her new surroundings. Like the last room, this one was dim and hazy, making it difficult for her to discern everything around her. But she could tell that this space was less cluttered than the last, with a small table in the middle on which sat her new "clothes."

Clothes was a generous term for them. Burn picked them up and considered them for a moment, running her hands over the rough pants and battered shirt. She briefly contemplated not following their orders but dismissed the idea just as rapidly. Pants – even ones as torn and stained as these – were easier to move in than a ballgown. Or easier to run away in, at least.

She changed hastily, slightly afraid that the men would come bursting back in. But as she listened outside, she heard them travel down the hall and into a room on the other side of the building, shutting a door behind them. Burn grabbed the shoes that had been placed next to the rags and crammed her feet into them, wincing as her battered toes curled to fit into the too-small space.

Burn balled up the dress and placed it on the table where her "new" clothes had sat. She felt a pang of guilt for the state of it, ripped in places and covered in blood and dirt in others. It had been such a beautiful gown, and now it was forever ruined, irreparable. She dreaded explaining the outfit's demise to Symphandra – but quickly realized that that was the least of her worries. What was a ruined dress compared to almost certain death at the hands of a tyrant?

Burn glanced down at herself, considering her new look. The shirt was more of a sack, hanging loosely against her small frame, and the pants were much the same. Altogether the clothes had the distinct effect of making her appear homeless and possibly deranged. That was probably exactly the look they were going for. The smell was powerful, as well, reminding her of some combination of onions and singed hair. She wondered briefly who had worn the garments before her – and what had happened to them – but ultimately decided that she didn't want to know.

As she tested her range of motion in the new attire, Burn kept tabs on the room across the hall, listening for any hint of conversation. It was quiet at first as the men poured one another a drink, settling themselves in chairs in what seemed to be the office. But they couldn't ignore their business dealings for long.

"Are we almost ready?" the large man asked Cross, sounding impatient with him. "I thought we were done with our tests. Then you bring me another one!"

"Patience, Wight," Cross said languidly, pausing to take

a sip of his drink.

Wight. Her jailer had a name. Burn hurriedly rifled through her memories trying to place the name, but it was foreign to her. She filed it away with the rest of the bits and fragments she'd learned.

Cross continued, "Two days. Give me two days and everything will be in place."

Wight sounded like he wanted to protest but stopped himself. It was clear that Cross had the upper hand in their dealings. He was in charge and Wight was simply one of his pawns – just like Burn.

"You still haven't told me how it's all going to work," Wight ventured timidly. Cross remained silent, so he went on, gaining volume and speed as he spoke. "I mean, how does my ManniK fit into your war? We've done the tests, and it works well for small-scale disruptions, but one or two mutants on rampages aren't going to do much damage against a quarter of the population."

The mention of ManniK sparked something in Burn's memory, and she flashed back to the night before. The papers in the desk, the ones about testing ManniK on mutants. It was all part of their plan after all. And she was going to be one of the test subjects. Her blood went cold at the realization. They were planning to dose her with ManniK then set her free in the city to terrorize innocent citizens, just as they'd done with dozens of people before her.

An image of herself blind with rage and hatred, unable to tell friend from foe, crept into her mind. Who knows how many people she would hurt before someone stopped her? Would some of them be friends? The Lunaria? Scar? Burn couldn't imagine herself harming her own sister, but then again she wouldn't truly be herself anymore, would she? The drug would take her over and she'd become someone else entirely – or some*thing* else. It was a chilling thought.

"One or two, Wight?" Cross asked, his voice bordering on amusement. "You think too small. You've always thought too small. That's why your drug *empire* has never even made it past this godforsaken level."

"So your plan is to use more of them?"

Cross sighed, obviously frustrated that Wight wasn't quick on the uptake. "No, Wight. My plan is to use everyone. All these people. All the lowlifes and cretins and complete wastes of space down here. There are enough mutated humans in this cesspit to ensure mass hysteria and carnage."

"But...I don't understand," Wight stuttered. "How... how will that even work? How can you dose so many people? And once you do, how can you contain them?"

A bark of laughter escaped Cross' mouth. "Contain them? Why would I want to contain them? I want them to spread into every corner of the lower levels, leaving panic and bloodshed in their wake. I want them to *destroy* these poor, insufferable areas – and the people in them! And whatever they don't destroy, we will. We'll make the problem then use it as an excuse to cleanse the city of its demons.

"This city has been far too crowded for decades, the poor and downtrodden leaching off of us, bringing us down to their level. These people, they're society's burden, freaks who should never have existed in the first place. And once they're gone, everyone will be better off. Cleaner air. More jobs. Less crime. It's the perfect solution."

A lengthy pause followed as Cross basked in his own genius. Wight, on the other hand, coughed and stammered, trying to make sense of everything Cross had said. Burn was in a similar boat, her mind overflowing with everything he had let slip about his plan – and everything that was about to happen in the city.

With the silence stretching, Cross spoke again. "And the best part is, they'll blame it on the addicts and the dealers. 'They should have controlled themselves,' they'll say. Or, 'They deserved what they got.' And we'll be the heroes who put the whole thing to a stop, saving countless lives in the process."

"But what about me?" Wight squeaked, concern apparent in his voice. "You're not going to lay the blame on me, are you? I thought we'd agreed…"

Cross interrupted him, cutting off the end of his statement. "I'm a man of my word, Wight. You'll be adequately compensated for your assistance and get a brand-new compound on one of the highest tiers. Unless, of course, you screw this up. In which case you get nothing."

Silence fell again as both men drank heavily from their glasses, Wight downing his in a few long gulps. "Sir…" he began, then stopped. His voice was wavering, and Burn could imagine his fat little hands shaking as he gripped his empty glass.

"What?" Cross barked, nearing the end of his rope.

"It's just that…I still don't understand how you're going to do it. How you're going to dose all those people at once, I mean. I gave you an adequate supply, but not one big enough for an entire city."

"Once again, Wight, you think too small. I'm tempted to make you wait and see. But then I wouldn't get to see your face when you finally figure it out, and what a shame that would be." He took another sip of his drink, enjoying the suspense. "Fine, fine. The truth is, we're not dosing them at all. We're gassing them."

"Wha...What?" Wight's stuttering was getting worse.

"We're gassing them. We've made your lovely little formula into an aerosol, which my troops will take down in canisters to the lowest tiers. With the hideous amounts of pollution down here, no one will even realize until it's too late. And we'll have all the exits locked down so there will be no means of escape. Anyone who tries to flee...well, let's just say we'll be armed and ready." He let out a self-important chuckle as he congratulated himself on his ingenious plan.

"Now, it's time to get to work," Cross said, standing. "I have to get to the station. And you have a job to do." With that, he let himself out of the office and walked down the stairs and out the front door.

Back in her little room, Burn fumed. It was a massacre they were planning alright. A massacre of tens of thousands of innocent citizens – maybe even more. Their only crime? Not being born to wealth or privilege or being born "different" – different than the norm, different than the rich, different than their ruling class.

It was ironic, she thought, looking back on all she'd learned. She had tried so hard to figure out what they were planning and had discovered next to nothing. Now, here in this place, she knew it all – and couldn't tell a single soul.

Burn sighed, inhaling a lungful of the polluted air, then

coughed repeatedly to rid her lungs of the vile poison. Once again, just like in her basement cell, the sound bounced back at her from around the room, hitting its various surfaces and reverberating toward her highly attuned ears.

Her mind struck on that, abruptly changing course from Cross' disturbing conversation. Burn could hear the room – not just the sounds within it, but the actual layout of the space.

Burn tested it again, closing her eyes and making a small clicking sound. As she traversed the room, a picture of it grew in her mind – where the furniture was, where the walls were, where the soft fabric sat on the table, absorbing parts of the sound.

This could work, she thought, a bubble of hope rising in her chest. She would have to be quick and precise, but it might work.

She didn't know how much time she had until Wight came back, so she moved swiftly, getting everything in place as efficiently as she could. She tore a few strips of fabric from her now-ruined dress, tying them together to form a long rope.

Then she unscrewed the single light in the ceiling, loosening the bulb until its rays just started to flicker. She secured the rope of fabric tightly to the base, creating a makeshift cord with which she could yank out the bulb and extinguish the light.

Burn's plan wasn't perfect. So much could go wrong. But she had no other choice. She put herself in position, stowing her body as best as she could behind the door, and waited.

It seemed like an eternity. Wight moved sluggishly

through the house, his girth no doubt impeding his progress. He walked with heavy footsteps first down the stairs then up them again, pausing on each landing to catch his breath. Then he entered another room on the top floor – a room that Burn later gathered was the bathroom, based on the uncomfortable noises issuing from it.

Finally he started toward her. Burn waited with bated breath as he made his way down the hall, pausing to unlock the door with a touch of his finger. This was it, Burn thought nervously, mentally steeling herself for what she was about to do. This was her chance – her only chance – at freedom.

The door opened slowly and Wight waddled in, scanning the room for her. He took one step, then another, his eyes catching on the cloth rope affixed to the light bulb. Sensing that something was amiss, he began to back up, but it was already too late.

Burn slammed the door shut, trapping him in the room. At the same time, she pulled with all her might on the rope, shattering the bulb and sending glass flying through the air. The space was instantly consumed by darkness, and Burn gripped the rope hard in her hands as she began making a low clicking noise with her tongue.

Once again, an image of the room resolved in her mind – and Wight was in the center of it. She acted swiftly, almost without thinking, jumping onto his back and ripping off his goggles. Wight flailed instinctively, like a bronco trying to buck off a novice rider. Within seconds, he had grabbed hold of her arms and torn them from his neck, sending her sprawling backward.

Burn landed hard on the cold floor but didn't have time

to assess her injuries. She jumped back up, the rope still clutched in her hand. Her clicking revealed that Wight was headed toward the door, and she leapt again, vaulting onto the table and wrapping the cloth cord around Wight's throat.

He clawed at it, but she held tight, steadily choking the life out of him. In an attempt to free himself from her grasp, Wight lunged forward, throwing all of his weight to the ground. It worked, yanking Burn off the table and sending her flying forward to land on top of him. She scrambled to her feet before he had a chance to grab her, positioning herself between him and the door.

Her rope, the only weapon she'd been able to fashion, was now in his possession, and he lumbered to his feet, unwrapping it from his neck. Burn froze in the darkness, trying to form a new plan as she stalked his slow movements.

Thankfully, the all-encompassing darkness was doing its job. Wight had no idea where she was, and he turned around cautiously, grabbing blindly at the empty air around him.

"Don't make this worse for yourself, little girl," he said as he moved. "I will find you, and once I do, you will regret this. I will make you PAY for this!" She didn't respond, not wanting to give away her own position in the darkness.

Burn knew she was small, with far less power behind her than this oaf of a man. But she was quick and, more importantly, had the element of surprise on her side. She made up her mind and sprang into action, running forward and jumping into a kick, which she aimed at his midsection.

The move worked, sending Wight sprawling backward into the table before he collapsed on the floor. Burn recovered in an instant and ran around to his head, stomping with all her might in the direction of his face. She heard a loud crunching sound as his nose gave way under her foot. He shouted with pain and anger, grasping at his now-bleeding face.

With the rope now free from his clutches, Burn took possession of it once again, dropping to her knees as she wrapped it once, then twice around his beefy neck, pulling with all her might. Wight clawed at her, more feebly this time, but she kept her grip on the cord. She felt him scratch her face along one side, but she didn't relent, the pain only adding fire to her anger.

Wight tried to cry for help, but all that came from his throat were small choking noises as he struggled to get air into his lungs. After a minute, his flailing arms slowed, then stopped entirely, dropping to his sides. Still high on adrenaline and panic, Burn kept her grip, fearing that the man would jump back to life and turn on her.

But he was still and silent, the fight gone from his body. Once she realized this, Burn relaxed, slumping back onto her heels. She had no idea if he was alive or dead and didn't care to listen closer to detect signs of breath.

Instead, she crawled to one side of his massive form and felt for his hands, bringing the left one up to her neck. It took a few tries to place his finger correctly on the locking sensor, but she finally managed it, hearing a small beep as the metal collar relaxed around her throat.

Burn breathed deeply, enjoying the feeling of the air on her neck. She stayed there, panting, for several moments, trying to make her heartbeat return to its normal rhythm. She knew she didn't have much time, that it was possible people had heard the commotion and were already on their way toward her. But for some reason she couldn't move, trapped in a state of aftershock that sent shudders down her spine.

Finally willing herself to act, she ran her hands along Wight's flabby waist until she found his pockets, which she emptied, stuffing the contents into her own. Then she tentatively reached up to his mouth, unwrapping his mask and tying it onto herself.

With that done, Burn began a quick search for his goggles, which she'd flung off somewhere near the door. On her hands and knees, she felt around for the leather of the band, hoping that they hadn't been damaged in the fall. Near the entrance, her fingers closed around their worn fabric, and she brought the goggles up and over her hair. The goggles themselves seemed to be intact, and she adjusted the band to fit her much smaller head, enjoying the feeling of opening her eyes without the sting of pollution.

She carefully got to her feet, wincing slightly as her myriad injuries sprang to life and protested her movements. Inching closer to the door, she found that it had automatically locked, trapping both her and Wight inside. Guessing that his fingerprint would once again be the key, Burn gritted her teeth and returned to the body. She put her hands under his arms, dragging him to the door in rough, halting movements. Once there, she brought his hand up to the keypad, pressing a finger to the scanner.

The accepting beep was music to her ears, and she was about to push the door open when a thought came to her. She immediately backpedaled and grabbed the collar that had so recently held her captive. She clamped it around

Wight's neck, squishing some of his flesh together so his entire girth would fit inside the metal circlet. She put her finger on the collar's scanner, imprinting her biometric data as the key code, and let his body fall back to the floor. If he was still alive, that would at least slow him down if he planned to come after her.

Listening closely to her surroundings, Burn heard no hint of footsteps outside the door, so she opened it gently, creeping out into the hall. The brightness temporarily blinded her, and she blinked as the house came back into focus. Making sure the door to the room was securely shut and locked, Burn made her way down the central staircase and out the front door.

# CHAPTER 19

It felt like a miracle that she hadn't run into anyone else – staff, family, drug-seeking clients – but she didn't have time to dwell on her luck. She needed to get out of there, wherever *there* was, and return to the city above – and to Scar.

Scar. The thought made Burn freeze in her tracks. What if Cross had already gotten to Scar? She knew he would have no qualms about targeting her sister, even if Scar hadn't had anything to do with Burn's plans. Images of her sister bound and gagged, at the mercy of Cross and his cronies, threatened to break through Burn's focus, but she held them at bay.

She had to hope, had to believe that Scar was safe, that Cross hadn't had time during his busy schedule of drugging and murdering people to find Scar and punish her for Burn's crimes. It was a small ray of hope, but it kept Burn moving.

The portion of the city in which she found herself was bleak, as were the people within it. Even worse than in Wight's home, the pollution here was thick and heavy, making progress difficult despite her new goggles and mask. The roads were composed of packed dirt that swirled around the people as they walked, mingling with the smog to create a thick haze of filth.

The stories she had heard about this place were right, at least in part. The road was flanked by makeshift homes and buildings comprised of boards or metal siding or even just thin fabric, anything people could find. But what she hadn't imagined was the true starkness of the place, the lack of life or joy or even light. Lamp posts were staggered here and there, but half of them didn't even function. The rest did their best to cut through the grime and darkness, but the meager rays weren't enough.

Despite the desolation, this zone was teeming with people. Children sat, playing in the dirt, as adults swarmed past in herds, going to and from their menial jobs or searching for anything that would get their family through another day.

Burn merged with the crowd, blending in with her raggedy clothing. She had feared that someone would notice her wounds or comment on the blood still matted to her head, but she shouldn't have worried. No one looked up. No one cared. Down here, she was just another faceless entity beaten down by life and trying to keep moving.

Without her tab, she had no way to search for directions back to the zones she knew. So she followed the crowd, hoping that the masses would lead her out of the darkness and up through the city.

As she walked, she considered her options. Hale had no doubt turned the Lunaria against her, whispering in their ears about her traitorous ties. Convincing them to listen to what she had to say, let alone trust her, was going to be a difficult feat. Maybe her sorry state and her sad tale would move them, but she doubted it. She would have to find a way to back up her claims, to prove what she had heard.

Maybe she could use something she'd taken off Wight. Looking around to make sure no one was watching, she reached into her pocket and pulled out the handful of items she'd managed to steal. An old-fashioned key. A wad of money. A vial of something white and viscous.

Burn looked closer at the vial, her curiosity piqued. Was this the ManniK that he'd planned to dose her with? If so, she might be able to use it to prove her innocence – or at least back up her claims about Cross' plan. It wasn't much, but it was something.

Gradually, her progress down the dark lane slowed, then stopped entirely. A crowd of people 80 or 90 strong stood in a pack blocking her way. She took advantage of her somewhat smaller stature, weaving through gaps in the chain and ducking under arms and between bodies.

The farther she got, the louder and angrier the people seemed to be – not at her, but at whatever barrier stood in their way. She craned her neck, trying to get a look at what was holding them there, but she couldn't see over the crowd. Continuing onward, her progress slowed, becoming harder and harder until she finally reached the front of the gathering.

From her viewpoint, Burn could at last make out the roadblock that was keeping these people trapped, barring them from their destinations. It was an actual roadblock, comprised of armed Peace Officers standing shoulder to shoulder blocking the passage of anyone up or down.

The crowd was incensed, screaming profanities and insults at the immobile officers. Burn was equally infuriated. How could she get back to her sister if they wouldn't let her out? How could she save this place if she couldn't escape it?

Then one of the Peace Officers spoke, quieting the crowd. "We have reason to believe that a dangerous criminal has escaped and is now on the loose in this part of the city. This man is armed and dangerous. Until we have this man in custody, no one will be allowed to travel between tiers."

Bullshit, Burn thought acidly. They were trying to keep the people where they were, sequester them in the lower tiers and foment a roiling anger. It was no doubt all part of Cross' plan: create an environment of hostility and anger, then dose them en masse, creating a bloodthirsty horde.

Burn had to get out of there. Anger and frustration fueled her on, and she made her way parallel to the blockade, traveling down the lane and out of the congestion. The more distance she covered, the fewer the people that stood in her way, and she was soon free of the crowd altogether. Before long, she found herself alone in a disused side alley, a dark passage that reeked of mud and filth.

Her mind was spinning, looking for any loophole that would help her get out. She could try to bribe one of the officers with the money she'd gotten off Wight. But they would never accept a bribe in front of so many people. She could scout around for another alley or secret passage up to the next tier. But Cross was thorough. He would have every route blocked – on this level and the ones above it. She was going to have to get creative if she wanted to get out of there alive.

A noise sounded at the other end of the alley, and Burn jumped back, hiding herself in the shadows. She glanced around, searching for a weapon, and her eyes landed on a large dislodged brick a few feet away. Without thinking, she lunged forward and grabbed it, hastily retreating back into the darkness.

She waited for a moment. Then two. Nothing happened and no one came down the dark lane. Yet she stayed where she was, silent and ready.

Then, through the darkness and haze, she heard footsteps. They sounded uneven and clumsy and were followed by loud crashes, like the person was injured – or drunk. Burn held her breath as the figure approached, emerging from the smog into the low light.

It was a Peace Officer. And he was clearly smashed, off his head on drugs or alcohol or some combination of the two.

Burn didn't even think. Instead, she jumped out of the shadows and swung, smashing the heavy brick into the officer's head. He dropped like a stone, hitting the dirt and staying there without so much as a twitch.

Her brain panicked at what she'd done, but she quickly recovered, pulling the body into the shadows alongside her. This was her chance – her one chance – and she wasn't going to let it pass by. Working swiftly, she stripped the officer of his gear, putting it on over her rags.

Despite the man's small frame, his tactical apparel still hung loosely around her limbs. It would have to do, though. She fastened his weapons belt around her waist, feeling the comforting weight of a loaded gun hanging against her leg.

Looking down at the unclothed officer lying in the dirt,

Burn couldn't even muster a hint of remorse for leaving him. She threw the brick down at his side, turning her back on him and returning the way she had come, back into the fray.

As she walked, she secured his goggles and mask around her face, carefully concealing any trace of her identity. It would be one thing to be caught sneaking through a road-block, but another thing entirely to be caught impersonating an officer. That was an offence you didn't come back from. She would have to tread carefully from there on out, being deliberate with every word and every action.

She tried to stick to the shadows as much as possible. Being a fugitive among Peace Officers was dangerous, but being a Peace Officer among protesters was doubly so. While her new garb would guarantee safety among fellow officers, it would also ostracize her from the masses, positioning her as an enemy of the people.

At first, as she traipsed through the disused alleys, no one stood in her way. In fact, no one even seemed to notice the lone officer creeping through the shadows. But as she neared the blockade, the tension around her mounted and people began to take notice. Some stood in her way, daring her to make them move. Others threw scraps and garbage as she passed. Yet more hurled insults her way, calling her a monster, a tyrant, a traitor.

"Move aside," Burn shouted at the crowd, adding authority to her words by grasping the weapon at her side. She tried to channel her father, tried to find his conviction and strength within herself and mold it into a character she could play. With a straight back and a straight face, she pushed onward, her eyes trained on the passageway that would allow her to escape.

She was close, but not close enough. A scream of rage erupted from someone behind her, and before she could turn to locate the source, she felt an enormous weight strike the middle of her back, knocking her to the ground. The breath escaped from her lungs as she landed hard on the packed dirt, her face bouncing painfully against the cool surface.

The crowd surged, gaining energy and purpose from one individual's act of bravery. They started advancing on the row of officers, their combined anger stripping their individuality and forming them into a joint force with one thought and one goal: to make their oppressors pay. And right now, Burn was one of those oppressors.

She tried to get up, tried to stand, but was knocked down again and again as countless pairs of feet trod over her, stepping on her legs, her hands, her back. Tears streamed from her eyes, fueled by pain and frustration and utter hopelessness. She had escaped one prison just to die in another. The taste of blood and dirt mingled in her mouth, threatening to choke her.

A sudden shot rang out, breaking through the bedlam and stopping the protesters in their tracks. Another shot followed, this time accompanied by screams. Still pinned to the ground, Burn couldn't see what was happening. But she could hear.

"He's dead! Oh my god, he's dead!"

"Stand back, unless you want to be next! Step aside. Go home."

"They shot him. I can't believe they actually shot him."

Gradually, the crowd surrounding Burn parted, and a

dark figure approached her. She lifted her head to find a Peace Officer standing before her, holding out his hand.

"Are you alright?" he asked, helping her gently to her feet. "Is anything broken?"

"I'm fine," Burn said, her voice wavering unsteadily. She took a step, but her legs no longer wanted to hold her weight, and the officer had to catch her to keep her from falling back into the dirt.

"You're not fine. Those animals did a number on you. But don't worry, we got the guy who started it. He won't be hurting anyone else."

His words didn't penetrate Burn's fog, only serving to confuse her further. But the sight of a body lying in the road surrounded by a pool of deep red liquid – that got through. It was the man who had hit her, she was sure of it. And now he was dead, shot through the head.

She stumbled again and bile rose up in her throat, threatening to spill over onto the street. His death was her fault. His life had been snuffed out in an instant because of her stupidity. Burn imagined his family, picturing daughters and sons whose lives would be forever altered, forever damaged.

But she had to keep going, another voice chimed in, pushing the grief into a corner of her mind. If she didn't make it back, if she didn't tell the Lunaria what was about to happen, it wouldn't just be the death of one man on her conscience – it would be the death of thousands. She couldn't let that happen.

"I got her! She's fine," the officer holding onto Burn yelled to his colleagues. A small cheer went through the ranks as they approached, and she received more than one pat on the back. Burn found herself unable to speak, so she merely nodded at the men, hoping it was enough to pacify them.

"Let's get you out of here, shall we," the officer said to Burn, less a question than a statement. "I'll escort you back, make sure you get through the rest of the blockades without issue."

"Thank you," Burn managed to get out, her voice still wavering slightly. She decided silence was her best option for getting out of this alive, so she kept her mouth shut as they walked, concentrating on putting one foot in front of the other.

Her whole body felt broken and bruised, and it was a struggle to keep moving. She wanted to sit down, put her head back, and go to sleep. She was certain she would have, too, if it weren't for the surprisingly strong officer at her side who kept her upright.

As they made their way upward, the man chatted genially, but Burn was unable to focus on his words. The conscious part of her brain wondered how she was going to ditch him so she didn't end up back at the Peace Station and back in Cross' clutches. The other, not-so-lucid part kept replaying the atrocities of the last day on a loop, starting with Cross' attack and ending with the man lying facedown in his own blood.

"…would love to lock them all up and throw away the key," the officer was saying. Burn heard the words, but they didn't penetrate the thick fog in her mind. He went on, "Of course, boss says we need the cells. They're overcrowded as it is. Gonna have to toss some of 'em out, if you know what I mean."

Burn must have fallen into a daze because the next thing she knew they were walking through another checkpoint and up into a higher tier. The air was steadily losing its viscosity, and Burn took several deep breaths to clear her head. It worked and some of the fuzziness floated away, leaving a renewed clarity in its place.

She slowly started to take her weight off the officer, testing her own strength. Her legs were shaky at first, but the more she moved the more her muscles responded, and she soon found that she could hold her own weight.

They had passed the final blockade now and were a few tiers away from the station – and from Scar. The shops and houses were now tinged with familiarity, and Burn knew she could find her way back on her own.

"I can take it from here," she said. "Thank you for your assistance, but you should get back to the team. It's clear they need you." She tried to put as much conviction into her voice as she could muster, and she hoped it was enough.

"Are you sure?" came his reply as he looked her up and down, assessing her myriad injuries.

She nodded, and without waiting for his response she walked on, leaving him behind in the street.

The journey back to her house was longer than Burn had anticipated. Every step sent a shock wave of pain through her limbs and up her core. But her stubbornness outweighed her agony and she kept moving, kept working her way closer and closer to Scar. The thought of Cross and what he would do to her sister if he had the chance was enough to propel her onward.

Finally, what seemed like hours later, she caught sight of her house. It stood there clear and bright, beckoning her forward. It felt like it took her an eternity to reach it, but she finally did, pressing her finger to the scanner to gain entry.

The door swung open and Scar – glorious Scar – turned to face her sister, her eyes wide with surprise as Burn removed her goggles and mask to reveal her identity.

Burn looked up weakly at her sister, willing the words to come out. "Cross is coming," she managed to whisper. "We have to go." With that, the world dropped out from under her and everything went black.

# CHAPTER 20

Burn woke up with a start, panic coursing through her veins. They had to get out. They had to flee. They had to find somewhere safe to hide.

"Scar!" she called out, frantic and confused, not even taking the time to process the world around her. "Scar!"

"I'm right here," came her sister's voice, calm and reassuring. Burn turned, eyes wild, to find her sister seated next to her on a low stool.

"We have to go. We have to get out. Cross could be here any minute." She spoke hurriedly, the words coming out in a jumbled stream. But Scar didn't seem worried. She was concerned, yes, but she made no move to get up or start packing or do anything else to indicate that she understood the severity of their situation.

"Calm down, Burn. It's OK. We're safe," Scar said, rubbing her cool hand against Burn's hot face. The gesture felt strange and foreign, and Burn flinched back from her sister's touch, retreating into the confines of the bed.

Bed. Something registered in Burn's brain, but she couldn't put a finger on it. Her thoughts seemed to be moving both too fast and too slow, creating a confused maze within her mind. Scar put her hands on Burn's shoulders, trying to keep her down as she struggled to rise.

"We have to go," Burn repeated, softer this time, pleading. Her sister shook her head, her strong hands keeping Burn from struggling.

A noise sounded in the hallway, and the door to the room creaked open, revealing another figure. Burn's mind jumped ahead, sure it would be Cross coming to take her sister away from her. But it wasn't. It was Symphandra.

Burn stopped her struggles, confused. She looked from Scar to Symphandra, not making the connection. She felt like she was lost somewhere in her own mind and was struggling to put the pieces of reality back together.

"We're safe," Scar said again, and this time Burn didn't protest. Instead, she looked around again, finally taking in some of her surroundings. This wasn't her bed. It wasn't her room either. Which probably meant it wasn't her house.

"Where...where are we?" she croaked weakly, looking up at her sister with a searching gaze.

"We're at Symphandra's," Scar said softly, removing her hands from Burn's shoulders and putting them back in her lap. Burn must have looked confused, because Scar explained, "When you collapsed, I grabbed your tab and messaged the last person you'd spoken to – Symphandra. I told her what happened, and she rushed over with the cart from her shop. We put you in, covered you with dresses, and brought you here."

As the words sank in, the panic in Burn's chest slowly abated and her breathing slowed to a more normal rhythm. They were safe, at least for the time being, and Cross would have no idea where to look for them. The sudden lightness made her feel giddy.

"Here," Symphandra said, coming closer to the bed and holding out a bowl. "Eat this. It will make you feel better."

Burn reached out, the movement causing her bruised arms to protest, and accepted the bowl. It was steaming, and she took a long sniff of the contents, breathing in the savory aroma of vegetable soup. The smell was enough to make her stomach growl loudly, and she realized that she hadn't eaten anything since the party. How long ago was that? Just a day? It seemed like a lifetime.

She carefully took a spoonful of the rich soup and brought it to her mouth, her hands shaking as she tested the temperature. Once she was satisfied that it wouldn't burn a hole through her tongue, she took a tentative bite, then another. The warm liquid soothed her throat, and each spoonful brought more clarity to her mind.

"How long have I been out?" she asked between bites.

"A few hours. It's evening now," Symphandra said, having returned to her post at the door.

Something nagged at the back of Burn's mind as she ate, and pieces of her disastrous exploits started to fall into place. Cross. Wight. ManniK. The massacre. She dropped the spoon into her bowl as it all came together.

"The Lunaria. I have to talk to them. Tonight. I know what Cross is planning."

Symphandra moved uncomfortably in the doorway, crossing her arms over her chest.

"Burn...about that," she said haltingly, trying to find the right words. "Hale told everyone you've been working for the other side, that you've been reporting back to them on our activities. He called you a traitor."

"But you knew what I was doing! Couldn't you have told them about my plan, what I was trying to accomplish?"

"I tried," she said apologetically, wringing her hands. "Honestly, I did. I think some of them believed me. But... Hale was convincing. And your disappearance last night was suspicious. It raised a lot of doubts about your allegiances."

Burn shut her eyes, considering her options. She could leave the Lunaria to their own devices, leave them to fumble alone in the darkness. Or she could try to convince them of the danger in their path, putting her own life at risk for the chance to save thousands. There was no contest. She knew what she had to do. Burn opened her eyes again and regarded the two women in front of her.

"Symphandra, you're going to have to call an emergency meeting. I can't do it since I'm blacklisted. And they'll be just as suspicious of Scar." Symphandra started to speak, but Burn held up a hand to stop her.

"We have less than two days to stop a war that will kill tens of thousands of innocent people. We need to work together or we'll have no chance of succeeding. Get me in front of the Lunaria and I'll do the rest. I just need the chance to tell my side of the story."

Symphandra and Scar looked at each other warily. It was clear that neither was a fan of the risky plan, but they had no alternatives to propose. So they each nodded slowly in agreement.

"Good," Burn said, trying to sound resolute. "Organize the meeting for an hour from now. That will give me time to clean up." She set the soup bowl on the table beside the bed and tried to hoist her legs over the side and onto the floor. She managed – barely – but found that her legs didn't want to support her weight.

Her sister appeared at her side, offering a hand. Burn took it, unsteadily getting to her feet and hobbling to the bathroom. Her body felt like it had been trampled – and she remembered, belatedly, that it had. Her arms and legs were stiff and difficult to move, and her stomach and ribs felt tight and restrictive. If she moved too fast or turned too far, a sharp pain blossomed in her chest, stealing the breath from her lungs.

Scar helped her get undressed and eased her into the tub, careful not to touch the large purple bruises blooming on her skin. It was strange, seeing this completely different side of her sister. Burn was used to being the caretaker in their relationship, the one who looked after the house and the money and Scar. But she was beginning to see that she may have underestimated her sister.

Still, Burn was an independent creature at heart, and she shied away from being bathed like a toddler. She told Scar she could manage on her own, and her sister went off in search of Symphandra.

Burn scrubbed at her skin with the soap, trying to erase not only the caked blood and dirt that covered her, but also the memory of how it had gotten there. Her cuts stung in the cool water and her teeth chattered as she worked, but she didn't rush. She could sense more battles looming on the horizon, and she wanted to savor this moment, this peace, while she could.

After removing the majority of the filth and debris, Burn hoisted herself out of the murky water. She dried herself off, then turned to the bandages that had been left out for her. She carefully wound one around her midsection, hoping to keep her jostled ribs in place, then used a few more to tie off some cuts that had opened back up on her arms and legs.

Once she was thoroughly mummified, she risked a glance at herself in the small mirror above the sink. The sight that met her was jarring. She barely resembled the Burn from last night, the one in the fine dress with the flushed cheeks and dark eyes. Now her eyes were dark from bruises and lack of sleep. A large brown and purple lump covered her cheek where Cross had struck her, mirrored on the other side by shallow slashes from Wight's fingernails. She looked away, not wanting to see more – or to remember more.

Feeling steadier on her feet, she left the bathroom and found some clothes laid out for her on Symphandra's bed – a flowing cream-colored shirt and loose brown pants. Burn struggled to get the shirt over her head, her arms protesting the increased angle, but she eventually managed it. Once dressed, she felt better somehow, more stable, and she went in search of the others.

Burn found them in the kitchen, huddled together in quiet discussion. Scar was smiling slightly at Symphandra in an expression that Burn had never seen before, and the whole scene felt warm and intimate. She hated to interrupt them, but she knew that time was not on their side.

"Thank you for the clothes," she said in an attempt to break them out of their reverie. It worked and they looked up, both wearing a small smile.

"No problem," Symphandra said, waving her hand. "I'm just sorry I had no time to hem them." The pants were indeed long on Burn, but as long as she didn't have to run for her life, she didn't foresee that being a problem.

"Oh! I almost forgot," Burn said in a rush. "What did you do with my old clothes?"

"Well, we considered burning them but thought the fumes might attract attention," Scar said wryly. "They're over there." She pointed to a pile near the door.

Burn rushed over and rifled through the clothes, quickly finding the pants and grabbing the contents of the pockets, including the vial of ManniK. She also took the Peace Officer's gun, slinging its cord across her back.

"Ready?" she asked them, feeling somewhat stronger. The two nodded, and they all donned masks, goggles, and cloaks before walking out into the cool night.

Burn pulled up her hood and tucked her hair under it, hiding as much of her face as she could. She wasn't sure if she'd been declared a fugitive yet, if Cross had figured out that she'd escaped and put a price on her head, but she didn't want to take any chances.

Together, the three women glided through the dark streets. Well, two of them glided and Burn hobbled after them, trying to keep up despite her injuries. Even with her impaired state, though, they made good time and soon found themselves outside the safe house. Symphandra used her finger to gain access, and Burn and Scar followed her into the unassuming building.

Just as they had planned, they were the first ones there, and the two sisters tucked themselves into the darkness to await their scene. One by one, the Lunaria started to appear, quietly taking their seats. The mood was different from their last meeting, subdued and serious, with no laughter or chit-chat to distract them from the matter at hand.

Hale was the last to arrive. At his appearance, Burn felt a sliver of anger shoot through her chest, but she clamped down on it, urging herself to stay calm. He wasn't the enemy, she reminded herself. Their goal was the same. And, more importantly, she needed him on her side if they were going to win this – or at least stand a chance.

The room sat in eerie silence as Symphandra stood, walking purposefully to the center of the circle. She addressed the gathered crowd, her voice low and serious.

"Thank you for coming on such short notice. I would like to get straight to the point. I have recently received intel on the Peace Force's plan, and it is grave news indeed. My source, who has gone deep within the organization, has suffered greatly to get this information back to us, nearly losing her life in the process. I urge you to listen to what she has to say and to heed her warnings. She speaks the truth, and I can vouch for her integrity."

She paused, gauging the reaction of the room. They sat in rapt attention, their faces grim. "I would like to invite Auburn Alendra to the floor."

With that, the room erupted in whispers. Burn emerged from the shadows and limped through the circle to join her friend. They stood arm to arm, together against the crowd. Upon seeing Burn, Hale rose and began to approach them, but Symphandra put a hand up to stop him.

"I know you've all heard certain accusations regarding Burn and her allegiances, but please allow her to say her part. If you are not satisfied with her explanations, you are free to do with her as you please. But I hope you take her words to heart. Countless lives hang in the balance."

Burn's heart pounded in her chest as Hale stared at her, his mouth twitching. After a few seconds, however, he sank back into his chair, and a small portion of Burn's anxiety eased. She stepped forward into the light so that the full extent of her injuries could be seen by the gathered crowd.

"After our last meeting, I formed a plan to infiltrate the Peace Station in search of more information, using my father's old contacts. This plan failed. Not only did I hear nothing of value, but I was discovered by General Cross and his suspicions were raised. I knew that any other attempts to gather this information would have to be done outside of the Peace Station and would require incredible ingenuity."

The crowd stayed silent as she spoke, hanging on her words. She couldn't tell if they believed her – or were simply biding their time until they could finish her off – but she kept going, nonetheless.

"Through an incredible turn of luck, an acquaintance – the same one I was seen with last night – approached me and invited me to the Peace Force ball. This acquaintance, an officer, has no idea where my real allegiances lie: with the Lunaria. He merely saw me as a romantic interest, and I encouraged his attentions in order to get closer to the truth."

Burn felt a pang of guilt when speaking about Kaz as if he were merely a means to an end. But it was the truth. She had used him – and then thrown him away.

"I attended the ball in search of answers. With the help of Symphandra and my sister, I was able to infiltrate their inner sanctum and discover more about their plan. I learned that it involves those of us born with gifts, as well as the street drug known as ManniK, which they've been testing on us. And I learned that it will result in innumerable casualties. But once again I was discovered by Cross. This time I couldn't escape."

Burn shuddered at the memory of Cross' hot breath on her face and his body pressed up against hers. She closed her eyes and swallowed, trying to rid her mouth of the sour taste that had appeared at the thought of his touch.

After a moment, she pressed on, explaining where Cross had taken her, what she'd learned from Wight, and how she'd escaped. She withdrew the vial from her pocket, passing it around as proof of her claims. She glossed over the painful details of her ordeal, knowing that the bruises on her face and the injuries across her body would tell the story better than she could. When she reached the end, she paused, considering her audience.

"We have the chance to stop a terrible atrocity," she continued, her voice grave. "I don't know how we're going to do it – or even if it's possible to succeed. But I do know that we only stand a chance if we work together. Thank you."

Done with her speech, Burn limped over to an empty chair and sat, her legs weak from the effort of standing. Symphandra once again stood alone in the center of the circle and addressed the quiet room.

"You've heard the whole story and must now understand the dire situation in which we find ourselves. It's up to you what we do next. The fate of the city, of so many innocent lives, lies in your hands. What would you like to do?" She addressed the question to everyone assembled in the small room, slowly rotating to meet their upturned eyes.

Hale was, of course, the first one to speak. "How do we know she's telling the truth? This could all be an elaborate plot to lure us out into the open. How do we know we can trust her?"

"You're right," Burn answered from her seat, causing Hale to frown in confusion. She wasn't supposed to agree with him. She was supposed to fight back. But she knew that fighting with him would do no good. "Trusting me is a leap. Trusting anyone, especially someone with ideas so different to your own, is never going to be easy." Her mind flashed back to what Scar had said only yesterday. *I think some people are just scared to trust those with different ideas.*

"But the simple fact is that we need each other. I need you and you need me." She addressed this directly to Hale, unblinking. "I've never let you down before, and I don't intend to start now. I'm one of you. And it's us against them now."

She continued to stare at Hale, daring him to fight back. But to her surprise, he didn't. Instead, he gave a small nod of approval and stayed silent. Burn let out a quiet sigh of relief. That was one less battle she would have to fight.

Several more of the Lunaria raised questions, but each dealt with the details of the plan, seeking additional information or clarification instead of probing her veracity. Burn answered each member calmly, laying out the plan to the best of her knowledge. It was clear that she didn't know all the details – like what time they planned to start, where they would be setting off the ManniK, or even how much of the force would be involved. But her intel was considerably more than they'd had before, and it put them far closer to an even playing field.

The conversation gradually shifted, morphing organically from a discussion of the Peace Force's plan to how the Lunaria was going to combat it. Hale and Ansel, an older man with the potent gift of manipulating fire, naturally got into an argument about firepower, while Symphandra, Scar, and an elderly woman talked heatedly about the likelihood of finding another drug to lessen the effects of ManniK.

"The problem is that we don't have enough people," Ramus interrupted, leaning forward in his seat. "Even if we all called in our favors and sources and operatives, we're only looking at a couple hundred people at the most. The Peace Force has thousands – and they're armed."

"We could try to recruit more," suggested Brindle, a younger girl whose powers involved the manipulation of light. "Start grabbing people off the street and telling them what's happening."

"They'll never believe us," Ramus countered. "And even if they did, that would take far too long. We don't have time to recruit and train an entire army. It's not possible."

"What we need is more people like us, more individuals with gifts," said Scar, jumping into the fray. "Then, even if we don't have the advantage in terms of numbers, we'd have the upper hand when it came to strength. Think about: a gifted army. It's what they're afraid of. That's why they arrest us and vilify us and keep us down. So, let's give it to them! Let's make their fears a reality."

"That's a fine idea," came Hale's voice from the other side of the room. "But how do you suggest we go about that? Our kind prefer to stay in the shadows. They're safer in the dark. They don't tend to stick out in public or congregate in easy to find groups."

"Unless they've already been brought together for us," said Burn, something sparking in her mind. It was such a strange statement that no one else quite knew what to say in response. Burn held up a finger, silently asking for a moment to think as she parsed through her hazy memories of the day.

The officer who had saved her from being trampled, the one who had escorted her past the barricades, he had said something about prisoners and overcrowding. His words came back to her slowly, as if she had heard them in a dream. *Gonna have to toss some of 'em out, if you know what I mean.* She hadn't known what he'd meant at the time. But she certainly did now.

"They're planning to throw a bunch of them – a bunch of us – into the Pit. They're trying to free up the cells. I bet whoever they don't kill during their little massacre they're going to toss in jail and label enemies of the state."

Hale latched onto her thought process, a hint of excitement creeping into his voice. "That means there'll be a prisoner transfer, probably sometime tomorrow. If we can find out when it's happening, we can intercept them. That could mean scores of new allies – people who already have a grudge against the Peace Force."

"I can use my intel on some of the officers to find out when the transfer will be," Burn said, her excitement matching his. Their previous animosity seemed all but forgotten, and they moved closer to one another, feeding off of each other's energy. "Then you can put together a team to ambush them and bring them back."

Hale nodded, already mentally forming his crew. Meanwhile, the rest of the Lunaria looked on, stunned at their sudden camaraderie yet hopeful that this plan might work.

They stayed late into the night, hashing out the details. It was still a long shot, and everyone knew there was no guarantee of success. But having a strategy, a purpose, and a team of people alongside them fueled each member on. Even Burn, whose injuries and exhaustion threatened to overwhelm her, felt invigorated by the solidarity.

Still, the time came when her fatigue got the better of her, and she found herself nodding off despite the frenetic energy. Struggling to stand, her legs having long since stiffened, she hobbled to find Symphandra and her sister, who were huddled with a small group discussing battle strategies. Burn beckoned them to leave and they followed, waving goodbye to their compatriots. Together, the three women walked out into the night, the promise of another meeting already on the horizon.

# CHAPTER 21

Burn's sleep was uneasy, filled with images of violence and pain. And Cross. She couldn't tell if they were memories, warped by her subconscious and twisted into narratives where she couldn't escape, or fears of what the next two days might bring.

She awoke early, her head clear but her muscles stiff and her chest aching. Her tab was next to the bed, salvaged from their home by Scar before their escape, and she grabbed it, hoping to wipe away the remnants of her dreams with work.

Before settling down to business, she scanned the Peace Force-sponsored news, checking for any reference to her or ManniK or what had happened down in Wight's lair. Thankfully, either Cross didn't know or he was choosing to cover it up, because there was no mention of the events among the headlines.

That done, Burn got down to the matter at hand: blackmail. Specifically, blackmailing Cross' officers into revealing the time of the prisoner transfer. She scanned her database of secrets, looking for something serious enough that someone would risk their job to conceal it. Infidelity? No. Gambling? No. Extorting money from a violent criminal in exchange for keeping him out of prison? A serious contender.

Burn didn't know which officers would be in charge of the transfer, so she spread her net wide, selecting individuals from across the organization to threaten. Although in this case, she reflected, it wasn't just a threat. A bit of chaos on the force would be useful in the coming war. So if they didn't give her what she needed, they'd soon find themselves facing up to their past indiscretions – and Peace Force punishments were never pleasant.

She sent her messages with the swipe of a finger. It was so easy to ruin lives, she thought, so simple to send their worlds up in smoke. A normal person would feel guilty, a small voice said in the back of her mind, but Burn had long since become desensitized to that. She knew that to fight fire, you had to find some fire of your own. This was hers.

Reluctantly, she lifted herself off the bed and onto the floor, shuffling to the bathroom. Looking in the mirror, she saw that her bruises had blossomed, bringing yellow and brown tones to the watercolor of injuries across her skin. The pain still lingered, but the memories were fading little by little, shut out by the balm of her present safety and the looming presence of something far worse on the horizon.

Ambling to the living room, she caught sight of Scar and Symphandra still asleep on the couch, arms twined around each other as if each could protect the other from the cruelness of the world. Not wanting to wake them, Burn tiptoed into the kitchen to fix herself a cup of tea.

A short while later, tea in hand, she heard a ping from her tab and snatched it from her pocket to check the message. It was a refusal. Someone thought themselves immune to blackmail. Well, Burn thought, someone had to be the example to the others, a lesson on what happened when you didn't comply. With a few taps of her fingers across the screen, she ruined his life.

Satisfied with herself, she sat down to wait. And wait. And wait. Scar awoke, followed closely by Symphandra, and the two prepared a breakfast of eggs and toast, all the while conversing in whispered voices and laughter. It was refreshing – laughter and love in the face of so much darkness – and it was contagious, easing some of Burn's tension.

What seemed like hours later, but was more akin to 30 minutes, Burn's tab lit up once more. Success. An eager hopefulness washed over her as she scanned the message.

"The transfer is happening in two hours," she said, reading aloud. "There'll be 10 guards and more than 30 prisoners." Without waiting for a reply, she encoded the message and sent it ahead to Hale, drumming her fingers on the table as she waited for a reply.

This time, the response was almost instantaneous. "Message received. Ambush set. Stand by for updates." Burn exhaled a breath she hadn't realized she'd been holding. They were one step closer to being able to stop this, one step farther along the road to winning a war.

But compared to the utter relief of discovering a crucial piece of intel on your enemy, waiting around for someone else to act on it was agonizing. Burn was used to being the one in charge and was unaccustomed to sitting back and watching as someone else took control.

She felt fidgety and anxious, and not even Scar's talk of robotics and weaponized tech could pull her thoughts away from the coming action. Time ticked by sluggishly, but it did tick by. Burn occupied herself by pacing and, when that became too painful, sitting on Symphandra's couch and tapping her fingers in time with the beats of the clock.

She couldn't see how Symphandra and Scar were so calm, how their stomachs weren't tied in an array of tiny little knots and thrust up into their throats. Unlike her, they seemed so relaxed, like they were certain of a positive outcome. Maybe it was because they had each other, a tangible source of solace in the sea of unknowns. Or maybe it was because they hadn't gone through what she had and didn't know firsthand the atrocities that were coming.

Scar brewed her a cup of tea and made Burn drink it, but the hot liquid did nothing to calm her nerves. She sat then stood then sat again, uncomfortable with every position. Once again seated on the couch, she put her head back, trying to calm herself. Her eyes felt heavy and she closed them, concentrating on her breathing, which suddenly seemed labored. Without warning, she dropped into a deep and dreamless sleep.

Burn awoke feeling groggy and out of sorts. She knew that she was supposed to be doing something, but for the life of her she couldn't remember what it was. It was as if the cogs in her brain were spinning but the movement was producing no discernible output.

Her tongue felt thick and her mouth fuzzy, and she reached out in front of her, searching for something to quench her thirst. Her hands closed on the teacup she'd been drinking from, and she brought it to her parched lips, sniffing. Something wasn't right. Her foggy brain took too long to process the fact that there was another smell accompanying that of the tea, something chemical.

"You drugged me," she said to no one in particular. Her thick tongue made the words slur and blend together, so she tried again, this time turning to address the kitchen. "Why did you drug me?"

Scar popped her head out, a small smile playing on her lips. "Good, you're awake. You've been out for a few hours. Have a good nap?" She was playing innocent.

"You drugged me," Burn tried again, hoping the same accusation would produce a different response.

Her sister stared back for a beat, choosing her words carefully. "You needed sleep. And you were never going to get it by pacing around. You also weren't going to help the Lunaria by wearing a hole in Symphandra's carpet. So we gave you a sleeping draft, just enough to help you relax and take your mind off the prisoner transfer."

"The transfer!" That's what Burn had been trying so hard to remember. "What happened? Has there been any news?"

"Not yet," Symphandra said, coming in from the bedroom. "We expect to hear something soon, though. It's been over an hour since the transfer. We've been keeping an eye on your tab in case you got any messages."

She tossed the tab to Burn, and it landed with a soft bounce on the cushion beside her. She flipped it open, confirming Symphandra's words, then settled herself back into the couch. As much as she hated to admit it, she did feel better. Some of the anxiety in her chest had dissipated, and a bit of the stiffness in her limbs had eased. She wasn't in fighting form, but it was progress.

Scar convinced her to eat a bowl of porridge – although, having learned her lesson, Burn made her sister take a bite first before she went anywhere near it. The gooey substance stuck to her throat going down, but it restored a bit more of her energy and wiped the lingering fog from her brain.

She took a quick shower, hastened by the icy water, before getting dressed, borrowing yet another outfit from Symphandra's closet. This one was also practical but favored ease of movement above all else, with tight black pants and a snug shirt. She entered the living room again, alert and ready for action.

A short while later, her tab buzzed. The message was short and succinct. "Mission successful. Prisoners at safe house B." Burn was nearly out the door before remembering the two other people in the house. She updated Scar and Symphandra in as few words as possible and waited by the door like an eager dog until they were ready to depart.

Safe house B was located deeper in the city than their previous meeting point, but it offered a convenient perch from which to fight a war on the bottom of Kasis. It also had room for more people – a necessity when you were gathering an army. Still, the trip was long and tiring, especially considering Burn's recent injuries, and an increased time on the streets meant an increased chance of them being discovered.

Their precarious situation was not lost on the trio, and they walked as swiftly as they could without drawing attention. The lower they went, the more the tension seemed to rise, not just among them but around them. They weren't yet to the levels of the blockades, but they might as well have been. People scurried past, heads covered, whispering and glancing around as if danger was hot on their trail. The atmosphere was rigid, afraid, like they knew something big was on the horizon.

Arriving at the safe house was a relief. They glanced around before entering the unassuming space, checking yet again to make sure they hadn't been followed. From the street, this safe house seemed like a small flat, only one or two rooms, the same as the houses around it. In reality, it spanned across and down, encompassing the building next to it and the one below.

The house was already buzzing with activity. There were people everywhere, set on every surface with even more overflowing onto the floor. Some were hurt and some were just dazed. Lunaria members that Burn knew, along with many that she didn't, scurried through the rooms tending to the injured, making food, or ferrying supplies to and fro.

Burn stood for a moment trying to get her bearings. The smell of blood and antiseptic stung her nose, and the porridge in her stomach gave a weak lurch. Typically a little blood wouldn't phase her, but the sheer number of wounded people, paired with her own recent bloody experiences, had the distinct effect of making the room feel like it was spinning.

She focused her attention past the commotion, searching for Hale. Such a large man should have been easy to spot, but he was nowhere to be seen. Burn moved farther into the house, past the front room with its bloody people laid out on couches and into the kitchen, where slightly less bloody people were propped up on chairs and counters.

She located Brindle near the end of the first floor and paused to inquire about Hale. Brindle pointed toward the subfloor, and Burn descended a creaky wooden staircase to the lower level. It was darker down there, and fewer people padded through the halls. She glanced into a few secluded spaces to find people sleeping, passed out on beds, chairs, and rugs. She closed the doors quietly, not wanting to disturb them.

Then she heard him. Hale, with his low voice, was in a room near the end of the hall talking briskly to someone. No, that wasn't right, Burn thought as she got closer. He was threatening someone.

"Hale?" she yelled in question, not wanting to walk in on something she clearly shouldn't. He stopped talking to whomever was in the room, pausing for a second before coming to the door. Seeing it was her, he squeezed out and shut the door hurriedly behind him, like he didn't want her to see past him into the room.

Burn looked inquisitively at him, raising an eyebrow in question, but he didn't seem inclined to explain, so she asked simply, "What happened?"

He stood there for a beat, shoulders tense and arms crossed, before replying. When he did, his voice was brusque. "Your source was right about the time. We staked out the area around the Pit and caught them on their way to dispose of the prisoners. We got 'em all without casualties. Well, without casualties on our side."

"And the other side?"

"Confiscated their gear and tossed them in the Pit." He said it so nonchalantly, like killing men for following orders was something he did every day. It sent a chill down Burn's spine.

Hale continued to look at her, his brows furrowed. There was something else, something he wasn't telling her. His attitude toward her had changed again, reversing course from friendly camaraderie to a cold indifference. She thought back on the few words she had said to him but couldn't discern what had brought about the change.

Then he glanced ever so briefly toward the door. Burn followed his gaze and listened, her ears tuned for any sound coming from the room beyond. There was someone in there alright, someone bound and gagged. Someone struggling.

"I thought you said that you'd killed all the Peace Officers," Burn said, a hint of accusation in her voice. He merely nodded but refused to elaborate. "So if they're all dead," she said, continuing her thought, "then who do you have tied up in there?" She pointed to the room he had just left, eyeing his face for any change in expression.

For a split second, Hale's face contorted into a sneer, a look full of malice. An instant later it was gone, replaced by his usual scowl. "It's just one of the prisoners we freed," he said curtly.

"He doesn't seem free to me."

Hale considered this for a moment before replying.

"He's dangerous."

"Dangerous?" Burn was taken aback. "Hale, most of the people in this house are dangerous. That's why they were locked up in the first place. We don't even know what most of them can do. So how is this man more dangerous than the rest?"

"He's dangerous in a different way."

Burn let out a loud sigh of irritation. Talking to Hale was like talking to a brick wall. She could see she wasn't going to get anywhere with this line of questioning. So she tried something else entirely: She tried to get past him.

Now, pushing past a guard wasn't something Burn was typically good at. But it was all the more difficult when the guard in question could pick you up and set you back down again without breaking a sweat. Which was exactly what Hale did.

Burn slapped at his hands, her body cringing at the unwelcome touch. He let go of her waist and stood there, staring at her. She stared back, putting all of her anger and frustration into the glare. They stayed there, eyes locked, for a few tense seconds before Hale sighed and stood aside, reluctantly giving her access to the door.

"Don't let him go," was his only warning as she scanned her finger and pushed into the dim room.

It took a second for her eyes to adjust, but when they did, she caught sight of a crumpled figure in the far corner of the room. He was lying on his side, curled up like a scared animal in the presence of a predator, and he held his head in his bound hands. Burn approached slowly, afraid to startle him.

As she got nearer, his features started to come into focus. He had thick dark hair, some of which was obscuring his face, and he appeared young and lean. He was wearing dark clothing that had once been nice but was now ripped and covered in blood. Whether it was his blood or someone else's, Burn couldn't tell.

She stopped a short way away from him, uncertain of how to proceed. She didn't want to frighten him further, but she needed to know who he was – and why he was there. She cleared her throat, hoping it might get him to raise his head, but he remained motionless.

"I'm not going to hurt you," she said, crouching down to his level. "I just want to talk."

The figure stirred at the sound of her voice, struggling to sit up. He kept his head down, though, and his hair continued to conceal his features. He remained silent, as if waiting for her to speak again.

"What's your name?" she tried, hoping that a direct question would spur him to talk.

The figure let out a short bark of laughter, followed by a painful coughing fit that sent him doubling over. Burn wanted to go to him, to help him, but she resisted. If he was as dangerous as Hale had said, she couldn't take any chances.

Then the figure started to speak, his voice low and raspy. "I would have thought you would know that by now."

Burn froze, her blood going cold. Then she rushed to him and pushed back his hair, taking his face in her hands. It was Kaz.

# CHAPTER 22

One eye was swollen shut, and he had a large gash over the other eyebrow, which had bled down over his face. His lip was split and bleeding, and Burn could make out various other injuries down his neck and across his body.

Kaz flinched at her touch, pulling his face out of her hands. She moved back, uncertain.

"What happened?" she asked insistently. "How did you get here? Who did this to you?" Her heart was suddenly pounding, and confusion and rage warred in her brain.

Another laugh from Kaz, this one quieter. "You're one of them." He shook his head before looking up at her. "You're a rebel, a traitor." He stared at her with a look Burn had never seen before, something between hatred and sadness. It was betrayal, she realized with a shock.

"What happened?" she tried again, gentler this time.

"You happened," he said coldly. The sharpness in his voice cut through her like a knife, and a sudden deep pain blossomed in her chest.

"Two of my fellow officers grabbed me after the ball," he continued, no longer able to make eye contact. "They said it was on Cross' orders. They told me that I had been found guilty of consorting with a criminal. You, of course." He spat at the mention of her, and Burn could see blood mixed in with the saliva.

"They chucked me in a cell and left me there. No food, no water, no light. And all I could think the entire time was that they were wrong, that you could never be a traitor. I mean, your father worked on the force, for god's sake."

He looked up at her again, fire in his eyes. "I wasted what might have been my last breaths worrying about you. And you couldn't have cared less about me. You used me. I was just your way in, wasn't I?"

"No," Burn choked, shaking her head emphatically. "That wasn't it at all."

"Oh, save it," he cut her off. "You've been lying to me since we met. Chased by thieves? Yeah, right. I was an idiot to trust you. I should have turned you in the second you came through my door."

A wave of emotions rushed through Burn, threatening to overtake her. He was right, of course. She had used him, just like she used everyone else: as a pawn in her own game. She was just like Cross. Hot shame rolled over her as the accusation struck, burrowing under her skin.

She had done this to him. Even if she hadn't been the one to hit him or throw him in the cell, his blood was still on her hands, staining her with guilt. She tried to speak, but her throat felt dry and cracked.

"I…I never meant for this to happen. You have to know that. You weren't supposed to get caught up in this." She searched for a way to make this right, something she could say that would make him stop looking at her like she was the devil incarnate. "I'm sorry," was all she could think to say.

"Sorry? Sorry for what? For using me? For making me think that you cared? For sending me to my death? Or for betraying Kasis and your father and everything he worked for?"

That struck a nerve and Burn's emotions spun, swirling from shame to anger to rage. Fire poured through her, coursing in her limbs and loosening her tongue.

"Betrayed Kasis? Kasis was betrayed long before I got here. It was betrayed by officers like you who thought they were gods and could do whatever they pleased to its citizens. It was betrayed when innocent people were locked up and killed because they were different. And it's about to be betrayed again! But this time we'll be there to stop it."

Kaz shook his head, brushing off her words. "You're just saying that to justify your own war. You lie to yourselves so you can feel like saviors when you cheat and kill and work to undo everything we've put in place. You've deluded yourselves into thinking that you're making a difference, when in reality you're just making a mess. And we'll be the ones who have to clean it up."

It was Burn's turn to laugh without feeling. Deluded? She wasn't the deluded one in this conversation. Kaz had been so brainwashed by the Peace Force's company line that he couldn't see what was happening right in front of him. It would be her pleasure to inform him, she decided.

"You have no clue what's happening in this city. Cross is planning a massacre. Tomorrow, in fact. It's part of his plan to 'clean up the city,' getting rid of trash like me. In fact, he already tried to get rid of me by handing me over to a ManniK dealer to use as twisted test subject. You're not the only one who's suffered here. If I hadn't escaped, I'd already be dead."

She shuddered again at the memory of Cross' hands on her, of being collared and chained like an animal, and of barely escaping with her life. As if responding to her thoughts, her bruises began to throb, keeping time with the pounding of her heart.

"If we do nothing, Cross will lead his men down to the lowest tiers, guns in hand. They'll dose entire zones with ManniK and watch as the people they're supposed to be protecting succumb to chaos and death at each other's hands. And if anyone tries to fight back, tries to defend themselves and their families, they'll be gunned down in the streets. Population control at its finest. If that's not betraying Kasis, I don't know what is."

They were both silent for a minute as Kaz processed what she had said and Burn tried to rein in her mounting frustration. She was suddenly aware that Hale was outside the door and had almost certainly overheard their conversation. He was probably taking pleasure in it, she thought acidly. He had warned her not to get involved with the Peace Force, and now here she was, dealing with the fallout.

Kaz was the first one to break the silence. "Trash like you? What do you mean by that?"

Burn sighed. Time to come clean. Really clean. "I'm

gifted. And so is Scar. And we can't stand by and watch as people like us are rounded up and punished just for being born. Or cursed at in the streets – called monsters and freaks and shunned because people buy into the Peace Force's lies. My dad used his position on the force to help people like us, and he was killed because of it. So now I'm doing what I can to fight back, to show the world this isn't how it has to be."

Burn took a deep breath and looked Kaz in the eye. "I'm sorry you got hurt. I truly am. But I'm not sorry for what I've done or what I'm going to do next. Maybe one day you'll understand and forgive me, but I can't wait around for that."

She took a step toward the door, then paused with her hand on the knob. Without turning to face him, she said, "After this is over, I'll make sure you're released, and you can return to whatever is left of your life. And if you ever want to talk…well, you know where I live." With that, she walked out of the room.

Hale was indeed in the hall, listening at the door just as she had expected. Except the look on his face wasn't one of superiority, but one of concentration. Burn made a move to pass him, no longer in the mood to talk, but he stopped her with a light touch of his hand on her arm.

"You told him we would let him go?"

Burn sighed, rubbing her head. She suddenly felt exhausted and wanted to find somewhere quiet to think, but she stayed, answering calmly, "He's burned his bridges with the force. If we win, he won't pose much of a risk to us. If we lose…" she trailed off and gave a shrug. "Well, if we lose, then it won't matter either way."

Hale nodded and released her arm, but Burn stayed

where she was. "Hale?" she asked, looking up into his dark eyes. He gave a grunt of acknowledgment, which Burn took as her cue to continue. "Please don't hurt him." With that, she started back the way she had come.

Her brain was full and her head was pounding as she made her way through the halls, but she could have sworn she heard a murmured voice behind her. "I won't," it said, low and somber. Burn kept going, leaving the voice and the man who possessed it behind in the darkness.

She didn't have much time to dwell on the situation, however, since the instant she reached the top of the stairs, Scar pounced on her.

"They have a healer!" she almost shouted into Burn's ear. Burn was so surprised by her sister's sudden presence that the words didn't fully penetrate.

"Who has a what?" she asked, shaking her head in an attempt to clear the previous conversation from her thoughts.

"One of the prisoners they rescued can heal people," Scar said, slowing her words to a more normal pace. "And he says he'll take a look at you. Come on." She grabbed Burn's hand and dragged her into yet another part of the maze-like house.

"Scar, wait," Burn tried to say, but her sister was on a mission. "I'm sure there are people far more injured than I am. He should see them first."

Like others with such extraordinary gifts, it was likely that this healer had a limited charge and could only help so many people before his abilities were drained. Glancing around at the people they passed, Burn couldn't help but think that they deserved his attention far more than she did.

In fact, she didn't feel like she deserved much at all at that moment.

"Nonsense," Scar responded, continuing her efforts to pull Burn along. "We need you in fighting form if you're going to lead an army into battle tomorrow. Besides, you look like death." Scar's bluntness was abrasive, yet somehow reassuring. Then her words sank in.

"Wait, what? I'm leading an army?"

Scar looked back at her sister with a look of utter bewilderment, as if she had asked what year it was or some other equally absurd question. "Of course you are. This is your plan. You discovered what Cross was up to. You thought to free the prisoners. Everyone kind of assumes you'll know what to do next."

Until that moment, Burn hadn't given any thought to what her role in the battle would be. She assumed, if anything, she would be just another soldier sent into the fray, taking orders from Hale or someone else with more experience in combat. She had never dreamed that she would be the one giving those orders.

Suddenly, Burn felt a huge weight descend onto her shoulders – the weight of others' expectations and of countless human lives – and the pressure built until she could barely breathe. She didn't know the first thing about war – about troops and battle plans and formations. What if she failed? What if their entire cause went up in flames because she made the wrong decision?

As the panic mounted, Scar continued leading her sister through the house. Almost without her notice, she set Burn down in a chair and went off to find the healer. She returned a minute later flanked by a painfully skinny man with a smooth bald head and a round pair of glasses that magnified his eyes. The effect was like looking at a bug. As Burn considered him, his head moved back and forth in sharp movements as if to reinforce the resemblance.

"This is Crete," Scar said by way of an introduction. "He's already taken care of the seriously injured and says he has just enough energy left for you." She gave a nod to the pair as if to say "my work here is done," then walked back the way she had come.

Left alone with the strange man, Burn tried to protest, saying that others in the house needed his help more than she did, but he didn't listen. Instead, he gently took her hands in his and knelt down in front of her, closing his eyes.

A warm tingling sensation appeared in her hands, then worked its way up her arms and into her chest. The energy seemed to poke and prod at the sore spots along her body, kneading them softly until they relaxed and the pain began to dissipate. Crete worked methodically, as if combing her for injuries with his mind. The feeling was so soothing that Burn found her eyelids fluttering shut.

Sometime later, maybe minutes, maybe hours, the tingling faded, pulled back from her body and out through her hands. She opened her eyes, expecting to see Crete suffused with some kind of ethereal light, the source of the tingling sensation. Instead, she was horrified to see that he was even more emaciated than when he had knelt down. It was as if by helping her, he had drained all of his own energy and was now left with only the shell of a body.

He got up slowly, and Burn was afraid that his now-feeble

legs might collapse under him. She started to get up, started to offer her strength in place of his, but he stopped her. Putting a surprisingly firm hand on her shoulder, he pushed her back into the chair.

"Rest now," he said in a melodic voice. "We both need rest." With that, he left her.

She wanted to get up and go after him, to make sure he found somewhere safe to lay his head, but a sudden drowsiness came over her. It wasn't the same as when her sister had spiked her tea. This was more of a pleasant fuzziness that gradually dulled her thoughts and numbed her worries, like a salve for her mind.

One minute the world was there, painful and complicated in ways she couldn't untangle, and the next it was gone, replaced by a world of dreams.

Burn awoke feeling content, as if her dreams had contained the answers she'd been trying so hard to seek. She tried to hold on to them – and to the feeling they gave her – but the harder she tried the faster they slipped away.

Finally reaching full consciousness, Burn looked down at herself, cautiously flexing her limbs and testing her injuries. She wasn't completely healed, but she was far better than she had been before, as if weeks of healing had taken place in mere hours. Her bruises had lost their deep purple and brown hues, mellowing to golden yellow in some places and disappearing completely in others.

She found with surprise that her ribs no longer protested

when she moved, and her legs felt strong and sturdy. She pulled up her pant leg and unrolled her bandages to discover that even the gash there had faded, now resembling an old scar from a long-ago injury. Even her mind felt calmer, less tumultuous than it had when she'd drifted off.

Burn felt a small pang of jealousy for Crete's amazing gift, but then the image of him pale and weak came to her. She made a mental note to thank him for his sacrifice in whatever way she could. But how could you repay someone for such a selfless act?

As she stood, Burn realized that the house had grown quiet. She glanced around to find people asleep on chairs and couches, sprawled out on the floor and propped against each other for comfort. She tiptoed over bodies, careful not to wake them. Tomorrow was going to be a nightmare, she thought sadly. At least let them have their dreams tonight.

Her sensitive ears picked up a whispered conversation from the front of the house, and she made her way toward it. Nestled in the front room, a small gathering of people were crowded in a circle with their heads together in fervent discussion. Burn drew up an empty chair and placed herself on the circle's edge. The group parted, a silent invitation to enter the ongoing deliberations.

"So what can all these newbies do?" asked Ansel in a whisper.

Hale, who was situated across from Burn, started ticking them off on his hands. "Well, there's Crete, the healer. He does good work but has limited power. Has to recharge after a couple of sessions. He might help us save a few people, although he should probably focus his efforts on the most powerful among us."

Burn was struck by the callous remark, the nonchalant way he talked about human life and whose lives to prioritize. Yet she kept her mouth shut, reminding herself that a war room was no place to discuss ethics and a battlefield cared nothing for your moral code. It was power and cleverness that would ultimately matter.

"Then there's Innoxia, who can manipulate the dead," Hale continued. "Could use her once we kill a few officers to turn them on their own teams. She reckons she can manage 15 to 20 at one time. Lore can control rodents, which could make a good distraction. Pierce has a poisonous touch, but he has to make contact with his victims to use it. And Coal can impersonate anyone. It's like he becomes them, or at least fools you into thinking he has."

"Don't forget Dormaline and Shaw," added a familiar voice to Burn's right. She looked over to find Meera, whose friendly face was a comforting sight. As the rest of the circle turned to look at her, she explained, "Dormaline can walk through walls. She basically dematerializes, or at least that's how she describes it. And Shaw has this really hard skin. He's basically impervious to bullets."

"Hmm, that could be useful," Hale considered, trying to fit these new individuals into his evolving battle plans.

Something was nagging at Burn and she spoke up, drawing all eyes to her. "Are all these people OK with being used as weapons in our war? They've already been through so much. Is it fair to throw them out there, especially against such uneven odds? We don't even know what we're up against."

"They know the stakes," Hale said, his face betraying no emotions. "They've had their chance to leave, and they've chosen to stay, to fight. They've suffered more than most at the hands of the Peace Force. Most of them see it as their duty. Besides, they're fugitives. There's no place out there for them. Not yet, at least. That's what we're fighting for." Burn nodded in understanding, as did the others around the circle.

They continued talking strategy late into the night, plotting movements and stations and scenarios, debating ways to stop the Peace Force before they released the ManniK on the bottom tiers. Burn was relieved that the weight of leadership hadn't fallen entirely on her shoulders, that these people would bear the win or loss together, sharing in the thrill of victory or the pangs of defeat. It was a strange kind of comfort, this fellowship of war, but for the moment it united them, bringing them together across tiers and backgrounds and beliefs to fight under a single cause.

Eventually, the circle dispersed, having established a tentative plan and contingencies to accompany it, and only Burn and Hale were left. They looked at each other, neither knowing what to say or how to start. Finally, Hale broke the silence.

"Are you ready?" It was a simple question, but the answer was far more complicated than a mere yes or no.

"How can you ever be ready for something like this?" Burn asked honestly, with no hint of sarcasm or malice in her voice. "We could die tomorrow. All of us. We could so easily lose the battle – and lose everything we've been fighting for along with it."

She looked up at Hale, hoping he'd have the answer. As

a man accustomed to fighting and violence, to facing his own mortality along with that of those around him, maybe he had a way to look at it that didn't seem so terrifying.

He sighed and looked down at her, giving her a long, lingering look. "You can't. Be ready, that is. But you can have faith – in yourself and those around you. Sometimes that's enough." With a nod, he bid her goodnight and disappeared into the back of the house.

# CHAPTER 23

The Lunaria and their new recruits rose before dawn to prepare. It was a quiet affair, everyone lost in their own thoughts and worries, but the rooms still buzzed with anticipation. People ate slowly, forcing themselves to choke down pieces of toast or bits of egg despite their roiling nerves. Others changed into dark clothes or light armor, depending on the part they had to play.

Burn found the lack of conversation disconcerting. As someone used to the ever-present hum, its absence seemed like an omen. She wished someone would burst into song or embark on an impassioned speech, just to break the tension that had settled like a blanket over the house.

Finding herself in need of company, she meandered through the halls until she found Scar, who was hard at work on a pile of electronics. It was another comforting sight, a bit of the familiar to fight off the unease. She settled herself down next to her sister, who noticed Burn but didn't pause to greet her.

"What are you doing?" Burn asked, despite the fact that she knew full well what her sister was up to. She just wanted a bit of time to feel normal before the world tilted on its axis.

"Upgrading comms units," Scar replied instinctively. "Everyone out there today will have one. So we'll all be connected. We'll all know what's happening throughout the city."

We. Burn flinched at that. She had begged her sister to stay behind, to stay where it was safe. Her gift wasn't one that was well-suited to the battlefield. But Scar wouldn't hear of it. She needed to be part of the fight, she'd said, needed to stand alongside her brethren. It didn't help that Symphandra had signed up to fight, even though she had no gift to speak of. Both women were crazy as far as Burn was concerned, but that wasn't going to stop her from doing everything in her power to protect them.

She sat with her sister for a while, chatting about nothing and everything. For a few minutes, at least, their lives were normal and comfortable, just two sisters facing the world together like it had always been. Burn got them both a plate of food and made Scar eat bites in between soldering wires and fixing microchips. And Burn forced herself to eat, as well, pretending that her stomach wasn't doing flips and threatening to send every bite back up.

Physically, she felt better than she had in weeks. She was well-rested and awake, and her injuries had healed even more overnight, leaving her with barely a scratch. Yet underneath her skin, an electric current buzzed, and she wondered if this was how Scar felt all the time – like a live wire was threaded through her muscles.

Then, far too soon, it was time to go. Deeming that it would be suspicious if a large group of armored citizens flooded the streets at once, they instead left in small groups, finding their way down to the lower sectors in twos and threes, draped in cloaks to conceal their weapons and gear.

Coal was the first to slide out into the darkness, but he wasn't really Coal, not anymore. Instead, he had slipped on another face and another body. The effect was eerie. Now, instead of the squat, balding man that he had once been, he stood tall and lean, his dark hair slicked back in a harsh mockery of someone Burn knew so well: Cross.

Wearing the gear of one of the officers whom they'd dispatched during the prisoner release, he looked almost exactly like the dreaded general. With dark eyes and an arrogant sneer, the disguise would fool anyone outside of Cross' closest confidants.

Burn had learned of the plan the night before, even helping shape the details of the plot, but it couldn't prepare her for walking into the front room and seeing Cross standing there. She had frozen, her mind clicking into panic mode before the rational part of her brain could catch up.

If you looked closely, you could see differences, errors in the copy. His edges were blurred and fuzzy, and if you concentrated long and hard, you could almost see through the shell to the man within. But it was good enough for their purposes, and Coal was more than happy to use his skill to take down the very man he was impersonating.

Coal was their key to getting through the barricades. Armored guards still manned every entrance and exit to the lower tiers, now acting as a damn rather than a provocation, keeping the poor in place in preparation for the day's brutal festivities.

These cronies, the lowest in the Peace Force pecking order, would be surprised when Cross turned up to temporarily relieve them of guard duty, but as he was their superior, they wouldn't be able to refuse a direct order. That would give the Lunaria enough time to trickle down tier by tier, putting operatives in place on each level.

Since the element of surprise was key to their plan, the original officers would need to be back in place when the real Cross started his campaign. So it was imperative that they tread lightly, raising no suspicions as they went – and harming none of the real officers along the way. Or, at least, only a handful. That was where Ansel came in.

Ansel was their backup plan, their muscle in case Coal failed. Accompanying Coal and posing as his right-hand man, it was his job to "clean up" any situation that got out of hand. If any suspicions arose, if any officer failed to comply with their orders, they would face Ansel's fire. Then the Lunaria would place their own members at the post.

It was a dangerous plan, as Cross might spot impostors in a minute and just as quickly have them dispatched, but it was the best they had. And, as their last resort, hopefully they'd never have to use it.

Burn watched as Coal and Ansel walked steadily into the darkness, starting their descent. She felt butterflies come to life in her stomach as the house gradually emptied and her turn approached. She wished now that she had more time, a few more minutes to mentally prepare for all that was to come.

Maybe she should have given a speech, she thought belatedly, a rousing soliloquy to bolster the troops and raise their spirits. She could have used such a morale boost, something to convince her that they stood a chance in such a mismatched fight, and she imagined that the rest of the Lunaria felt the same. Instead, there'd been only a hushed gathering as each member learned the plan and their part within it. No moving words or inspiring homilies. Just: "Good luck. Stay safe. Try not to die." Encouraging words, indeed.

With a nod from Hale, who was manning the door and would ultimately bring up the rear of their company, Burn and Scar readied themselves and walked out into the predawn gloom. They kept silent as they moved, but their footsteps still echoed from the walls and platforms above them, sounding too loud in the otherwise still streets.

Each group took a different path to their destination, spreading out through the city's streets and alleys like a spiderweb of spies. The sisters moved briskly, trying to keep their pace above a walk but below a full-out run. The cold and the excitement spurred them on, however, and more than once they had to slow each other's quickening gaits.

Eventually they came to the first checkpoint. Burn observed with a rush of relief that Coal and Ansel were there and that they were alone, with no dead soldiers or fire damage surrounding them. The sisters darted through the gate, sending a curt nod to the faux guards as they passed.

Coal gave a quick smile in return, and Burn found it strange to see such an uncalculated expression pass over Cross' face. She had almost gotten used to the disguise, but decided then that it would never be something she could stomach for more than a few minutes. Cross' body brought with it too many memories and too much pain, no matter whose soul was inside it.

Having fallen behind, Burn now trailed Scar on the way to their temporary hideout. Each team had a predetermined place to wait as the rest of the Lunaria made their way onto the tier. Once they were all in place, some would stay behind to guard the level while others would press on, down and down until they reached the bottom of the city.

That's where Scar and Burn were headed: to the depths. They'd pieced together that the main campaign would be waged at the bottom of Kasis, where disease and pollution raged rampant and the poor and defenseless would be the easiest to wipe out. So that was where the Lunaria was focusing their efforts, stationing their most powerful troops throughout the area.

The others, situated above them, would be fighting any additional units and clearing the way for innocent citizens to flee upward. Their plan was simple: to stop Cross before he set off the ManniK, freeing the people before taking out the army that had been tasked to kill them. What could possibly go wrong?

Waiting in the shadows for their signal to move was agonizing. Fired up by the movement, Burn wanted to keep going, keep moving. Instead they sat, the seconds ticking by like minutes and the minutes like hours. The adrenaline that had been pumping through her veins faded, leaving her drained.

She looked across to Scar whose face was unreadable

in the darkness, wondering – not for the first time – if they would both make it out of this alive. Burn didn't want to think about it, didn't want to consider the possibility of such a grim fate, but the thought kept worming its way back into her mind.

"Scar?" she whispered to her sister, who was seated across from her in the narrow drainage tunnel. Scar moved her head slightly to show that she was paying attention, but she didn't speak. "You don't have to do this, you know. There's still time to leave, to go home. No one would think less of you."

Scar tilted her head, an odd expression on her face. "Of course I have to do this," she said, like it was plainly obvious to everyone but Burn. "Cross took our dad. He's seeded the city with hate and revulsion for our kind, especially people like me. And he almost took you. What kind of big sister would I be if I let him get away with that?"

Burn felt a lump rise in her throat. She swallowed it down, trying to get control over her emotions – and failing miserably. So instead she simply reached across the space and took her sister's hand, squeezing it.

"If anything happens…" Burn tried, then found herself unable to continue. "I love you," she finally managed to get out.

Scar nodded, squeezing her hand in return. It was enough.

A short while later, a crackly voice came through the comms. "Everyone's clear," said Ansel in a low tone. "Moving on to the next level."

It took only a few minutes for them to travel to the next

barricade, then the whole process began again. Wait. Hurry through the streets. Cross the blockade. Hide. Wait. Repeat.

They were down to the second-last barrier when their luck ran out. Maybe the officers saw through Coal's disguise. Or maybe they knew something the Lunaria didn't. Either way, they declined to vacate their posts, even for a few minutes. With time running out, Ansel made his move, encompassing the area and the people within it in a quick but deadly ball of fire, burning them to a crisp within seconds.

Burn tried not to look as she passed through, but it was difficult to block out the scene. Two crisped bodies being dragged away and hidden. Smoke billowing around them. The stench of burnt flesh.

Thankfully, they passed the last barricade without incident. Burn felt her skin tingle as she once again descended into the bowels of the city. The smell and the haze and the atmosphere of discontent clung to her, forcing her mind into places that it didn't want to return. She stuck close to Scar, fearing that they'd get separated in the smog and be unable to find each other in time.

The trek to their post wasn't a long one. They were situated in the middle of the city, as far up as they could go without hitting the next platform. Burn found the building without trouble, and the two climbed a rough metal staircase along the side to reach the top, three floors up. There, they set themselves up to watch.

They were the sentinels, the eyes and ears of the operation. Well, mainly the ears. The Lunaria were counting on Burn's gift to discern the Peace Force's movements through the city, to detect where Cross sent them and how many men made up their ranks. Her gift made her a good spy, but an even better general, allowing her to direct the Lunaria through the city like a conductor at the stand.

Atop their perch, the pair watched – and listened – as the others took their places. The world was just starting to awaken, and the first signs of life were appearing throughout the city. People began to emerge from their makeshift dwellings and started going about their day, blissfully unaware that it might be their last. People ate their breakfast, kids played in the road, and the world went on the same as it always had, giving no signs that today would be any different than the day before or the days to come.

"Is everyone in place?" Burn asked into her comms, taking up the mantle of leadership for their ragtag misfit militia. Affirmative replies trickled in from all sectors, crackling through her headset one by one.

"We're all set here," replied Hale, the last to check in. He was situated at ground level in the heart of the city, the likely epicenter of Cross' attack. With his strength and combat know-how, he had volunteered to lead the front line into battle.

Burn's heart constricted as she considered how much danger he and the rest of the combat forces would be in once everything kicked off. She prayed that it would go smoothly, that they would be able to circumvent the massacre with minimal bloodshed, but she knew better than to expect that outcome. Cross wouldn't accept defeat easily. If it was a bloodbath he was after, he'd do everything in his power to bring it about.

Burn slid down against the half wall that bordered the

roof, dropping out of sight of the street. The noises from the city were growing, and she concentrated on the sounds she was searching for: marching feet, the clatter of weapons, Cross' cold voice barking out orders.

Once again, the waiting felt like torture. Her mind replayed everything that had led her to this position, this place. And no matter how hard she tried, she couldn't stop herself from envisioning the future – friends and allies lying dead in the streets, their sightless eyes staring out at a scarred battle-field drenched in blood.

Nearly an hour passed as they waited, tucked into the shadows in the depths of the city. And then she heard it: footsteps, marching in unison, making their way downward. Hundreds of them, far outnumbering the Lunaria's forces. It was time.

# CHAPTER 24

Burn signaled the troops, alerting them to the imminent arrival of Cross' men. She listened intently as their enemies descended, spreading themselves out across streets and levels, setting their traps.

Their movements were well-coordinated and precise, honed by years of training and guided by Cross' firm hand. Down they came, one army with one aim: to do as much damage as they possibly could. In a fair fight, the Lunaria wouldn't stand a chance, with most of them possessing no formal training and only an odd assortment of miscellaneous weaponry. Then again, they didn't intend to fight fair.

"They're coming," came a short burst, this time from the faux guards they had put in place one tier up. The static from the comms seemed to fizzle throughout Burn's entire body as she readied herself for her part in the deadly drama.

For the first time, she wished she were on the ground with the rest of her comrades, preparing to fight alongside them. She wanted to get her hands dirty, to channel the anger and frustration and helplessness she felt into concrete action. Yet she knew that with her gift, her place was above it all, choreographing this dance of death.

The Peace Force was getting so close now that Burn could just make out the short, barked orders that were driving them on. "March. Left. Straight on. Halt."

"They're getting into position," Burn informed her squadron. "They're focusing their attention on the center of town, just like we planned."

It was a good sign. It meant they might be able to stop the massacre before it even began, blindsiding the Peace Force and swiping their ManniK before they had a chance to set it off – and set off a war along with it.

Burn peered above the half wall, adding a visual aspect to the soundscape in her head. She couldn't see any troops yet, but she knew they were there, hiding behind walls and crouching around corners. Waiting for the signal.

"GO!" she heard from the ground, kicking off a flurry of movement. Almost simultaneously, Burn released her own signal, urging her troops onward.

That's when the darkness fell. Brindle stole the light from the street, causing a flood of blackness to drench the area around them. Automatically, Burn's goggles switched to night mode, a feature which Scar had installed on all of the Lunaria's eyewear.

But even with her goggles tuned to the darkness, Burn couldn't make out the action through the dense morning smog. She knew the plan by heart, though, and listened with bated breath as it began to unfold before her.

As Brindle continued to hold back the light, Dorma-line would use her gift to run straight for the center of the city, through walls and buildings and people, grabbing the ManniK as she blew past and taking it with her through the safety of building after building. Shaw would be there too, a safeguard in case of open fire, and his skin would block the girl as she fled, protecting her from harm. The Lunaria occupying the other levels would do the same, using their own gifts to steal away the ManniK before it could be released. That was the plan, at least.

Burn heard the small footsteps as Dormaline ran, heard her grab something, heard a shot fire and then another. Then the darkness lifted as Brindle's grip on the light slipped, and Burn saw the aftermath of what had taken place. An officer on the ground. Shaw standing above him. Dormaline and the cannister of ManniK nowhere to be seen.

A sharp trill of hope went through Burn as she realized that their plan had worked. They'd stopped it, held back the enemy before they could harm a single soul. They'd won.

And then Burn's heart, which had been floating in her chest, dropped like a stone. Five more officers, each carrying a cannister exactly like the one the Lunaria had just stolen, walked out into the street. Burn barely had time to shout an order before the soldiers dropped their loads, sending clouds of mist into the air around them.

"Masks on!" Burn screamed as the ManniK rapidly wafted through the streets, finding every alley, every home, and every person within them. The Lunaria had planned for this, adopting masks with superior filtration to protect themselves against the aerosol threat, but they could never be completely safe from it. If their masks slipped or were damaged, or someone knocked them off, they'd be at the mercy of the drug and the rage it spawned, adding yet more crazed mutants for the Peace Force to put down.

Burn instinctively reached up to secure her mask, making sure it was tight and immovable against her face. Then she checked on Scar, who was standing immobile at the wall beside her, watching with horror as the drug began to take effect on the citizens. She didn't even flinch as Burn tested her mask, tightening it as far as it would go on her sister's head.

Then Burn turned her attention to the ground. The Lunaria had abandoned their hideouts and streamed onto the street, positioning themselves for a war on two fronts – one against the Peace Force and one against the citizens they'd just poisoned.

The people of this tier, with their ragged clothes and thin masks, coughed and doubled over as the drug-infused smoke entered their systems and took effect. With a scream of rage, a man in a dark blue tunic ran toward the Peace Officers, his arms raised above his head in preparation for an attack. A shot rang out, loud and clear, and the man went sprawling backward, a deep red fluid gushing from his chest. And then all hell broke loose.

The people in the streets turned on their neighbors and friends, grabbing anything they could find to use as a weapon. They advanced on the Peace Officers and the Lunaria alike with no concept of friend or foe, enemy or ally. They were blind, the rage consuming their thoughts and their reason, leaving them as empty shells bent on destruction.

The gifted among them fared even worse, as the ManniK heightened their aggression and strength, creating monsters out of men. They began tearing signs and light posts from the street, hurling them into the crowd and pinning people to the ground. Others picked up their friends and neighbors, holding them over their heads before chucking them in any direction they saw fit.

The Peace Force rallied, shouldering their guns and preparing to fire at will into the crowded street. And the Lunaria stood between them, with an army on one side and a riot on the other, danger pressing down on them from all directions. With no other choice, they began to fight back.

Thick brown ropes started growing from the ground, wrapping themselves around officers and residents alike and binding them tightly, their arms and legs trapped against their bodies. It took a moment for Burn to realize that they weren't ropes at all, but vines, and that Ramus was controlling them, calling them forth from beneath Kasis' surface.

As he worked, Innoxia searched the ground, combing the battlefield for souls that had already been lost to the war. One by one she crafted her own army, positioning the dead like a barrier between the soldiers and the people they were supposed to protect.

"Take cover!" Burn yelled through the comms as she heard the Peace Force give the order to fire.

The first volley of shots rang out and more citizens began to drop, the drug suppressing their fear of bullets and death. Innoxia's wall of corpses held back most of the fire, taking more damage than any living person could handle, but they weren't invulnerable. As they dropped, Innoxia worked fervently to replenish their ranks, drawing from the ever-increasing pool of bodies littering the road around them.

Meanwhile, Shaw was taking a more personal approach to battle. Knife in hand, he walked through a hail of gunfire toward the soldiers, his skin impervious to their bullets. By the time they realized that their guns had no effect on him, it was already too late – his knife had already slashed their throats, sending them to the ground in a shower of their own blood.

Pierce stalked around the edges of the troop's formation, picking off errant men with a touch of his finger. He wasn't impenetrable like Shaw, so he kept to the shadows, catching his targets unaware. His poison worked quickly, so before the soldiers even had time to turn around, they had already lost control of their limbs and crumpled to the ground. His progress was aided by the nearby Brindle, armed with a gun, who sent small parts of the street into darkness so she could fire on the officers with advantage.

From her position, Burn narrated the battle as best she could, sending her troops this way and that as the tides changed. As the riot of citizens began to coalesce and descend en masse, she dispatched Ansel and Hale to stop them, hoping they could form a barrier between the two sides before more chaos could arise.

Ansel conjured a wave of fire that set the street ablaze, drawing a flaming line in the sand that set apart the two camps. Despite their MorniK-addled brains, the citizens drew back, something within them still recognizing the danger of the inferno. Hale tackled any that were brave enough – or high enough – to test the fiery line, sending them flying to the ground and knocking them out with a punch.

More of the Lunaria, including Symphandra and Meera, did what they could from the sidelines, picking off enemies from strategic perches behind benches and around corners. Together they held the line, keeping both the citizens and the Peace Force at bay.

Despite all the odds, they were winning, forcing the army back through the streets and steadily gaining ground against their mighty foe.

Then Burn's ears pricked, catching on a sound from a nearby street. It sounded like...marching. Troops. Peace Force reinforcements were coming, and they were coming quickly. Burn bellowed through the comms, warning the Lunaria of their imminent company, but she couldn't tell if it even registered amidst the madness.

And then they descended, a second horde shoring up the first, bringing new energy and fresh weapons to the raging battle. Burn watched in horror as Innoxia's dead army faltered, then fell, dropping too rapidly to replace. Pierce and Brindle moved to help, a cloud of darkness billowing around them, but a sudden burst of shots sent the darkness flying. In its place were two figures on the ground, immobile and bleeding.

Ansel turned his fire on the Peace Force in an attempt to block their progress, but they kept moving forward, their gear immune to his flames. Burn glanced around hastily, trying to find someone to send in to help, but her troops were scattered across the battlefield, either pinned down or too far away to help.

Five men had grabbed Shaw and brought him down,

tying him tightly to a nearby post so he couldn't escape. And Ramus had been cornered by one of the local mutants, his vines no match for the man's razorlike teeth and claws.

The tide was turning against them, and all Burn could do was watch. She felt a frustrated powerlessness rise up in her chest and threaten to overtake her. She wanted to dive down, to join her brethren and fight, to smash the Peace Force's weapons to bits, but she couldn't. Her gift was no use in battle. She couldn't help them.

And then Scar screamed. It was a bloodcurdling scream, one that went straight through Burn and pierced her heart. Turning on her heel, she immediately scanned her sister for injuries, fearing the worst. But she saw no bullet wounds, no fire damage, no hint of physical injury that could explain the sound. Then she saw where her sister was looking.

Down on the battlefield, Symphandra lay face up, unmoving in a growing puddle of dark red blood. Burn stepped closer to the edge of the building, staring unblinkingly at the body and willing it to move. But it didn't. She didn't. Burn's heart sank, tears threatening her eyes. She gulped, swallowing the lump in her throat, and turned to Scar. She didn't know what she was going to say, but she had to say something. Only Scar wasn't there.

Burn heard the clatter of the metal staircase and ran over to the ledge. She just caught sight of her sister's dark gear before Scar leapt off the stairs and into the street, running at full speed into the fray.

Burn didn't even think. In fact, she couldn't think. Her mind had ground to a halt the instant Scar had left her, leaving one thought in her head: She had to save her sister.

She leapt from the building onto the stairs, the weak metal groaning under her sudden weight. Taking the stairs two at a time, she all but flew down them, all the while searching for her sister in the crowd. Her heart raced as she ran, but she couldn't spot Scar's wiry red curls anywhere amidst the commotion.

Reaching the bottom of the building, Burn dashed to the mouth of the alleyway. While fervently scanning the area, her eyes locking on every bit of red in the crowd, she withdrew the gun that she had strapped to her back, holding it tightly against her body. Its weight felt strange in her hands, and she prayed she wouldn't have to use it on another living soul. When it came to finding her sister, though, she would do what she had to.

Taking a deep breath, she left the safety of her hideout and entered the fight.

It was unlike anything Burn had ever experienced. Watching the action from above was nothing like being in it, down amongst the fire and the bullets and the bodies. The acidic iron smell of blood penetrated her mask, tinged with hints of smoke and dirt and burnt hair. The haze that had covered the sector was thicker than ever, mingling with the smoke to create walls of misty fog.

Burn stumbled on something in the road but caught herself before she fell, looking down to see what had tripped her. To her horror, she saw a woman's body, the face and arms charred past recognition and the hair still smoking. Bile rose in her throat, and she had to concentrate to force it down.

Despite the shock, she kept going. And going. Past citizens who were intent on killing each other with their bare hands. Past injured officers screaming for help. Past Lunaria who lay unmoving on the ground. She saw Crete bowed down over one of them, his hands to their face, concentrating. He already looked so gaunt, so weak, that she wondered how many more people he could possibly save, how many wounds he could heal before he, too, was just another casualty of the war.

She pushed the thoughts away, pressing onward toward the front line. That's where Symphandra had been, so that's where Scar would be headed. Yet navigating the battlefield was more difficult than she had anticipated.

A loud bang rocked the street. Burn turned to see that one of the citizens, crazed beyond sanity, had pulled down one side of a building, sending showers of heavy bricks raining down on top of him and the nearby crowd. Screams erupted as people tried to flee, taking off in every direction in search of a safety that didn't exist.

Burn continued onward, her ears ringing from the noise. All around her, screams and gunshots and sounds of warfare clouded her consciousness, dampening her ability to hear the world. Disoriented and panicked, she lurched forward, no longer certain where she was headed.

Suddenly, something hit her from behind, knocking her to the ground and forcing the breath from her lungs. Before she had time to react, another blow struck her, sending a shock wave of pain through her body. Knowing she had to move, she rolled blindly, just missing another swing.

She glanced up to see a burly man, his eyes wild, standing over her with a plank of wood gripped tightly in his hands. He was preparing another strike, and Burn rolled again, this time managing to get her feet under her. She shot upward, dodging his attack, and rapidly searched the ground for anything she could use to defend herself.

She didn't want to shoot this man, this innocent citizen operating under the effects of a terrible drug, but she needed something to incapacitate him. Spying part of a metal signpost poking out from beneath the prone form of a woman, she resheathed her gun and dashed to grab it. Her hands closed around it an instant before the wood plank came sailing back into her vision.

This time, however, she wasn't quick enough to avoid the blow entirely. It clipped her left shoulder, and a numbness temporarily immobilized the limb, followed by a sharp pain that caused her to swear loudly. The next time a blow came, she was ready, holding up the sign fragment in front of her like a shield. The wood slammed against the metal, sending painful reverberations through her wrists and up her arms.

The two stood there, weapons locked, battling it out with pure strength and force of will. And Burn was losing. Her muscles were straining to keep the plank of wood away from her body, but it was inching closer, her small frame no match for the man's drug-fueled rage. She couldn't hold on much longer, the weapon now only inches from her face, and she felt her grip on the metal sign starting to slip.

She had to think of a plan, a way out of his grasp, but for some reason her brain didn't seem to be working at its normal speed. It inched along, unable to find an avenue of escape or a way to distract him. Pure terror washed over her as the plank's rough edge grazed the side of her face.

Another loud shot echoed through the street, this one

nearby, and the man's eyes went wide. He loosened his grip on the plank and staggered forward, grabbing Burn's shoulders. Unable to stop his momentum, she lost her footing and fell, the man's staggering weight landing on top of her with a sickening thud.

Pinned under his enormous body, Burn struggled to free herself as blood started to pump from a gaping wound on his chest and spill out over her torso. The warm metallic taste filled her nose and mouth through her mask, threatening to choke her. She squirmed as she tried to free her arms and legs from beneath him.

Through the pain and the terror and the thrum of battle, Burn made out a heavy pair of footsteps headed in her direction. Still trapped beneath the body of her assailant, she had no way to know if it was a friend or foe coming toward her. So she froze, willing herself to stiffen, fighting against every instinct that was telling her to run.

The steps grew closer and closer, coming to rest an arm's length from where Burn lay. She held her breath, worried that even the slight movement of her chest might cause him to shoot. Through squinted eyes, she could just make out a pair of Peace Force-issued boots and dark pants. If she had wanted, she could have reached out and touched him, but that would have been a death sentence.

He stood there, towering over the pair, admiring his kill. He gave a rough kick to the man on top of Burn, chuckling sadistically as the body lurched. For good measure, he aimed a kick at Burn, too, hitting her in the same shoulder as the wooden beam had just moments before. She bit her lip to keep from screaming, forcing her body to remain limp and pliable. The officer seemed satisfied because he sauntered off, shouldering his weapon as he re-entered the fray.

As soon as his footsteps receded, Burn doubled her efforts to free herself. She writhed painfully, making slow progress as she pulled first one arm then the other out from beneath him. Her top half now free, she was able to drag herself the rest of the way out, panting from the exertion.

She knew she had to get up, had to find her sister, but the thought of moving seemed like too much for her already ravaged body. It was the idea of Scar, hurt and alone, that ultimately spurred her forward, and she pulled herself to her feet. With the gun once again clutched in her hand, she strode back into the fight, ready to do what she had to in order to survive.

Through the haze to her left, another Peace Officer emerged, gun drawn. Burn didn't hesitate. She pointed and pulled the trigger, a kick knocking her back as the gun erupted, blasting a bullet directly into the man's chest. She watched as he collapsed, a sudden numbness encompassing her thoughts. After the terror and panic that had been racing through her brain, the lack of feeling felt soothing. She relished it, embracing the detachment from everything and everyone around her.

Suddenly everything seemed quieter, like the action had been muted and the harsh soundscape dulled. She walked like a zombie through the field of the dead and dying, her mind focused on one thing: Scar. She had to find her sister, had to save her.

As she wandered through the hushed landscape, the image of Scar's face and the memory of her voice permeated

Burn's brain, sinking into every corner of her consciousness. It was as if her ability had been completely reversed; instead of hearing everything, she heard nothing, her mind scanning the void for the one thing that mattered. And then, like a beacon shining on the darkest night, Scar's voice broke through the haze.

"Stay with me," Scar pleaded, the whisper pulling Burn through semi-collapsed buildings and over piles of debris. "Don't leave me." Burn knew the words weren't meant for her, but they burrowed into her soul, nonetheless, spurring her into a run.

Dodging people and weapons and objects flung blindly through the smog, she followed the voice, listening with rapt attention as it begged. It felt like a cord had been tied around Burn and she was being reeled in, closer and closer with each step. She scrambled over a mound of rocks and rubble, one of the jagged peaks ripping through her pants and into her flesh, but she didn't stop, couldn't stop.

Minutes later – minutes that seemed to span days – she spotted Scar's red hair, her head bent low as she crouched over a form on the ground. Burn put on a burst of speed, rushing to her sister's side to grab her, to protect her.

That's when the world slowed and time seemed to stop. A bang broke through the silence in Burn's head, and a bullet sped straight for her sister's heart. It felt like she was running through water, pushing her legs as fast as they could go but getting nowhere.

Burn screamed her sister's name, the single word imbued with such anguish and heartbreak that she thought it might tear her apart. Scar looked up just as the bullet pierced her skin, her eyes widening in shock as they met Burn's. And then she dropped, time falling back into place as she hit the hard, packed earth.

Burn slid to her sister's side, shaking her in a vain attempt to rouse her, but she wouldn't wake, wouldn't move. She just lay there, broken, like a small china doll. A fire so hot it would melt stone erupted in Burn's core, coursing through her veins like molten lava.

She looked up, scouring the area for the monster who had done this. Her eyes alighted on a hooded figure, his gun still raised toward her, ready to fire. Without thinking, she barreled toward him, knocking the gun out of his hands before he had the chance to pull the trigger.

Instead of staying to fight, the man turned and fled, Burn trailing behind him as he swerved and ducked across the battlefield. He took a sharp turn down an alley, skittering on the loose stones and debris rolling under his feet. Burn couldn't react fast enough to his sudden change in direction, and she collided with the wall on the far side of the entrance. Pushing off of it, she resumed her chase, the man still within her sights.

The bedlam of the battle faded behind her as she ran, her vision clouded with red. The man made another sharp turn, then another, weaving through the dirty back streets and dingy alleys. Burn kept her eyes trained on him, following every movement he made. Her legs ached with the effort and her lungs burned, but she kept going, swerving to follow him into yet another dim lane.

As she turned the corner, a hand reached out from behind the wall and slammed into her face, knocking her to the ground. Before she had time to react, the man had kicked her gun away, leaving her defenseless. She sprang to her feet, crouched in a fighting position, and stared straight into the eyes of Illex Cross.

# CHAPTER 25

A growl sprang from Burn's throat, low and guttural, an animalistic drive overtaking her senses. She stood, weaponless and alone, before the very man that had caused this devastation, this travesty of justice, and she wanted revenge. She wanted to make him pay for the lives he'd ruined, the chaos he'd crafted. And for Scar. Smart and loyal and beautiful Scar.

"I was hoping we'd meet," Cross said with a self-satisfied air, as if he'd coordinated this entire encounter. As if he, too, wasn't alone and weaponless in a dead-end alley. "I was disappointed in Wight for not killing you, of course. But then I realized that I would have the pleasure of ending you with my own bare hands. And that is going to be so much sweeter."

They circled each other slowly, like two fighters in a ring. Burn wanted to reply, to tell him what she really thought of him and the sadistic Peace Force he had curated, but her mind remained feral, consumed by need and hate.

"Fuck you," was all she managed to snarl before taking a wide, clawing strike at his face.

He lunged backward, easily avoiding her attack. As she withdrew, he aimed a kick at her midsection, sending her staggering into the opposite wall. She reeled slightly but regained her balance in time to sidestep another kick. This one hit the wall instead, propelling Cross backward.

Burn took the opportunity to punch Cross as hard as she could in the face, his head snapping back with a satisfying crunch. She followed it up with a kick to the groin, which caused him to groan involuntarily. Not wanting to lose the momentum, she pinned him to the wall with one hand, readying another punch with the other.

Before she could make her move, Cross thrust his knee into her stomach, knocking the wind out of her and sending her stumbling back several paces. His body now free, he returned the punch she had given him, slamming her head into the wall behind her.

Dazed, she stuck her hands out in front of her to protect herself as her vision swam. She somehow managed to parry another blow, then kicked out blindly, making contact with his leg. He fell to his knees and Burn descended on him wildly, striking his face and torso with both hands as she raged.

Finding himself unable to rise amidst the fury of her blows, Cross grabbed her midsection, pulling her down next to him. She screamed as her injured shoulder struck the ground, sending waves of pain through her body. Cross noticed and capitalized on her weakness, pressing down on her damaged shoulder as she writhed.

Burn kicked and clawed at his face with her free hand. After a moment of struggling, she made contact, her nails ripping ragged strips of skin from his cheek. He bellowed in pain as he brought his hands up to his ruined face, freeing Burn from her prison.

She staggered to her feet, her left arm now hanging uselessly at her side. Ignoring the pain, she aimed a low kick at Cross, but he rolled away, narrowly avoiding the strike. As she recovered, he got to his feet, his right leg visibly paining him.

Both panting, the two stared at each other in revulsion. By this time, Burn had recovered enough of herself to piece thoughts and sentences together in her mind.

"Why?!" she shouted at him, the words echoing off the walls around them. "Why did you have to do this? What have we ever done to you?"

"Look around you!" he screamed in reply. "Look at what you're fighting for. It's nothing. These people are nothing. Kasis will be better off without them – and without you."

"Go to hell," Burn ground out through gritted teeth, her eyes fixed on Cross.

"This is hell," he replied quietly, without artifice.

With that, he lunged at her, hurling his body toward hers and knocking them both to the ground. Burn thrust her palm upward toward his face, making contact with his nose and feeling bone crack. Blood began to gush from the wound, spilling onto her mask and covering its filter, blocking the flow of oxygen.

Without thinking, she reached up and peeled off the mask, gulping in lungfuls of the thick, soupy air around her.

It was only then that she realized what she'd done. Traces of ManniK still hung in the air, bound in the ever-present pollution that infected the tier. And she had just inhaled it in large gasps, filling her body with the poison.

The effects were instantaneous. Her heart rate and breathing increased, and she could feel her pupils dilate, brightening the world around her until it hurt. A shiver went through her as the drug rushed into her system, filling every muscle, every molecule with power. Her pain faded to the background as the energy took hold.

The tightness in her chest – the pain of losing Scar and Symphandra and so many others – faded, too, replaced by something so pure and powerful that it blocked out every other emotion, every other feeling. Rage.

Burn let out a terrifying scream as the drug took over her. In an instant, she surrendered everything she was, giving herself over to the madness. It felt amazing. And for the first time, Cross looked scared.

Burn started to laugh, a manic, uncontrollable laughter that filled the alley with sound. Filled the alley with *her*. She wanted to take up as much space as possible, to own the world around her and everything in it – and to burn it all to the ground. Starting with Illex Cross.

As soon as he'd realized what was happening, Cross had scrambled off of her, retreating to the corner of the alley like a scared little rat. Burn advanced on him slowly, savoring his terror.

"What's the matter, Cross?" she heard a voice say. Her voice. It sounded different, lower and less human, like she'd become something else entirely. She walked closer, a predator cornering her prey. He reached the end of the alley, his back against the wall, and she leaned in, whispering in his ear, "Are you afraid of one of the monsters you've created? No? Well you should be."

With that, she swiped a hand across his face, giving him another set of scratches to mirror the first. He reacted instinctively, grabbing a handful of her hair with one hand and hitting her as hard as he could with the other. The pain barely registered as her head shot back, and she recovered in a flash, lunging at him with ferocity.

The woman who was no longer Burn wrapped her hands around Cross' neck, gradually squeezing the life out of him. Before she could complete the deed, however, he managed to get a foot up and kick her back, and she lost her grip on his throat. She laughed hysterically at his futile attempt to stop her.

Diving toward him once again, she used her newfound strength to throw him against the opposite wall like a rag doll, his body hitting the stone with a delicious thud. He slid down the wall and landed on his feet, his legs now struggling to support his weight. He took one step away, then another, attempting a slow and pitiful escape. After a few more steps, he collapsed, his arms splayed on either side of his battered body.

Burn smiled a wicked smile, the taste of victory already sweet on her tongue. She stalked forward, licking her lips as she contemplated the kill. Then Cross twisted on the ground, turning over to reveal a gun. Her gun. He'd managed to collapse on top of it without her even noticing.

Her instinct for self-preservation warred against her

need to tear him limb from limb. A voice within her head, a small voice lost in the darkness, told her to run, to hide, to let it go. But that voice was so quiet, so far away that it barely grazed her consciousness.

The haughty smile returned to Cross' face as he leveraged himself up, keeping the gun trained on her. Unable to choose between attack and retreat, Burn merely stood there, watching him. Her brain was moving sluggishly, crawling along through the muddled haze of the ManniK, but she couldn't figure out why he wasn't shooting. He just stood there, pointing the weapon at her heart.

"What's stopping you?" the voice that wasn't her voice asked, curiosity tinging the abrupt question.

His smile widened. "Nothing," he said sweetly.

The instinct to attack finally won out, and Burn lunged to the right a split second before a shot rang through the air. She felt something sharp bite into her shoulder, but the ManniK dulled the impact, allowing her to focus her energy on her target.

The world moved in slow motion again as she leapt, crossing the distance between them in a bound. She collided heavily with his solid form, knocking him to the ground. Hands and elbows and knees made contact with flesh as they grappled in the dirt, fighting for control.

Cross trapped one of Burn's arms under his own, pinning it to the ground. Burn retaliated by kneeing him in the stomach. She moved her free hand to his face, her fingers searching for his eyes, but he turned away, thwarting her attempt. In his distraction, however, Burn managed to free her other hand and it flew up to his chest, where it held him down. She struck him once, then again, stunning him long enough to grab the gun and push herself off of him.

Panting, she heaved herself to her feet and looked down at Cross. Unlike him, she didn't hesitate to pull the trigger.

Burn left him there, alone in the alley. Her thoughts were steadily returning as the ManniK left her system, but so was the pain. She struggled to maintain consciousness, holding onto the wall as she walked and using its support to keep herself upright.

Her only goal now was to get away – get away from what she had done, from who she had become. She didn't want to be found there, next to him. She wanted to find the battle, find her friends, and fall alongside them.

The sounds of combat started filtering back into her mind, quieter than they had been before, less frantic. She couldn't tell if it was because the fighting was drawing to a close, one side claiming its victory, or if her brain was shutting down, no longer able to process the stimuli. She headed toward it, nonetheless.

Her shoulder was starting to burn, and she looked down to find it dripping with blood, the bullet having ripped a gaping hole through her skin. Her blood mingled with that of Cross and the large mutant who had attacked her, soaking her clothes and smelling of iron. She vomited then, the stench of death pairing with the ManniK withdrawal to turn her stomach inside out.

She kept walking, her steps getting smaller and smaller,

but she finally came to the opening of the alley, returning to the battlefield. Burn looked around at the city spread out before her. It was burning. With that thought, she lost her tenuous grip on consciousness and fell into the darkness.

# CHAPTER 26

Burn struggled in and out of consciousness. Or, rather, she struggled to remain unconscious. Because she didn't want to go back to that world – the world with so much death, damage, and destruction. The world which she'd helped to destroy.

In the dark moments, the moments where she couldn't hold herself under and rose to the surface, she saw flickers of life and faces and turmoil. The first time, she heard someone call her name, followed by quick footsteps, then someone shaking her. She wanted to tell them to leave her, to let the world fall down on top of her, but they didn't. Instead, they picked her up, strong arms encompassing her, and carried her away.

The second time she awoke to searing pain. She imagined they were torturing her, punishing her for the part she'd played in ruining their world. Opening her eyes, however, she found that someone was digging into her arm with sharp metal instruments, clawing through her ravaged skin to get to something beneath it. Yet it wasn't long until the pain took hold, thrusting her back into the darkness.

At one point, she could have sworn that someone was holding her hands. But that didn't make sense. There was no one left that cared for her like that. It must have been a dream. Still, she felt it, the warm touch sending her down into a peaceful abyss.

When consciousness came for real, she fought it, attempting to bury herself in dreams. But it didn't work, and reality fell around her, consuming her. She kept her eyes closed for some time, blocking out the light and the harsh truths that would come with it. Eventually, though, she opened them, taking in the room around her.

It was small and enclosed, with no windows and only a single door. She was relieved to see that it was not a prison cell, at least not the kind she was familiar with. It was just a bedroom, albeit a small one, with a bed and a nightstand and a single chair in the corner. A chair that was currently occupied.

The man in it was out cold – sleeping, she hoped, not knocked unconscious…or dead. He looked the worse for the wear, with deep purple bruises under his eyes and cheekbones so pronounced that he looked gaunt. He was clean, though, dressed in simple white and tan garments that bore no blood stains or streaks of dirt.

Looking closer, Burn realized that she knew the man. It was Crete, the healer. So someone had been holding her hands while she slept after all. It had been him, sending his power into her.

It comforted her to know that he was still alive, that he had made it through the battle. That meant that there was hope, that maybe others had made it through, as well. She didn't kid herself into believing that they had won, of course. She had seen the tide of the battle change against them, seen them beaten back by the second wave of Peace Officers. But maybe some of them had gotten out. Maybe they had saved themselves when they realized that they could no longer save the city.

Her eyes stung at the memory of the battle. All those people fighting and dying for nothing, just pawns in someone else's game. It wasn't fair. She brought her hand up to wipe away the tears and found it wrapped in bandages. Thinking back, she couldn't even remember what she'd done to it. Or she didn't want to remember.

Leaning her head against the back of the bed, she heard footsteps coming down the hallway, heavy but quick. She swung her head around to face the door, the movement sending a jolt of pain down the left side of her body. It was a moment before the door opened, but when it did a large, familiar form stepped into the room. Hale.

He didn't even notice Burn, going straight to Crete instead. He shook the man lightly, saying his name in a low but urgent whisper. Crete finally came around, his eyes red but alert, and he blinked at Hale, surprised by his sudden presence.

"Has there been any improvement?" Hale asked anxiously, squatting down to Crete's level.

Crete blinked a few more times before glancing over at Burn. The two made eye contact, and Crete's eyebrow moved up slightly in an expression of light amusement.

"Ask her yourself," he said, raising his hand weakly to point in Burn's direction.

Hale spun around, a look of surprise evident on his face. Burn merely sat there, watching him, which was all her stiff body would allow her to do.

"I didn't know you were awake," he said, stating the obvious. He stared at her, as if expecting her to respond, but she just sat there, waiting.

"We didn't know if you were going to wake up," he said after a few beats of silence. "You lost a lot of blood."

Burn had a sudden vision of herself standing on the battlefield, drenched in blood. She closed her eyes, trying to fight back the bitter taste in her mouth.

"Most of it wasn't mine," she said, her voice raspy.

Another moment passed, neither wanting to speak or even knowing what to say. Burn finally broke it, asking the question that burned in her thoughts but terrified her beyond measure.

"What happened?"

Hale sighed, running a hand through his short-cropped hair. He glanced back at Crete, who nodded in understanding and left the room without a word. Hale grabbed the now unoccupied chair and brought it closer to the bed, taking a seat before beginning.

"What's the last thing you remember?"

Burn thought back. The memories wanted to stay hidden, buried in her mind, but she dug them out and brushed them off, sifting and sorting them until they resembled a coherent story.

"The second wave of troops came in," she said, almost like a question. Hale nodded, urging her on. "We'd been winning, or at least keeping them back, but...there were too many of them. Then Symphandra went down and Scar..." Burn broke off, unable to put the rest into words.

"I left my post," she went on after a minute. "I didn't see what happened after that."

Hale nodded and looked away, his eyes flicking back and forth as he fast-forwarded through the battle in his mind, queuing up the right part so he could fill in the blanks. It felt like a parent picking up where they'd left off in a bedtime story, although Burn imagined that this tale was not going to be suitable for children.

"First, we have to go back to the beginning, back to what happened on the other levels," he said, sounding as if he'd told this particular story many times before. "Three of the other levels we staked out were attacked. None of them were allocated quite as many troops – or as much ManniK – as our tier. It looks like they planned to wipe out the worst of the 'problem' first, then work their way up.

"Our teams managed to steal the ManniK on two of the levels, preventing the attacks entirely. On the third level, the one above ours, the Peace Force released a limited quantity of the drug, infecting some of the citizens rather than all of them as they had planned. With support from the first two teams, our squad was able to contain the damage and beat the Peace Force back."

He took a deep breath then, as if coming to the difficult part in the story. "While they were fighting, however, the first two teams of Peace Officers were called down to the bottom tier as reinforcements. That's who you saw coming down as backup, the 'second wave.' Instead of one battalion, we were suddenly up against three. That's when we started to lose ground – and people."

He looked down into his hands, and Burn wondered what he was seeing in them. Probably the same thing she'd see if she looked into her own: blood.

"It was bad," he finally said, a sliver of emotion working its way into his voice. "We lost a lot of good people, but they went down fighting. And, by god, they took some of those bastards down with them."

He seemed to come back to himself, shaking his head to rid it of the images. "We thought we were done for, especially after we lost contact with you." Burn felt a hot wave of guilt roll through her chest and up into her cheeks. She tried to speak, tried to apologize, but Hale held up a hand to stop her.

"Let me finish," he said gently. "What we didn't realize was that we had reinforcements of our own. Once our teams had finished cleaning up the third tier, they made their way down to us. When they appeared on the field…well, it was just what we needed. We rallied and gave those sons of bitches everything we had."

He smiled grimly at the memory. "It was around then that the ManniK started to wear off. Then Coal noticed that Cross was nowhere to be found and no one was giving the men orders. So he did his thing. He picked up a comms unit from one of the fallen officers and gave the order to retreat. In the commotion, none of them even questioned him. They just picked up and ran. It was like they'd been waiting for the signal to fall back.

"By that time, there weren't a lot of them left anyway, so we let them go. We had a lot to deal with, what with so many of us injured. Not to mention the civilians who'd been caught in the crossfire."

It took Burn a few moments to process everything he had said, but when she had a little bubble of hope began to blossom in her mind.

"So...we won?" she asked tentatively, not fully letting herself believe it.

Another sigh from Hale. "Yes and no," he replied cryptically. Instead of extrapolating, he pulled out his tab and navigated through a few screens. Then he handed the device to Burn. It was a video, an official Peace Force bulletin issued to all citizens.

"Earlier today, a violent terrorist organization set off a chemical attack on the base levels of our city," said the official male voice, which was superimposed over images of the destruction. "The mysterious substance, believed to be a derivative of the drug ManniK, was released into the air in gas form in an attempt to dose the entire population of the lower levels. Their intent appears to have been to create as much chaos and bloodshed as possible, especially among the large number of mutated humans that reside there.

"Thankfully, our brave Peace Force raced to the scene to fight back against the radicals. With their selfless actions, they managed to contain the attacks and save the city. It is our sad duty, however, to relate that General Illex Cross perished while fighting bravely for his city. The Peace Force will mourn the loss of this great man and leader.

"An interim general will take his place as our esteemed

senior officials consider the next steps for Kasis. The public is warned that several members of the terrorist sect known as the Lunaria are still at large. If you have any information regarding this group or their whereabouts, it is your duty to come forward. As always, your safety and welfare are our highest priority."

The broadcast cut off abruptly. Burn sat there silently, staring at the now-dark screen for a time before looking up at Hale.

"They blamed it on us?" she asked incredulously. She couldn't believe it. After everything they'd done, everything they'd worked for, they'd been labeled as terrorists, enemies of the city.

Instead of getting angry, Hale smiled. "It was bound to happen," he said calmly. "They couldn't have it look like they'd been plotting against their own citizens. We were a convenient scapegoat." He let out a long breath before continuing.

"Most of the citizens out there know the truth, though. Or they at least suspect it. And they want to help us fight. The Peace Force is weak. They've lost one of their highest-ranking officials – and a lot of their men. And some of the officers that remain are starting to question their allegiances. We finally have the opportunity to rise up and fight for a better life."

Burn closed her eyes and rubbed at her face with her battered hands. She was sick of fighting, tired of the bloodshed and pain. She wanted it to be over, to go home and find Scar there, working on her harebrained creations like always. Scar. The thought of her sister sent a silent sob through her body, filling her with pain. Scar was gone. And she was never coming back.

Another moment of silence lapsed, then Hale spoke, his voice gentle. "Listen, you don't have to be a part of this. You've done more than enough already. The Peace Force doesn't know our identities. They can't pick us out with any certainty. If you want, you can go home and leave all of this behind."

Burn couldn't even process his words, not because they didn't make sense but because she couldn't envision a future for herself, not one without Scar in it. They had been a team for so long, just the two of them against the world, that she didn't know what she would do now that it was only her.

Instead of responding to his statement, she asked quietly, "What happened to them? The ones that didn't make it. Did you bring them back? Or...did you leave them?" She needed to know.

Hale cleared his throat, thrown by the question. "We were able to bring some of them home. Like Pierce and Brindle. But we had to leave some of them behind. Like Shaw. And Ramus." His voice broke for the first time as he said their names, acknowledging their sacrifice.

"And Scar?" Burn's voice was so quiet that it was barely above a whisper. She closed her eyes, dreading his response. Neither scenario would make her feel better, but if she could see her sister, maybe hold her one last time...maybe it would lessen the pain. Nothing would ever fix it, she knew.

A few tense seconds passed, but Hale didn't speak. Burn opened her eyes to find him looking at her, his head cocked and a strange expression on his face. He opened his mouth to say something, but closed it again, like he wasn't sure how to tell her. Instead, he got up from his chair and walked out of the room, leaving her alone in her confusion.

Burn was stunned and hurt. Why couldn't he just tell her? Each second she dwelt on it, it became more and more difficult to bear, threatening to crush her. A few tears escaped as she fought to keep control.

Then she heard his footsteps returning, this time accompanied by another pair. She looked up as he re-entered the room. But it wasn't Hale. It was Scar.

Burn's heart broke and healed and broke again a million times in the blink of an eye. She couldn't believe the sight in front of her, and her brain tried to convince her that she was still in a dream. Or that Coal was playing a terrible trick on her. But it was Scar. It was really her.

"How?" she breathed out, choking back the tears that threatened to fall. "How are you alive? I saw Cross shoot you in the heart. I held your body."

Her sister smiled, and it was enough for the tears to break through and begin streaming down Burn's face. It was Scar, alive and smiling and right in front of her, close enough to touch.

"I'm tougher than you know, little sister," Scar said. With that she pulled down the hem of her tunic, revealing where the bullet had struck her. It had indeed been aimed at her heart. And there, marring the smooth surface of metal that covered her chest, was a dent.

Burn found herself smiling through the tears. Her sister truly was tougher than she had known. She opened her arms as wide as she could, beckoning her sister forward into a hug. Burn squeezed her tightly with her good arm, relishing the feel of Scar's cold metallic skin against her own.

After a time, when all the tears had been shed and Burn's mind had finally accepted that her sister was well and truly alive, they sat together on the bed and talked. Scar filled her in on the parts of the battle she had missed, adding color and detail to Hale's story.

They talked for a long time before Burn finally had the courage to ask about Symphandra. She watched as her sister's face fell, an expression of deep sadness and pain contorting her features.

"She didn't make it," Scar said, her head bowed. "By the time I got to her, it was already too late. She was gone." Burn reached out a hand and placed it on top of Scar's in a gesture of silent consolation.

Her heart was also heavy with loss, but she couldn't even begin to imagine what Scar was feeling. To finally find love then to have it ripped away so soon was a cruel trick of fate. She closed her eyes and saw everything the two could have had, everything they could have shared if things had been different.

It was in that moment that she decided to keep on fighting. It wasn't a sudden choice – or even one she was aware she had made – but from that moment on, she knew she couldn't sit by and watch the people she loved suffer. She had to take a stand, to do what she could to save Kasis and the people in it. Even if she had to burn this city to the ground to do it.

# EPILOGUE

A few hours later, when she'd regained enough of her strength to get to her feet and walk around unassisted, Burn made her way down the hall. They were once again in the Lunaria's secondary safe house, which had been transformed into a pseudo hospital to treat their injured troops. Burn was only one of the many individuals currently receiving care under its roof.

She trekked down the hallway slowly, her body protesting the movements. Crete had done as much as he could, with assistance from a few on-site medics, but she still had a long way to go before she'd be back in fighting form. So she took her time, pausing halfway down the stairs to gather her strength before continuing her descent. She reached her destination – the door at the end of the hallway – and paused before scanning her finger on the pad to gain entry.

Kaz looked worlds better than he had the last time she'd seen him. He had washed and changed, and his wounds had been treated and wrapped in bandages. His room, too, was unrecognizable, with a bed and a wash basin and a cozy chair draped in a blanket.

He didn't look up when Burn entered, his face buried in a book as he lay on the bed. She made her way carefully to the chair, settling herself down and considering him. After a beat, he looked up, putting a marker in his book and placing it on the bed beside him. Sighing, he swung his body around to face her.

Noticing her wounds for the first time, his face softened into a look of concern before he could put up his guard. She let him look for a moment, allowing him to take in her battered state before she spoke.

"I promised if we got through this that I would make sure you were released," she said, her eyes looking straight into his. "I'm a woman of my word. I don't know what's out there for you, but you're free to find out. We won't stop you."

Kaz looked dubious, as if she were trying to trick him in some way. His eyes narrowed as he said, "But I know who you are. I've seen your face – and others. Aren't you afraid I'll turn you in or something?"

"No," Burn said quietly but confidently. "I trust you." And it was true. Despite his past, despite the fact that he had been one of *them*, she did trust him.

"Why?" he asked, shaking his head in disbelief. "Why would you trust me?"

"Because you're like us," she said simply.

He cocked an eyebrow at her. "What? Are you implying I have some sort of hidden desire to free the people, to fight the power?"

She gave a light laugh. "Yes…and no." He waited for her to expand on this, a look of mild amusement on his face. "You're a good man. You want to do what's right – and you know that the Peace Force hasn't been right for a long time. Just like my dad knew it. You want to help people, to give them the protection you didn't have – or the protection your family didn't have." Kaz nodded, considering her words.

"But that's not what I meant when I said you're like us," she continued, looking for the right words to explain it. "You're…gifted."

His head shot up at that, a look of confusion written on his face. "I'm not…" he started to protest, stuttering. Burn held up a hand to stop him.

"I should have realized it the night we met," she explained, shaking her head. "I'm not an easy person to sneak up on. I can hear people coming from three tiers away. Yet somehow I could never hear you, even when you were right behind me. I would turn around and there you were, no sound, no warning.

"You said you grew up down there," she said, indicating the lower tiers. "It makes sense. Didn't you ever question why the man who killed your mom and sister didn't hear you – a man who was probably gifted himself? Or why you were such a 'natural' on the force?"

He shook his head, trying to shake off the idea that he was like her, that he was different, a mutant. Yet it all added up. She watched as he put the pieces of his life together, assembling them according to this new information.

"It's like super stealth or something," she continued. "The perfect spy. And it's only a matter of time before the force realizes it, too. And they'll either use you as a pawn in their game or lock you up with the other *freaks* and throw away the key."

"And what?" he asked, immediately going on the defensive. "You want me to use my powers for good? To join you so *you* can use me as a pawn against the Peace Force?"

"No," Burn said calmly. "I want you to leave." With that, she stood up and walked out the door, leaving it open behind her.

# AUTHOR'S NOTE
## & *Acknowledgments*

This whole thing started as a dream. An actual dream while I was asleep – one in which people with crazy powers battled each other to the death and a giant land-based octopus held me captive in an underground lair. Needless to say, I had to tone it down a bit for the actual book.

However, the real story of how this book came to be started with COVID-19, and it was far more difficult than a plot just coming to me in my dreams. Like thousands of people throughout the country, I was downsized when coronavirus struck, leaving me stranded. I didn't know what to do with myself each day, how to get out of bed and keep moving. My only other creative output, local theater, closed its doors due to the virus and left me without a place to feel at home. So I created my own.

I had always wanted to write a book. I studied journalism in school, wrote for national print publications, and helped companies tell their own stories through print and digital avenues. Of course, I always had a book or two on the back burner. But I'd never had the time or creative energy to fully invest in a story, to shape its characters and mold its plot in the way that I wanted.

Then this "new normal" came, bringing the world to a standstill, and I found myself with all the time in the world. I could no longer go outside, see friends, or do the things I loved. But through Auburn I could. Creating Kasis and its inhabitants allowed me the chance to go on an adventure, a journey that was denied to me in real life because of the threat lurking just outside my door.

As I wrote, striking similarities became clear between the world I was creating and the one in which I was living. It was a world where prejudice and discrimination flourished, where those in power used their positions to further their own goals instead of those of their people, where even the air was dangerous and wearing a mask was the only way to protect yourself. When these very same issues began to dominate the daily headlines, it became more important than ever that I finish what I'd started.

With this book, I hope people find a way to escape their lives and delve into something new and magical, a story that sweeps them away and inspires their imaginations. But I also hope that it makes them question what is and encourages them to consider what could be.

*Burn this City* would never have come to be without the constant support and encouragement of my husband, Robert. He believed that I could do it when I didn't.

Thank you to my friends and beta readers: Robert Herlache, Melissa Graham, and Kayla Suhm. Your feedback and encouragement helped bring this story to life and I will be forever grateful.

And thank you to everyone who has read this book. You have made my dream come true in more ways than one! If you've enjoyed the journey this book has taken you on, please consider leaving a review on Amazon. You can also join my mailing list on *glassfishpublishing.com* to be notified of events, contests, and new releases – including the next book in the *Burn this City* series!

# ABOUT THE AUTHOR

Brenda Poppy has spent more than a decade writing and editing for publications across the country, as well as lending her writing and graphic design talents to companies to help them craft their brands. With a degree in journalism and sociology from Marquette University, she loves to seek out unique stories and capture them for others to enjoy. When not writing, the Milwaukee native can be found acting in local theater, spending time with her adorable corgi, Darcy, or traveling around the world with her husband in search of craft cocktails, good food, and inspiration for her next novel.

**Connect with Glass Fish Publishing on Facebook and Instagram, or join our mailing list at *glassfishpublishing.com*!**

Made in the USA
Columbia, SC
27 October 2022

70097520R00181